Alya
Sometimes Hides Her
Feelings in
Russian

Nonoa

"Master ♥, Princesses ♥, welcome home!"

"One Cinderella
for the lady."

"What's wrong?"

Contents

Resident of Masachika's mind #2. Always returns no matter how hard you try to get rid of her.

Alya Sometimes Hides Her Feelings in Russian

6

Sunsunsun

Illustrated by Momoco

New York

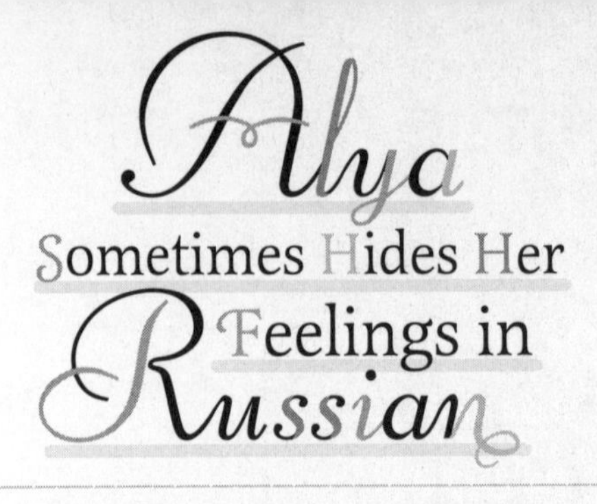
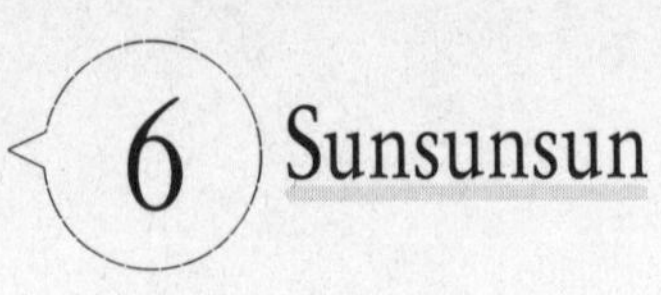

Translation by Matthew Rutsohn
Cover art by Momoco

TOKIDOKI BOSOTTO ROSHIAGO DE DERERU TONARI NO ALYA SAN Vol.6

First published in Japan in 2023 by KADOKAWA CORPORATION, Tokyo.
English translation rights arranged with KADOKAWA CORPORATION, Tokyo, through TUTTLE-MORI AGENCY, INC., Tokyo.

Yen On
150 West 30th Street, 19th Floor
New York, NY 10001

Visit us at yenpress.com • facebook.com/yenpress • twitter.com/yenpress
yenpress.tumblr.com • instagram.com/yenpress

First Yen On Edition: December 2024
Edited by Yen On Editorial: Leilah Labossiere
Designed by Yen Press Design: Liz Parlett

Yen On is an imprint of Yen Press, LLC.
The Yen On name and logo are trademarks of Yen Press, LLC.

The publisher is not responsible for websites (or their content) that are not owned by the publisher.

Library of Congress Cataloging-in-Publication Data
Names: Sunsunsun, author. | Momoco, illustrator. | Rutsohn, Matt, translator.
Title: Alya Sometimes Hides Her Feelings in Russian / Sunsunsun ; illustration by Momoco ; translation by Matthew Rutsohn.
Other titles: Tokidoki bosotto roshiago de dereru tonari no Arya san. English
Description: First Yen On edition. | New York, NY : Yen On, 2022-
Identifiers: LCCN 2022029973 | ISBN 9781975347840 (v. 1 ; trade paperback) | ISBN 9781975347864 (v. 2 ; trade paperback)
Subjects: CYAC: Language and languages—Fiction. | Friendship—Fiction. | Schools—Fiction. | LCGFT: Humorous fiction. | School fiction. | Light novels.
Classification: LCC PZ7.1.S8676 Ar 2022 | DDC [Fic]—dc23
LC record available at https://lccn.loc.gov/2022029973

ISBNs: 978-1-9753-8952-9 (paperback)
978-1-9753-8953-6 (ebook)

10 9 8 7 6 5 4 3 2 1

LSC-C

Printed in the United States of America

My Wizard

"You're such a hard worker, Alya."

Ever since I was a child, people have repeatedly given me this compliment, but it always made me feel weird. Why was I being praised simply for working hard? Putting everything into the tasks at hand was only natural. If anything, *not* putting in effort would be strange.

Even after realizing that I was the outlier, I didn't change. I continued to reach for the stars, working hard in pursuit of the ideal version of myself…

"If you've got a problem with how I do things, then do it yourself!"

I was nine years old when a classmate yelled that at me, and in that instant, I realized it didn't matter whether anyone understood my way of doing things. Others' acknowledgment and praise meant nothing to me because I knew that I was working hard, and that was what was most important to me. I was certain that I would continue this lonely path to better myself… That is, until my teacher asked us a particular question at school one day.

"What do you all want to be when you grow up?"

It was an extremely nonchalant question, but I was taken aback because I didn't have an answer. I didn't have any life goals. Although I strove to better myself, I had no idea what was beyond the stars that I was trying to reach, and with that realization, I started to doubt the way I was living my life. I felt like I was in a hot air balloon with ropes that had been cut. I could only go up. The farther I went, the darker my surroundings got, and the harder it became to breathe. However, there was nobody around to save me. There was no one I could ask whether I'd made the right choice when I chose this path.

I wanted someone to fly as high just as quickly as I was. My doubts would have surely vanished if I weren't alone, and having someone to compete with would make floating into the darkness less scary. There wasn't anyone, however, because I'd left everyone behind. Ultimately, I was the only one of my peers who'd decided to reach for the stars, and there was no going back now.

I gazed down at the ground below from my tiny basket, trembling in fear at the thought of falling, while continuously rising. I journeyed upward without a clear destination or without even knowing what was going to happen to me.

"Why do you want to be the president of the student council?"

When he asked me that day, I was able to immediately reply:

"Because I do. I'm aiming for the top. Do I need any more of a reason than that?" But even I knew that wasn't the whole truth. I answered as quickly as I could so that he wouldn't ask me any more about it. After all, I had a far more selfish reason for wanting to become the student council president. The reality was that I wanted someone to recognize how hard I was working. I wanted proof that I had chosen the correct path. After transferring to Seirei Private Academy and seeing how students respected and supported their student council president, I figured that this could finally be my chance to breathe again. My doubts would fade away, and I wouldn't be afraid to rush into the darkness any longer.

"I know you've been working hard."

He probably had no idea how much those words meant to me. He was like a wizard—a mischievous wizard who could freely fly the skies without the need for any vehicle, and he didn't seem to care how high or low he went. At times, he would even teasingly fly around my basket as I curled up in a ball inside and blindly headed further into the darkness. And at other times, he would soar high into the sky, as if to guide me.

He was not afraid of falling, or of the darkness. He was as free as a person could be, and that aggravated me, so I lectured him and told him off. But no matter how many complaints I muttered, he treated me like a child...and that aggravated me even more. I was annoyed, and yet I was having fun. Whenever he wandered off somewhere, I would feel so lonely, but at the same time, I was bitter about his whimsical reappearances at my side. I knew the truth, though. He was the only one there for me. He saved me. And that was why...

"So don't say a word and just take my hand! Alya!"

That was why I took his hand and dared to leap out of the basket. Then I saw just how small the world I once lived in was. Although I used to believe I was alone, I discovered that there were so many others flying in the clouds as well. They were all traveling the skies in their own ways, sometimes alone and sometimes with the help of others, but each method was fascinating. I discovered that my initial belief was merely a fantasy: Flying higher than others didn't make me any better than they were.

There were some places that were accessible only by flying extremely high, but there were also destinations that couldn't be reached and sights that could not be seen simply by trying to reach new heights. Moreover...

"You're such a good singer, Alya!"

"I really like the band name...so thanks."

"How does your throat feel? Please don't practice too hard. We wouldn't want you to strain your vocal cords."

"Yo, Alisa. Want some chips?"

Once I managed to build up the courage to take a step into the unknown, I found people who would actually let me fly alongside them, and he was the one who encouraged me to take that step.

However, he was not destined to settle on a single vehicle. He would fly onto one like magic, then freely disembark as he pleased. He would casually cross from vehicle to vehicle while he wandered the skies. He was a wizard who could go anywhere he wanted, and there was no telling where he would go next. Although he seemed to be carrying something, he would never show you what that something was, and when you tried to take a peek into his heart, he would crack a joke and hide it again. I always felt like this was his way of rejecting me, so I never tried to push the issue any further...but I wanted to know. I wanted to be closer to his heart. He was, however, a whimsical wizard, so if I forced my way in and got too close, then he would surely fly away, and that was why I couldn't ask him.

Hey, Masachika. What are you after? What are you carrying? How long do you plan on staying here by my side? When you look at me, what do you.........?

They're getting a little too into it.

"One mana potion and elixir, please!"

"Coming right up!"

After the trivia show finally came to an end, Masachika and Alisa headed over to their class to help with their booth. The two of them figured that they should at least assist as much as they could today, since the school festival committee would most likely be terribly busy tomorrow when the school festival was open to the public—or at least open to those with invitations, that is.

"Hi, Masachika. Looking good, by the way."

"Ha-ha. Thanks. This is a lot more embarrassing than I thought it would be, though."

"Unfortunately, you're going to have to put up with it just like the rest of us. I've already gotten used to it, to be honest."

"That's the chief for you."

"Pffft. Call me 'Guild Master,'" said a colossal, muscular student with a confident grin. He was a member of the judo club. He wore a flamboyant coat with large lapels, which, coupled with his fierce looks, made him look like the leader of a band of thieves…or perhaps even the master of his own adventurers guild.

The original concept was a café…but, well, I guess we could just pretend that this is a cosplay-themed café.

Masachika took a plastic bottle from a cooler while musing that there was hardly anything café-like about their booth. Working at the café today was relatively stress-free for him, since there weren't too many customers. Plus, all the customers were fellow students. The only minor issue was the fact that he was dressed like a wizard with a robe and pointy hat, which ended up being far stuffier and more of a pain in the ass than he'd imagined.

My robe touches the ground every time I squat, so I'm basically creating a small cloud of dust every time I stand back up…and this hat? If there's something it can get caught on or bump into, it will find a way. Like, this costume couldn't be any worse for dealing with customers.

Masachika frowned at his robe, which would tangle itself around his legs every chance it got, while he poured a drink into a paper cup and placed it on a tray. A female classmate dressed as a knight then promptly grabbed the tray and brought the drink to a customer's table.

The difference in quality is staggering…

The look on his face would be hard to put into words as he watched the knight walk off. Although her cape was clearly cheap and her armor and sword were made of paper and cardboard boxes, one of their classmates was clearly a perfectionist when it came to making costumes, so the armor was exceptionally high-quality. Masachika felt like a child dressed up for Halloween standing next to a professional cosplayer, and it was starting to make him feel self-conscious. It didn't help that the judo club member seemed like he was wearing something he usually wore in his spare time.

Eh. I guess it doesn't matter, since I work in the kitchen… Anyway, when's Alya getting here?

They came to the classroom together because they were supposed to work the same shift, but the moment they arrived, three female classmates grabbed Alisa and disappeared with her. Fifteen minutes later, they still hadn't returned.

Our shift started a while ago… Is everything all right? I mean, I'm not really having trouble handling everything alone, but…

When Masachika looked around the room, he noticed students—customers—were frowning after sampling their drinks.

"I'm sure there's some ginger ale in this, but what's that other flavor? I think I've tasted it before."

"Do you think this has cocoa in it? There's something really nostalgic about the taste…"

"Hey, is it just me, or do you guys taste a hint of pickled plum, too?"

"Wait. For real?"

They were trying to guess what was mixed into each of their drinks. While the original plan was to just serve drinks, a certain classmate came up with the idea to write the recipes on the back of the menu and make a game of guessing what was in the drinks for the customers. Although the game didn't offer any prizes, a quick glance at the customers made it clear that they were having fun.

Of course, a game like this would keep the customers in the café longer, which could potentially harm sales by preventing new customers from entering, but that wasn't really a concern. The reason the class went with a café was because it was simple and didn't require a lot of staff.

Nobody's really interested in the award for excellence or the special award, either...so this is perfect.

Student and non-student customers would vote for their favorite class, and the winning class would receive the award for excellence, while the special award would go to whichever class made the most money. However, while there were numerous classes and clubs that were seriously competing for these awards, Masachika and his class weren't even toying with the idea.

Besides, there's no way to get the special reward without connections. There's always some rich parent who manages to hook their kid's class up with the most ridiculously expensive, high-end booth that crushes its competition...

He thought about it for a few moments until the classroom door slowly began to rattle open...revealing an elf.

"Guh?" grunted Masachika. He wasn't the only one surprised. When every student, both customers and workers, shifted their gazes in the direction of the door, their jaws dropped at the sight of a visitor from another world.

"Sorry to keep you waiting!" a girl in the back exclaimed merrily, pushing the elf into the room. After taking a good look at the exuberant girl, Masachika realized that she was one of the three girls who had whisked Alisa away earlier. The other two promptly walked into the classroom while gleefully checking everyone's reaction as well.

"Ha-ha-ha! Look at their faces!"

"This made all that effort worth it!"

"Yeah, that was a lot of work..."

The three stood proudly, radiating a sense of achievement as Masachika timidly approached the elf whose face was twisted with bewilderment and embarrassment.

"...Alya?"

The elf, Alisa, glanced in his direction before immediately looking away. She was wrapped in a white-and-green costume dress that complemented her pointy ears poking out from under her silver locks. Even though that was about the extent of her cosplay, there was something otherworldly about her beauty, despite her not wearing makeup. Regardless, seeing Alisa dressed like this—

She doesn't even look human.

Masachika could only see her as an elf. It didn't help that her familiar and well-adored Western features made her look like someone straight out of a classic 2D fantasy, either. She was a nerd's dream come true. The pointed ears and fantasy-style clothing had completely transformed Alisa into an elf. After all, there was no way a real human could be this beautiful.

"<I gathered up the courage to step forward...and found myself in another world...,>" muttered Alisa cynically in Russian. Her downcast, almost spaced-out gaze instantly drew Masachika back to reality. After softly clearing his throat, he said:

"Anyway, you look great... You look...really beautiful."

The instant those words left his lips, the three kidnappers whistled playfully, and within seconds, every student in the classroom began crowding around Alisa. This, of course, left the whistling three girls with no choice but to stand around her like bodyguards.

"Whoa! She's really an elf! She looks like a real elf!"

"This isn't fair at all... How are Japanese people supposed to compete against this?"

"C-can I get a picture?! Just one!"

The three girls clicked their tongues and barked like thugs at the crowd of guys who were each trying to be the first to get Alisa's attention.

"Get back, ya bums!"

"Hey, no free pictures! If ya want a picture, then ya gotta pay!"

"Do you punks not know the rules of cosplay?! You take one picture without our permission and you're outta here!"

Incidentally, these three highly educated girls came from exceedingly well-off families and would usually not even think about speaking like this. That said, judging by Alisa's appearance, it would seem that they were very passionate about cosplay as well.

Wait a second… They're all members of the craft club, aren't they…? Now it makes sense. There are a lot of very passionate—crazy?—people in that club.

Masachika's eyes unfocused slightly as he thought back to various events involving the craft club in the past until Alisa suddenly covered her ears and looked at Masachika.

"S-stop staring… You're embarrassing me."

"…If you're embarrassed while looking this good, then how should I feel, dressed like this?"

Alisa glanced at his pointy hat and robe, and her lips curled into a smile.

"Oh, I don't know. You look fine to me."

"You're being sarcastic, aren't you?"

"Not at all. All you need now is a staff with a star on the tip, and you'd be perfect."

"Perfect for what? Trick-or-treating?"

Alisa placed a hand over her mouth and giggled, but that gentle smile of hers sucked the souls out of all the boys' bodies as their jaws dropped again.

"P-Princess Alya's…laughing…"

"She's so…cute…!"

"Hold up. I thought the solitary princess was supposed to be more cold… She's laughing like any ordinary girl."

"Dude, you have no idea how rare this is!"

After a second of silence, the room had erupted with bewildered and surprised cries. Although marginally embarrassed, Alisa frowned as if she were annoyed, before rearranging her expression.

"Aw, man…," groaned a few disappointed boys as the three guards from the craft club began to break up the crowd. While watching them from the corner of her eye, Alisa looked down at her attire and muttered:

"To be honest, I don't really even know who this elf-person is. What kind of character are they?"

"It's actually not a character but a race of creatures. Elves are very common in fantasy worlds. They're typically one with nature and live in the forest. They're known for having pointy ears, being beautiful regardless of gender, and despite living for hundreds of years, their unique bodies retain youthfulness, allowing them to look like they're in their early twenties. Also, they're known for being a very proud race, and they aren't really fans of humans. They often live closed off from the world and keep to themselves."

"...Oh."

Masachika noticed a somewhat melancholy note in her voice, and he suddenly realized something. After glancing at the three girls behind him from the craft club, he added a rambling whisper:

"Oh, but...I don't think they dressed you up as an elf because of your personality. Elves are everyone's go-to race when it comes to beauty. That's all. Besides, in many tales, elves are also vegetarian, dislike metal, and are proficient with a bow, which are all traits you obviously don't have, and..."

"...? What?"

Alisa turned a quizzical gaze on him after his sudden pause, but he instantly averted his eyes and promptly tried to come up with an excuse for his silence.

"And...elves usually have light-blond hair...so I don't think they put much more thought into it other than that... Yeah."

Even he felt he was a coward for not being honest with her, but there was no way he could say, "Good old-fashioned elves are usually very slim and not curvy like you!" Obviously, that meant he couldn't tell her there was particular slang in Japanese for elves with sexy, exaggerated hourglass figures, either.

But, well, elves are master archers, so being stacked would kind of get in the way...right?

"...You're not thinking about anything weird, right?"

"Not at all? Why would you say that? Oh, hey. We should probably get to work before the place gets crowded again."

Masachika tried to look natural as he promptly returned to his station, while Alisa watched him go with skepticism in her eyes. She was soon sent to the entrance to attract customers, but...

"Whoa?! An elf?!"

"Yo, yo, yo! Get over here! You've gotta see this!"

"Duuude!"

"E-excuse me! Do you think I could get a picture with you?!"

Not even a minute had gone by, and the hallway was already swarming with students, leaving the three girls from the craft club with no choice but to pull Alisa back into the café. The crowd eventually transformed into a line, and before long, there was complete pandemonium inside the café.

"The café suddenly got crowded, huh? What are we going to do about this, Guild Master?" asked Masachika, facing the chief, aka guild master, who looked smug.

"No clue."

"Seriously?!"

"Uh... What do you think about offering to-go drinks?"

"That's not going to work. We don't have lids for the paper cups. Plus, it's obvious everyone's only here to stare at Alya."

"Oh, lids... Right... Wouldn't want them spilling their drinks... Uh... How about we add a few more seats? Maybe we should impose a time limit per seat as well?"

"Good idea, Masachika! Get on it!" replied the guild master, without missing a beat.

"Hey?!"

The guild master's eyes were kind and gentle as he placed a hand on Masachika's shoulder.

"Masachika, I hereby promote you to vice guild master."

"I'm guessing you used to be an adventurer who worked his way up to become the guild master. Am I right? You're confident in your skills on the battlefield, but you hate doing mundane tasks."

"I'm counting on you, Vice Guild Master!"

""""We're counting on you, Vice Guild Master!!""""

"You guys, too?!"

Masachika glared at his classmates, who were more than happy to pile on him after the guild master tossed him the hot potato, but every single one of them immediately looked away, pretending not to notice his predicament. Even Alisa averted her gaze, with a somewhat awkward expression.

Wow... Even the future president of the student council... Then again, I guess this is actually something I'm good at.

After reconsidering his situation, Masachika accepted it and took over to fix their current issue.

"All right, let's have a ten-minute limit per seat for the time being... We can make a sign with the time limit written on it and have someone hold it in front of the line. Hey, you three demons who started this whole mess! Don't you dare think you can sneak off now. Take some responsibility for what you did and help us."

He stopped the craft club members just as they began to rush out the door with expressions basically saying, "What? This isn't our problem. Our shift isn't until later." He had one of them handle the line, tasked another with keeping time, and put the third in charge of guarding Alisa.

"What? You want me to time them? Don't you have stopwatches somewhere for that? Couldn't you use the timer app on your phone? We could have one phone per six seats—"

"Just start logging everyone's time when they first sit."

"You want me to do this with a pen and paper?! Analog style?!"

Although there was some pushback, the class managed to restructure their system before there were any customer complaints. Then again, everyone lined up in the hallway had a clear view of Alisa through the classroom window, so there was probably not a soul who would have complained, regardless.

"Yo, Kuze. Pretty crazy crowd you've got here."

"Yeah, thanks. Having a basketball club meeting here or something?"

"We're taking a break, so we stopped by."

Masachika tipped his hat at the older schoolmates as a few other members of the basketball club got seated and greeted him amicably as well.

"We watched the trivia match."

"What a show that turned out to be! That comeback came out of nowhere! I legit screamed."

"Thanks. I'm glad you enjoyed it."

"You were so cool, Alisa."

"Huh?! Th-thanks."

Alisa's eyes widened at the sudden compliment, but the basketball club paid no heed to the awkwardness in her bow while they passionately discussed the trivia showdown.

"That was incredible. I was honestly trying to play along, too, but I couldn't guess the answers right."

"Yeah, you were sooo confident when you first challenged us, and then you ended up doing the worst, but I'm happy because that's why you're paying for all of our drinks," one of the athletes said, ribbing their friend.

"Also proves how amazing Alisa is. She got all those answers right and onstage in front of everyone."

"Yeah, let's give another round of applause to the winner! Congratulations!"

Once one of them began to clap, the others at the table immediately followed suit. Like a ripple in the water, the other students surrounding them also began to clap and praise Alisa until the entire room was booming with cheers.

"Oh, uh…"

Showered with the friendly gazes of her schoolmates from every direction, Alisa shrank for a few moments before eventually bowing. She bowed a few more times, as though she didn't know how else to react. This girl was very different from the confident, strong woman she'd been onstage, and yet it was this innocence of hers that warmed the hearts of those around her.

"…Is it just me, or is there something different about her?"

"Right? I don't really know her, but, like, she seems to be a lot easier to approach than I thought she'd be."

"...Alya's always been this way. Everyone is just afraid to talk to her because of her looks," Masachika said.

"Wait. For real?"

"Yeah. She's not really the best communicator and has trouble talking to new people, but she'll talk if you reach out to her," claimed Masachika casually, resulting in the basketball club members' surprise.

"Seriously? I figured you were the exception, since you always seem to know the right things to say, Mr. Smooth."

"Who the hell is Mr. Smooth?"

"You, man."

"Yeah, you can make friends with anyone," one of the older classmates added.

"Seriously, look at you now. You're being extremely friendly with us like we're your classmates, even though we're older than you. Absolutely no respect."

"Who me? Nah, I respect you guys... Ouch. Ow."

The instant Masachika put on his innocent face, his older schoolmates quietly began to poke him until he escaped to the kitchen (which was what they called the area where they were keeping the drinks). A few minutes went by, then all of a sudden, he heard people buzzing in the hallway again. Although he continued to prepare drinks for the customers, his focus remained on the commotion until eventually, the source of the excitement appeared at the door.

"Oh, my... Are you all sure? I feel extremely guilty..."

"Please be our guest! If anything, we would love to keep watching from here!"

Someone was being pushed to the front of the line. It was Yuki, robed in a short *yukata* with frilly lapels and sleeves, and her black hair clipped into a ponytail on one side with a large hair ornament. She looked almost calculatingly cute in her outfit—like a handcrafted doll next to a high-quality figure (Alisa). Tension immediately rippled throughout the classroom, for no one was expecting the two to be reunited so shortly after their passionate battle onstage. As countless eyes watched in anticipation, it was Yuki who was the first to speak.

"Oh, my. Alya, you look beautiful. Like a fairy."

"Thanks… You look really nice in your outfit as well."

"Really? Thank you so much."

"Is that outfit for your class attraction? I remember hearing it was festival-themed?"

"Yes, I decided to keep it on for the rest of the day, since changing would take far too long. Furthermore, I figured I could use this as an advertisement for my class's attraction as well."

There didn't seem to be any friction between them. If anything, their conversation seemed cordial, but the surrounding students still watched with bated breath. Were they aware that they were being watched? Most likely. In fact, Yuki seemed to be talking to Alisa with a purposeful smile, as if she were performing for an audience.

"By the way, can I compliment you on your performance during the trivia show? I still cannot believe you pulled off that comeback at the end. I know I lost, but it was extremely exciting. It was like something out of a movie."

"Huh? O-oh… Really?" said Alisa hesitantly, not really knowing how a winner should behave toward the person she defeated. Nevertheless, Yuki softly giggled, as if she could see right through her rival.

"Oh, please stop that. Seeing you so uncomfortable is making me uncomfortable. We gave it our best, and you won, so you should be proud of yourself."

"Y-yeah…"

Alisa wasn't the kind of person who could boast in front of the person she defeated, though, so she just nodded ambivalently. However, Yuki just continued to smile, unbothered by the reaction. Anyone who perhaps didn't see their match would have had a hard time telling who'd won and who'd lost…and that was exactly what Yuki was going for. One universal truth, which could be applied to all competitions, was that people respected a loser who would gracefully admit defeat and praise the winner. Yuki may not have won the trivia match, but she'd won herself some new fans. On the contrary, people hated sore losers who insulted the winner, let alone even shook their hand, and Yuki knew this, which was probably why she wasted no time coming to see Alisa.

She's flaunting confidence and showing she's a big deal, despite losing... Alya's going to have a hard time up against her one-on-one like this.

However, butting in to back Alisa up would end up hurting her reputation, so Masachika decided that he would have to put a stop to the entire conversation by talking to neither Alisa nor to Yuki but to the girl in charge of keeping time.

"I think table three's ten minutes are up."

"Huh? Oh, y-you're right. Excuse me. I hate to bother you all, but your ten minutes are up."

Although the students at the table weren't thrilled about having to leave when things were getting good, they still reluctantly got up and left. Without a moment's delay, the female knight swiftly cleaned the desk and offered Yuki a seat.

"Thank you very much. Do you think it would be okay...if Alya were my server?"

"I—"

"Of course it would be okay! In fact, you two should sit together!"

"Huh?"

Alisa's own bodyguard had cut her off while quickly pulling out a seat next to Yuki and then practically forced Alisa to sit in it. It was as if she had changed her job class from bodyguard to tavern master as she tried to sit a new waitress down with a wealthy patron.

"Ah... It's like staring at a work of art."

The three girls from the craft club gazed at Yuki and Alisa, in a trance, but they weren't the only ones who had been enchanted. The eyes of every student in the classroom and in the hallway were drawn to the pair's unequaled beauty.

"But I have work to—!"

"I'll take care of it! Anyway, Yuki, what would you like to drink?"

The guard cut Alisa off before handing Yuki a menu, but after taking a quick glance, Yuki cheerfully smiled and asked:

"Do you think I could have a glass of milk?"

Immediately, a chill ran down the spine of every student in Class B, with the exception of Masachika and Alisa. The guild master slowly approached Yuki, placed his hands on the table, and said with a menacing growl:

"Young lady… This is a tavern. If ya want milk, then go home to your mommy to get some."

"This isn't really a tavern, though…?" Masachika interjected softly, unable to keep up with this strange turn of events. Yuki, on the other hand, stared hard into the guild master's eyes, still smiling. Seeing her face-to-face with the large, muscular guild master made her small stature that much more apparent, but even then, she didn't cower.

"My mother passed away on a beautifully moonlit night."

"No, she didn't…," murmured Masachika yet again as the guild master simultaneously let out a snort and grinned. He then walked to the back of the room, took what appeared to be a wooden box from a locker, and placed it in front of Yuki before installing himself in a seat as well. His movements were dramatic to build suspense, until he eventually opened the box, revealing a remarkable and elaborately decorated glass bottle.

"Looks like we've got ourselves the cutest little customer today… All right, here it is. It's all yours."

"Hold up."

Masachika unconsciously grabbed the guild master's shoulder over the coat's obnoxiously large collar, for he knew nothing of this mysterious bottle, let alone anything about this entire scenario.

"Seriously? What is this? What's going on?"

"Come on now, Masachika. Everyone knows taverns in fantasy worlds have backdoor businesses as well."

"Again, this isn't a tavern." Since the surrounding students were shaking their heads in disbelief and disgust as well, Masachika quickly set his eyes on Alisa to make sure that at the very least they were on the same page. "This is just like when I stopped by and helped with the taste test. Why do you guys keep leaving only Alya and me in the dark? Don't tell me you're handling dangerous goods that you don't want the student council to know about."

"Of course not. Everything here is legal."

"Only people selling stuff that isn't illegal *yet* say that! And I noticed you didn't even deny that this *thing* here is dangerous!"

"It's nothing dangerous."

"Then what's in the bottle?"

"Your mom."

"Seriously?"

Once he realized talking to the guild master was a dead end, Masachika shifted his gaze back over to Yuki.

"Anyway, how did you know the password when I didn't even know we had a password?"

"I heard rumors that you could get a mysterious drink if you said that password."

"...Uh-huh."

There was no telling where someone with a wide circle of friends like Yuki had heard that rumor, but that wasn't important. What Masachika really wanted to know was if it was safe to drink. After all, he learned firsthand during the taste-testing phase just how terrifying one of these concoctions could be.

"Hey, Guild Master. That drink isn't going to cause any weird side effects, right?"

"Beats me, kid. Drink at your own risk. My job is selling what the people want," replied the shady guild master while staying completely in character, so Masachika dug his fingers even deeper into his schoolmate's shoulder and repeated:

"There is nothing in this drink that can harm her, *right*?"

"Oh, uh... Right. It's perfectly safe."

The guild master ended up giving in under the pressure of an overprotective brother, but only after staring into his eyes for a few moments did Masachika finally let go of his shoulder. Once that was settled, the guild master grabbed the bottle from the wooden box, poured some of it into a shot glass, placed the glass in front of Yuki, then cleared his throat a few times to get back into character.

"Enjoy our tavern's most secret of drinks: amrita."

It would be nearly impossible to tell the drink apart from water, at a glance, and it had absolutely no traits that could serve as even the smallest clue as to what they'd mixed together to create it. And it wasn't just Masachika, either. Even Alisa seemed bewildered as Yuki grabbed the shot glass.

"Here goes nothing," announced Yuki, throwing back the drink in one gulp, then opening her eyes wide in astonishment. But after a few moments went by...

"This is...! A fragrance reminiscent of an autumn sky... The richness of the fruits of the earth condensed into one... If I were to describe this in one word, I would say it tastes like...," muttered Yuki while carefully examining the empty shot glass in her hand.

"Nothing."

"'Nothing'?"

"Nothing."

It apparently didn't taste or smell like anything.

"I will still be on break for a while, so I was wondering when you were going to be free, Alya. Perhaps we could enjoy the festival together?"

"Oh, I—"

But before Alisa could even finish replying to Yuki, the same girls from the craft club interrupted her again.

"You two are going to check out the other booths?! Alisa, do you think you could continue wearing the costume to advertise our tavern a little longer?"

"Honestly, the hallway is completely packed, so you might as well take your break early. Besides, having Yuki with you would be twice as effective in getting people interested in our tavern. Oh, hey. Why don't you take Masachika with you, too?"

"You're fine with that. Right, Guild Master?"

"Huh? No, I—" The guild master tried to protest.

"""Tsk!!"""

"Y-yeah, of course, I'm fine with that!"

Although their crude expressions were unseemly for three proper young ladies, they managed to essentially force the guild master to agree, allowing them to shift their focus to Masachika.

"You hear that, Masachika? The guild master said you can take your break with them, so let's get you another costume to match."

"Wait. There are more costumes?"

"Yep. You can be a noble or an orc. Which would you prefer?"

"Having either of those around an elf would be dangerous!"

"Well, you don't have to decide right now. We can think about it on the way."

Masachika was quickly taken away before he even realized what was happening, leaving Alisa and Yuki behind. Although the passionate gazes still made Alisa marginally uncomfortable, she managed to ask:

"Well, it looks like we're going to check out the other booths. Is there anywhere in particular that you want to go?"

"Hmm… I would enjoy seeing my friends' booths. What about you, Alya?"

"I'm fine with anything…"

"Really? Oh! Now that I think about it, I believe that Masha and Chisaki's class is doing a magician run bar."

"Yeah…," said Alisa. "I don't know about Chisaki, but I doubt Masha's going to be able to pull off any magic tricks."

"*Giggle.* It is hard to imagine her confidently cutting cards, isn't it?"

"She's too laid-back and dense for any of that," replied Alisa ruthlessly—only because Maria was her sister.

"Perhaps calling her 'easygoing' would be a better way to put it. Wouldn't you agree?" suggested Yuki in a slightly troubled manner, but Alisa merely shrugged. However, after another brief pause, the silver-haired elf's eyes widened as if she had suddenly remembered something.

"What about you, Yuki?" she timidly asked with a soft voice after checking her surroundings.

"Hmm?"

"Before, you said you had an older brother, right? What kind of person is he?" The moment those words passed Alisa's lips, her eyes widened again, for she had recalled being told that Yuki's brother had left home and was living somewhere else. Therefore, while she wasn't familiar with their situation, she felt she might have accidentally overstepped. "Oh, uh… If you don't want to talk about it, that's fine, too…," she added in a fluster, but her worries were met with a smile, as if to let the other girl know it was okay.

"*Giggle.* You do not have to worry about upsetting me. My brother and I still have a wonderful relationship."

"O-oh."

"Now, you wanted to know what kind of person he is, yes? Hmm…"

Yuki tilted her head, and her eyes wandered until she suddenly placed a hand over her mouth and chuckled. She then looked at Alisa from the corner of her eye and replied:

"He is extremely cute, for starters."

"He's c-cute?"

"Yes, very. I think you would really like him, too."

"Oh…"

The comment caught Alisa completely off guard, since she was expecting Yuki to say something like "He's nice," or "You can really depend on him," so she basically had to force herself to smile back.

He's cute…? He's a guy, but he's cute…

Alisa imagined a few of the music idols who were so-called "pretty boys" and always seemed excessively casual and flirty. In other words, they were the exact opposite of what Alisa was looking for in a person, since she strongly preferred independent, mature individuals.

Then again…being called "cute" by your little sister…

She immediately visualized a youthful boy with chihuahua-like qualities, delicate and of small stature like his sister. The trembling, hopeless boy wouldn't even be able to survive without Yuki, who took care of his every need. The scenario alone made Alisa grimace. At any rate, whether he was some cute yet cunning tease or a pathetic puppylike boy, it didn't change the fact that he was the complete opposite of what Alisa looked for in a person.

I feel bad, but I don't think I'd be able to get along with him. I'm sorry, Yuki.

Regardless, Alisa was sure there was probably no chance that she would ever meet him, so she was unconcerned and ambiguously smiled back at Yuki.

"Anyway, I think it's wonderful that you two really get along."

"Yes, I actually really hope I can introduce him to you one day."

"Yeah… I'm looking forward to it," replied Alisa, out of politeness, but when Yuki meaningfully smiled back at her, she suddenly felt as if Yuki could see right through her act, so she quickly looked away.

Anyway, does Yuki like "cute" boys or something?…Why? It makes absolutely no sense to me.

Alisa kept to her thoughts while pretending she didn't notice Yuki's mirthful smile, when…

"Sorry to keep you guys waiting," apologized a feminine voice with impeccable timing, filling Alisa with relief, as though the voice were here to save her. But the first thing she saw when she looked back were red trunk-hose—like the three-quarter pumpkin pants you would see a prince wear in picture books.

"Pfft!"

"…!"

"See? I told you they'd react this way."

Masachika already looked fed up after seeing Yuki's shock and watching Alisa cover her mouth and look away. But the pout on his face and the attire only made Alisa and Yuki work even harder to control their laughter.

"Ha-ha…! You—pfft! I apologize! You look—ha-ha-ha! You look wonderful!"

"You wouldn't be laughing at me if you actually felt that way. You really should work on your acting."

"I'm serious—pfft! You look…great… Right, Alya?"

"Y-yeah."

Alisa glanced at Masachika once more, but the fact that he now looked even more like a child whose mom had dressed him up for Halloween was unbearable, so she quickly averted her gaze again.

"…!!"

"Seriously?! Stop that! You're going to actually start hurting my feelings if you keep doing that! Hey?! Did you just take my picture?!"

Masachika, red in the face, glared at all those around him, but the costume just made him look like a little prince throwing a tantrum, eliciting even more laughter.

"<You're so cute ♡,>" muttered Alisa with a mischievous grin.

CHAPTER 2 All nerds dream of doing a chi blast.

"Now, where would you like to go first?"

Masachika, who had changed back into his apprentice wizard costume, replied:

"Anywhere with food would be fine by me. I still haven't had lunch… Same with you, right, Alya?"

"Huh? Oh, right…"

It was already past two thirty PM, but neither Masachika nor Alisa had eaten lunch yet, since they had been busy with school festival duties before the trivia show. It didn't help that all the excitement and anxiety from the competition had suppressed their appetite, either.

"I only had something light after the trivia show, so I am feeling peckish as well. Shall we find a booth serving food, then?"

"How about that place over there? Seems to have a bit of a line, though."

Where Masachika was looking, there was a joint project between the freshman students of Class D and Class F. It was a maid café, and its presence was overwhelming, spanning three entire classrooms. Class F's classroom was being used as a dressing room and a kitchen, while the other two rooms were the café itself. Incidentally, Class E had set up a booth in the schoolyard, so they didn't need to use their classroom. There were rumors that a selfish, stuck-up girl whined about not being able to do a maid café unless a certain "Saya" did it with her, so Class E ended up giving in to the pressure and were forced out of their own classroom. Nevertheless, Class E never filed a complaint, so there was no telling what really happened.

"What a wonderful idea. I was actually interested in checking out the café myself."

"I don't mind eating there, either."

After receiving their approval, Masachika got in line, and thankfully they didn't have to wait long, perhaps due to it being past the lunch hour already.

"Welcome home, Master and Princesses."

"H-hey."

A rather cute maid, who was working as the greeter, reverently bowed, catching Masachika off guard by how surprisingly authentic this was.

"Masachika, I see you are smiling from ear to ear."

"No, I'm not."

"<Pig…>"

The fact that I can't argue with that makes it even more frustrating. Oink, oink…

The unprompted verbal abuse from both sides started to worry Masachika, so he swiftly covered his mouth, which made the maid giggle.

Oh, no…

He could feel his lips reflexively curl into a smile under his palm.

What is this…? Don't tell me that… Do I have a weakness for maids?!

The young wizard figured he was used to maids, thanks to living with a real one, Ayano, for a decent portion of his life…but it appeared he was quite wrong.

Th-this is bad… If I'm getting this giddy at the entrance, then I'm probably going to turn into a sweaty, blushing nerd once I step inside, and to make matters worse, I'm with these two!

Yuki would probably never let him hear the end of it, and Alisa would most certainly stare at him with contempt. At any rate, the maid, who had finally suppressed her laughter, shepherded them into the classroom. Masachika's heart raced, as if being in the café unexpectedly put him in danger.

"Follow me, please. By the way, we charge two hundred yen per seat if you wish to dine at the neighboring classroom."

"Oh."

The scummy surcharge the cute maid announced wiped the smile right off Masachika's face. When he glanced at the two classrooms' windows, he realized that they had been completely blacked out, making it impossible to see what was happening inside. In other words, there was no telling what kind of maids were inside, so if the classroom you were taken to didn't have the maid you were looking for, then you would have to pay a fee to be moved to the neighboring classroom. Sketchy stuff.

All right, I'm not smiling anymore. I'm ready to go.

After rebooting his mind, Masachika stood in front of the sliding door, knowing that he was not going to drool over himself no matter what maid stood inside, so he confidently grabbed the handle and slid the door open.

"Master ♡, Princesses ♡, welcome home!"

You could almost hear a crystalline sparkling sound as the beautiful young maid flawlessly welcomed them inside. Covering her firm rear was a frilly miniskirt that hung over her long, smooth, snow-white legs, and her somewhat childlike wavy pigtails only complemented her innocent smile. You would be hard-pressed to find a maid this attractive even at an actual maid café.

Masachika didn't see the appeal, though.

"Blech."

Instead, he felt sick. It was Nonoa, after all.

"…? Is everything okay, Master? ♡"

"I could ask you the same thing."

His facial muscles twitched. She was acting like a completely different person, so he was taken aback.

"Oh my! ♡ What a beautiful little elf you brought along with you, too. ♡ You look so cute. ♡"

"Oh, uh… Thanks?"

Even Alisa appeared weirded out. Her eyes were wide in astonishment.

"Thank you for welcoming us to your café, Nonoa. You look lovely."

Meanwhile, Yuki, who acted like a gentlewoman while at school, did not even bat an eye in front of the maids. Her graceful smile didn't budge as she smoothly complimented Nonoa, making Nonoa clasp her hands together, place them against her chin, and bashfully swing her hips from side to side.

"Whaaat? For real? You have no idea how happy you made me. ♡"

...All she was missing was a calculating giggle sound effect in the background.

"Bff! Mmp."

The ominous sight was too much for Masachika's stomach to take as it twisted and turned with nausea.

"..."

Meanwhile, Alisa's brain had shut off. Nevertheless, Nonoa didn't seem bothered by her bandmates' reactions (because she probably wasn't), and she cheerfully winked before taking them to their table.

"E-excuse me! May I order, please?!"

"Oh! Be right there! ♡"

Right as they got seated, Nonoa immediately headed over to another table to wait on other customers. It was almost as if Masachika, Alisa, and Yuki were the only ones who found her behavior bizarre, because every other guy in the café seemed to be in love with her already. Even while she was taking the other table's order, there were countless not-so-subtle gazes ogling her slim waist and white thighs peeking out from under the hem of her skirt. There was no way Nonoa *didn't* notice, but she seemed totally composed. Perhaps she was used to being stared at, thanks to modeling. If anything...

"Oh my gosh! ♡ My eyes are up here, you know?"

"Oh, uh...! S-sorry..."

She even had the confidence to mischievously tease the patrons to get them to stop. The fact that she made it obvious that she wasn't really mad at them only made the boys bashfully blush and smile even more.

"Oof."

Masachika started to feel nauseated again but then another more traditionally dressed maid—at least compared to an Akihabara-style maid like Nonoa—approached them.

"May I take your order?"

One look at her was all it took for Masachika to instinctively mutter:

"Oooh! Th-the head maid..."

"...? Yes?" She pushed up her glasses and raised an eyebrow, as if she weren't the least bit fazed by their costumes. It was Sayaka, but unlike the other maids, she was taking business seriously and wasn't being the least bit flirty. She wore a maid uniform with a long, plain skirt, and her spectacles, which were reflecting a chilling light, drew a distinct line between her and the average maid. "May I take your order?"

"Uh... I'll have the 'spaghetti and meatballs made with tons of love.'"

"Today's special is curry."

"What?"

"Today's special is curry."

The head maid casually refused to take his order, so although he was mildly annoyed, he decided to go with the day's special. That is, until—

"Wait a second. You just don't want to boil the pasta because it's a pain in the ass."

"Oh, was it that obvious?"

"Of course it was. Who do you think checked all the food-related projects for the festival?"

All food being served at the festival had to be approved and inspected by the public health center, so the entire cooking process had to be monitored in advance, to make sure there weren't any glaring issues. Furthermore, Masachika was involved in the setup, so he knew that the curry was instant, which meant all they had to do was microwave a box of curry, then dump it onto a bowl of rice, which would take only minutes. On the other hand, they would have to boil pasta for the spaghetti and meatballs, which would take some time. Plus, the profit margins for the curry were far higher, to boot.

"Actually...the curry is pretty expensive. Even if this were homemade, a thousand yen for curry at a school festival is kind of outrageous."

No matter how wealthy some of the students' families were,

asking four digits for a single dish wasn't typical. Maybe if it came as a set with some extremely high-quality coffee, then it would be excusable, but even with the value added by claiming the curry was "home-maid-made," it was still just ordinary curry. The price seemed far too pushy. Nevertheless, there was no way this head maid would set the price so high without good reason.

"Have a look at the fine print. Everyone who orders the curry will be automatically entered in a drawing to win the chance to have their picture taken with a maid."

"A picture with a maid…?"

Although Masachika had never personally been to a maid café before, he had heard that some shops allowed customers to take pictures with the maids as long as they collected enough points. Winning a chance through ordering curry, however, reminded him of how certain idols did their raffles for meet-and-greets.

"What are our odds of winning, by the way?"

"That would be a secret for maids' ears only, Master."

"Oh, so you'll at least call me 'Master,'" unconsciously grunted Masachika, as if that had surprised him most of all. This prompted Sayaka to lower her gaze while quietly pushing up her glasses.

"…There is nothing to worry about. The raffle isn't rigged. Far from it, in fact."

"All right. I mean, I wasn't really worried that—"

"Excuse me! Could I get another order of 'lucky curry' over here? Hold the curry, please!"

"Me too!"

"Here are your raffle tickets. ♡"

"Uh… Sorry, but did I just hear an extremely shady transaction take place?"

"You must be hearing things."

"Then how do you explain that?! Look at their eyes! Those are the eyes of people who have become completely addicted to gambling!"

"We are not forcing them to do anything. All we wish to do is please our masters."

"…! Y-you know, it's really hard to argue with you when you put it that way, even though it's still wrong…"

Then again, it shouldn't be a surprise that the debate queen could make an argument for any situation. If anything, Masachika was impressed that she could shamelessly make excuses like this with a straight face. Even Yuki nodded to herself, as if she were struck with admiration.

"Interesting. It appears you make up for your café's poor customer traffic with higher average spending per customer."

"Wow… You really know how to ruin the mood with your analyses. This is a maid café—a place where people come to dream."

"Master, perhaps you need to wake up. It's only a maid café, after all."

"Can I get a new head maid over here?!"

After yelling at the head maid, who had ruthlessly crushed his dreams and ruined the mood, Masachika ordered the curry, even though he wasn't really interested in winning. Both Yuki and Alisa did the same, so they ended up ordering drinks and curry for three.

"As you wish. I shall be back shortly with your meals."

Once Sayaka left, Masachika surveyed the café. What surprised him, however, was the fact that each female maid was wearing a different type of maid uniform.

"The uniforms alone must have been stupid expensive…which is probably where most of the money went, seeing how simply they decorated the place."

"I don't know who hooked them up, but apparently, a student used one of their connections to rent all of these maid outfits for next to nothing."

"Seriously? I guess you would know, being the student council accountant and all."

But when Masachika faced forward to make eye contact with Alisa, he was met with a chilling glare.

"So… That's what you're into, huh?"

"What? Oh, no. It's not like I have a thing for maids or anything… I mean, I guess I think their outfits are cute? In a nerdy kind of way?"

"Oh?"

"But when we were at the entrance talking to…Ms. Mizoguchi, was it? You were grinning from ear to ear," Yuki said.

"What? No, I wasn't—"

"It sure looked like you were," Alisa cut in, immediately shutting Masachika up. He personally didn't believe he felt anything for the maid, but he needed to explain himself, so he desperately racked his brain for the right words…when Yuki suddenly began to giggle.

"I am joking. I was only teasing you, Masachika. After all, you never really are that interested in people when you first meet them, right?"

"I feel like you could have phrased that a little better, but…yeah, I guess," Masachika admitted bitterly, since Yuki's statement was more or less accurate. Masachika actually never found himself drawn to people he had no social interaction with. Meeting new people like the maid from earlier was no different from seeing a pop star or an actress on TV to him. Although he might have thought they were cute, or beautiful, or had a nice body, that was where it ended, and he wasn't interested in befriending them. Now, if he did start interacting with them for some reason or another, then perhaps he would start to find himself attracted to them. In fact, when he first met Alisa, he thought, *Whoa. She's really good-looking*, but he wasn't really interested in getting to know her any more than that. The only exception was Maria—"Mah," technically.

And I guess that would mean…it was love at first sight.

While Masachika was deep in thought, Yuki, who was sitting across from him, leaned toward Alisa and whispered into her ear:

"Alya, Masachika is thinking about another woman while completely ignoring us."

"Right? I was actually about to say the same thing."

"Hey, can someone explain to me, scientifically, how a woman's intuition works?"

Masachika glared warily at the mind-reading duo, but Alisa ignored the question and coldly pressed him for an answer instead.

"So? Who were you thinking about?"

"…Ayano. You know, since she's a maid and all."

"Oh? She really is cute, isn't she?"

"…You'd look really cute dressed as a maid, too, Alya," Masachika said.

Although he meant it, he also wanted to please her, to smooth things over. After another second went by, however, he suddenly tilted his head with bewilderment.

"Wait. Why do I get the feeling that I've seen you dressed as a maid before?"

"...It's just your imagination. You're probably thinking about something else."

"Really...? Oh... Well, if you say so," he agreed, albeit begrudgingly, which made Yuki's lips curl mischievously.

"Wow. You really do love maid uniforms, Masachika. Maybe I should start dressing like a maid, too?"

"Whatever makes you happy."

"...Masachika, why do I feel you have been treating me rather poorly lately?"

"What? Why would I care if you put on a cute costume? Right?"

Despite Alisa's fairly reproachful gaze narrowing at her frowning partner, a sense of superiority made her sneer. However...

"I'd admire you for a second, then take a picture, but that's about it."

"Oh my. How bold! ♪"

"I'm joking. Alya. It was just a joke, okay?" reassured Masachika after seeing the flash of pure chaos in her eyes. Of course, he wasn't really joking, because if Yuki actually were to dress up in a cute maid outfit, then he would take tons of pictures and admire her all day. But obviously, admitting that would only cause trouble, so he decided to claim he was joking instead.

Regardless, Alisa seemed convinced, even though she swiftly looked away with her nose in the air.

"What's that about? Ha-ha," he joked with a forced smile, because although Alisa looked slightly annoyed, there was no denying how she felt for him.

Then again, you could interpret it as her just being envious of her friend.

"<You never say anything like that to me.>"

...Or not. Yep. She definitely wants to be seen as a woman, not a friend.

And the fact that Alisa herself didn't realize this bewildered Masachika.

Maybe in her mind, she thinks she just wants her partner, me, to always view her as a cut above the rest? She loves to win, after all...

But the head maid returned with their curry and drinks before he could come to any sort of conclusion.

"I apologize for the wait. 'Home-maid-made lucky curry.' Enjoy."

"Oh, thanks."

After serving the food and drinks, Sayaka placed a box on the table with a hole in the top.

"These are the raffle tickets."

"Oh, so this is what's causing those agonizing cries of pain in the background."

"How rude. That master over there simply ran out of luck. That's all."

"I wonder if luck is really to blame."

Although Masachika didn't mention it, he was pretty sure that big bills were being spent, because when he strained his ears, he could hear dispirited voices saying, "I'll get it next time for sure," and "I can't spend any more than this." He could even hear Nonoa sweetly asking customers if they wanted another drink as well. But the instant these guys were seated, it was already over for them. They were going to be drained of every last cent they had. So sketchy.

Just saying these guys had bad luck makes me feel even worse for them...

That was the first thought that crossed Masachika's mind as he reached into the box, pulled out a piece of paper, and unfolded it... only to reveal the word "*Winner*" written inside.

"Huh?"

"See? It's all just luck," said Sayaka before loudly announcing to the room, "Congratulations! We have our first winner!"

The announcement seemed to have persuaded the other customers to give up, but right as they were about to get out of their seats, Nonoa immediately swooped in like a vulture.

"Would you like another drink?"

"...Yes, please. And one more lucky curry, please!"

"Mmm... Me too!"

"*Sigh...* Those pathetic fools have given in to the thrill of gambling once again..."

If they actually cooled off first and thought about it, then they would realize that they had an even lower chance of winning, since one of the winning tickets was now gone, but they probably weren't able to make rational decisions anymore. Though it wasn't truly a competition, there were probably more than a few people who didn't want to lose to someone who just came in and won on his first try.

Wait a second. Was it really a coincidence that I won? It can't be, he thought. *There's no way...* Masachika's win had actually rekindled the thrill of the game for these gamblers. Once the seed of doubt was planted in his head, he realized that the other pieces of paper were tightly folded shut while his seemed rather loose and easy to grab...

"Oh, mine says, '*Try Again.*'"

"Me too..."

Yuki and Alisa placed their losing tickets onto the table while Masachika stared hard into Sayaka's eyes, but she wore her soft smile like a mask, making it impossible to tell what she was thinking.

"Now, Master, it is time for you to choose the maid you wish to take a picture with."

"Huh? Oh, uh..."

"Nonoa is our most popular maid, by the way."

"Nah, anyone but—"

"Yes, I figured you would choose her. Nonoa! Our master here wishes to take a picture with you!"

"Are you even listening to me?!" Masachika yelled.

"Be right there! ♡ ...You called for me, Master? ♡"

"..."

Nonoa was still acting overly cute, which seemed to warrant a genuinely cold glare from Masachika, but she gracefully ignored his aggravation.

"Come on, Master. ♡ Let's go take a picture together over there. ♡"

Nonoa headed over to the blackboard, where hearts, flowers, and even ribbons were drawn all over it in every color of the rainbow, creating the perfect spot for a social-media-worthy picture.

"Oh… That's where we're going to take the picture?"

Masachika honestly didn't want to take a picture with this ominous creature, but asking for another girl would probably create even more issues and misunderstandings, so he decided to keep his mouth shut and stand.

"This can't be happening…"

"My Nonoa…"

He could hear the pitiful cries of brain-deprived boys coming from every corner of the room.

"I feel your pain. GG (good game), boys…," Yuki mumbled.

"'GG'?"

Masachika listened to Yuki's and Alisa's exchange while he stepped in front of the blackboard where Nonoa almost immediately held out a piece of chalk to him.

"This is for you, Master. Could you please write your name right here for me?"

"My name?"

"Yes. I want to have our names written together before we take the picture. ☆"

After taking a closer look at the board, he noticed something resembling an umbrella or cross drawn in the middle, with Nonoa's name on the left side of the line.

Oof. Just when I thought this couldn't get more embarrassing.

Even though this was supposed to be an extraordinarily wonderful experience for customers at maid cafés, it felt like a public execution to Masachika. The glares were like daggers in his back, and the grudges forming against him were palpable.

"Master?"

Hesitantly, he gave in to Nonoa's pressure and wrote his name on the board, but he didn't stop there. Underneath their names, he added: *"Fly High! We Are the Next Student Council!"* Unsurprisingly, Nonoa's face went blank for a few moments before her lips curled like a cunning cat's.

"*Giggle*. You're so funny. ☆"

But after her soft whisper, she smiled angelically.

"All right! We're ready over here!" she declared while turning to face Sayaka. Only then was Masachika able to sigh in relief, because at the end of the day, he honestly didn't have a humiliation fetish. All he wanted to do was emphasize that Team Kujou and Kuze were working together with Team Taniyama and Miyamae, and when you thought about it that way, it wasn't that embarrassing—

"Now, make a heart with your hands in front of your chest, okay? I'll count down, like, 'Three, two, one, and love beam!' Then we'll take the picture," the head maid instructed heartlessly.

Masachika died a little inside that day.

"The curry was really good, wasn't it?"

"Yeah, it had a lot of meat and vegetables in it, too. It actually ended up being a lot more worthwhile than I was expecting."

Masachika, Alisa, and Yuki got out of their seats, satisfied with the finely cooked curry that had exceeded their expectations.

"I'm not gonna give up yet! It's time to limit-break!" someone roared.

"No backing out now!" another cried out.

The trio headed over to the register to pay for their food while pretending not to notice the shouting victims who were far past the point of no return.

"Here is your picture from earlier. Congratulations."

"Wow, thanks..."

He honestly didn't want it. If anything, it would surely become an embarrassing reminder of today, so he wanted to throw it right in the trash, but he wasn't comfortable tossing it in front of so many people.

I guess I could just wait until I got home to throw it away...

Without even glancing at the picture, Masachika immediately tucked it away in his breast pocket, and after they left the café, they decided to follow the plans they'd made while they ate and head over to the schoolyard.

"Excuse me. ☆"

"Whoa."

Nonoa passed right by them, seemingly heading over to grab more food from Class F's classroom while every student in the hallway pursued her with their eyes. Regardless, the three didn't even have to peek inside the classroom to know what was happening, for when they were passing by—

"I know you have all been very busy, but I know you can do it! I'm counting on you. ♡"

"You can count on us! Men, let's do this!"

""""Yeah!!""""

Masachika stared off into space while listening to the voices of perfectly trained soldiers in the background. Alisa, on the other hand, glanced at the classroom with a twinge of surprise but soon nodded as if it all made sense to her.

"I was wondering why I didn't see any male students working at the café. It looks like they were all sent to the kitchen to work."

"Yeah, I'm guessing it had to be a guy who came up with the idea to do a maid café...but something about this seems off. It's like they created a world where men are at the bottom of the social ladder."

Maids were draining money from their male patrons while their male classmates did all the physical labor. Perhaps Sayaka's leadership skills were enhanced by Nonoa's devilish magic, because it almost seemed like brainwashing.

"Chef! We have trouble! We don't have enough pots to prepare all the food!"

"Tsk. Then go buy one, ya numbskull!"

"Wait. You want me to go buy another stockpot...?"

"What's the problem? The ladies out there are working hard to take care of our customers, so it's time for you to start taking your job seriously, too!"

"...! Yes, sir!"

The boys' exchange went beyond the average conversation between meatheads and sounded more like something one might hear in the military.

"...There's a lot of shady stuff going on at that café, now that I think about it."

"I know it is a little too late to be saying this, but I am starting to feel like Sayaka and Nonoa may have been real MVPs as student council president and vice-president in middle school, if we hadn't beaten them."

"It doesn't sound like they're forcing their classmates, either... Hell, if you wanted to put a positive spin on it, I guess you could say that they did a good job uniting these guys to work together?"

The three conversed with awkward, uncomfortable expressions while they retreated from the area. They went around checking the other classes' attractions and booths for the next thirty minutes until Yuki suddenly checked the clock and suggested:

"Oh, it appears I only have twenty more minutes until I have to return to my duties for the school festival committee, so I was wondering if we could go see my class's attraction."

After the other two agreed, they stopped by the freshmen's Class A room, which had been decorated like a traditional Japanese festival, with paper lanterns decorating the walls, yo-yo fishing, target shooting, and even a ring toss.

"Welcome to— A-Alisa Kujou?! Whoa..."

A boy near the entrance was wide-eyed with his mouth agape, rendered speechless by the sight of Alisa. The other students were no different when they looked in the direction of the astonished voice, only to be taken aback and tongue-tied as well. Even though this neighboring class was relatively used to seeing Alisa around, seeing her dressed as an elf seemed to be far too shocking.

"Good afternoon, everyone. I will be showing these two around, so please do not mind us," announced Yuki to her mentally numb classmates, snapping them back to reality. Time resumed, but even though everyone went back to work, they couldn't help but glance at Alisa every so often, despite being busy with other customers. Fortunately, the customers seemed to be having a hard time keeping their eyes off Alisa as well.

"So, Alya, is there anything you would like to try out?"

"Oh, uh... Well, I would like to try the yo-yo fishing, since I wasn't able to catch a single balloon at the last festival we went to."

The instant those words left Alisa's lips, the customer at the yo-yo fishing booth immediately moved out of the way, which, unsurprisingly, startled her.

"C-come! Try your luck yo-yo fishing, young lady!" stuttered the male student at the yo-yo fishing stall with clear delight and a sense of superiority in his voice while gesturing a welcome. However, before Alisa could timidly make her way over to the stall, Masachika took off his robe and handed it to her.

"...? What?"

"Tie it around your waist. Remember how soaked your legs got last time?"

"Oh..."

Unlike Masachika's robe, which was some cheap mass-produced piece of fabric, Alisa's costume was of exceptionally high quality and handmade, to boot, so getting it wet would be a shame. At least, that was the excuse Masachika was going with, since in actuality, all he wanted to do was make sure nobody could see her underwear when she squatted in front of the booth. After Alisa looked back at him sharply yet a little bashfully, as if she realized his true intentions, she thanked him softly while accepting the robe. Masachika then followed her to the yo-yo fishing booth, but it was only a matter of seconds before a crowd had formed around her. Masachika smiled wryly.

"Seriously? What about the other booths?"

Witnessing her classmates in charge of other booths abandoning their duties seemed to make Yuki scowl.

"Well, I suppose it is not that big of a deal, since all the customers have gathered around to watch... It would seem Alya's presence alone is bad for business."

"Yeah... By the way, should I crack a joke about the 'air' that has been following us around yet?"

"Please continue to pretend you don't see her. It seems to be a touchy subject for maids such as her."

"All right."

"At any rate, is there anything here that piques your interest? You are my guest today. Unfortunately, we cannot give you any prizes, though."

"No prizes?"

"Of course not. You would win every last prize and leave us with nothing if we allowed that, right?"

"Good point."

They spoke a little more casually with each other, since there was no one else around.

"Oh… But now that I think about it, I do believe that even you would have trouble winning *that.*"

Yuki pointed toward the middle of the top shelf at the target-shooting booth where a stuffed bear was placed. Unlike the other prizes, it sat firmly on the shelf, making it clear that it was going to take more than a few weak shots to knock it off.

"…I feel almost intimidated by it."

"That teddy bear is apparently one of a kind and was handmade by a famous craftsman for a very well-known brand in England, so you can imagine how highly coveted a prize like that would be among enthusiasts."

"Then why are you using it as a prize at a school festival?"

"Because this is Seirei Academy."

"Tsk. Good point," muttered Masachika while he headed toward the target-shooting booth, since above all, it was his duty as the older brother to never back down when challenged.

"It will be three hundred yen for five shots," Yuki said.

"You're gonna make me pay?"

"In return, I promise you can have that teddy bear if you knock it down," she vowed with a serious, calm expression. However, a devilish grin almost immediately appeared, revealing her true self, while she added in a whisper, "How about giving it to Alya, my dear brother? That way, she'll always have something to remind her of today."

After glancing over his shoulder seriously at Alisa at the yo-yo fishing booth, Masachika quietly took out his wallet.

"I'll take five corks."

"Here you are."

Once Yuki handed him the ammunition, he loaded the rifle as if it were second nature. Then he focused on the front sight to make sure it was aimed right at the teddy bear, and silently pulled the trigger, hitting the teddy bear directly on the head…

…only for the cork to bounce right off of it.

"What kind of peashooter is this? You couldn't make this thing any weaker."

"I told you that it was impossible."

"Sure, but even crane games are set where the arms are strong enough to make you think you have a chance of winning."

The beautiful shot to the forehead just barely made its head wiggle as it remained proudly perched on the shelf.

"…Hey, Yuki. How many rifles do you have?" asked Masachika, while observing how ever so slightly the teddy bear leaned forward.

"…? Four in total."

"Get them out."

Once Yuki lined up the four rifles on the table, Masachika took his remaining corks and loaded one into each gun.

"…Do you plan on firing all these rifles in a row? I highly doubt that is going to work."

"Yuki…" He muttered her name as if he were scolding her for hastily jumping to conclusions, then shifted his gaze back to the teddy bear. "I've actually been practicing my chi blasts lately."

"Yo, seriously? You're a real-life superhero."

Masachika snorted at his sister's inner nerd seeping out, then slowly lifted his chin while he got into position with the rifle.

"Watch and learn. It's all about how you channel your inner chi," Masachika claimed audaciously as he pulled the trigger. The cork flew right under the teddy bear, bounced off the blackboard behind it, then directly hit the prize on the back of the head. Without even checking to make sure he'd hit it, Masachika immediately switched guns and accurately hit the same spot again and again, slowly pushing the teddy bear forward until it fell onto the shelf below and knocked down those prizes along with it.

"Cha-ching."

"What do you mean 'cha-ching'? I didn't see any chi blast."

"That's because chi's invisible."

"Oh, shut up," said Yuki, sighing and rolling her eyes while she picked up the teddy bear.

"*Sigh*… I still can't believe you pulled it off. I was hoping to keep it around so it could be tomorrow's big prize, but well, a promise is a promise. Here."

Masachika glanced over at Alisa with a sharp grin while Yuki handed him the stuffed animal.

"Heh. Go on. It's time for you to both embarrass her and make her happy at the very same time ♪," jeered Yuki. However, Masachika handed the teddy bear right back to her.

"Hmm…?"

"It's yours."

"Huh?"

Yuki seemed genuinely baffled.

"You're allowed to have teddy bears now, right?" pointed out Masachika with sweet yet rather sorrowful eyes. Yuki used to have terrible asthma when they lived together as children, so she hadn't been allowed to have any stuffed animals or anything else that easily collected dust and germs. Even the stuffed animal she used to carry around as a baby was taken away, and she had to stay in an extremely simple, hospital-like bedroom where cleanliness was prioritized above all. That was why Masachika was never able to give her any of the stuffed animals he used to win at the arcade, and it was that regret that moved him to give her the prize.

"…"

Yuki squeezed the teddy bear tightly and lowered her gaze. Her shoulders trembled for a few seconds, as if she was trying to hold back her emotions, but she eventually lifted her chin and had a calm, composed expression on her face.

"Phew… That was a close one. I'm glad I caught myself before doing something dangerous in broad daylight. In my own classroom, to boot."

"What were you going to do?"

"*Sigh*. What are you doing, trying to raise my affinity even more? My affinity's already at max level."

"Just trying to maintain what I have."

"Tsk. How can my brother be this lovable?" muttered Yuki, burying her mouth in the teddy bear while bashfully swaying side to side.

"*Giggle*... Oh, come on... My dear brother, why are you my older brother?"

"Because I was born before you."

"That's it? Guess I don't need to respect you, then," replied Yuki with a surprisingly straight face.

"Where did that come from?" But after thinking about it for a moment, he came to a sudden realization and shot his sister a reproachful glare. "Actually, I can't even think of a single moment where you've actually shown me any respect."

"...You know what? Me neither."

"I rest my case."

"If you want respect, then you're going to have to show me that you deserve it."

"If you want me to be an older brother who you can respect, then you're going to have to show me that you deserve it."

"Do you have an issue with having the cutest little sister in the world?"

"Well, I do have an issue with her sudden mood swings."

"I felt someone watching me, so I had to switch back to 'lady mode.'"

"What kind of superpower is that?"

"Pretty cool, huh?"

"Pretty weird if you ask me."

But after tittering elegantly, Yuki slipped and cracked another goofy smile.

"Thank you, Masachika."

"You're welcome."

He almost reached out to rub her head, but immediately caught himself and nodded instead. Nevertheless, Yuki gently smiled as if not even a movement as subtly aborted as that could get by her. Sibling love was in the air...until a cold gust of wind blew by, making both of them flinch.

They immediately looked for the source and found Alisa glaring right at them through the crowd. The surrounding students backed away, intimidated by her ominous aura as she stood like a ghostly revenant. Parting the crowd like Moses in the story of the Red Sea, she approached and smiled at Masachika with dead, joyless eyes.

"You look like you're having fun."

"Y-yeah, you too. I heard everyone cheering."

"Yes… It wasn't easy, but I finally caught a balloon."

"Really? That's awe—!"

"So? What were you two doing while I was struggling all by myself?"

She tilted her head and grinned mirthlessly, making it obvious that she would kill him if he even joked that they were flirting, so he decided to stick to the truth instead.

"…I was shooting targets," he stated matter-of-factly.

"And?"

"Yuki said I couldn't get the grand prize…so I decided to prove her wrong."

"Oh? Then?"

"I won the grand prize…but, well…I didn't really want the teddy bear for myself…so I gave it to her."

"Is that so?" said Alisa.

At that moment, the other students in Class A seemed to realize the development as well.

"What the…?! Hold up! Did he knock the teddy bear off the shelf?!"

"No way! I can't believe I missed it!"

"Nah, man. There's no way he could have done that. Was nobody watching?"

However, Yuki turned to a corner of the classroom and asked:

"He won fair and square. Right, Ayano?"

Ayano, who had been indistinguishable from air the entire time, took a step forward.

"That is correct," she agreed with a blank expression, blowing the minds of every student there. Cries of agony immediately filled the air. Some were voices of disappointment, while others were panicking about the rest of the festival, since they didn't have a grand prize anymore. The room was swallowed by utter chaos until Ayano, as if rather proud and full of profound emotion, suddenly announced:

SHAVED ICE

"It was truly an incredible display of superhuman skill. To be able to see his chi blast—"

"Wait, wait, wait!" shouted Masachika in a panic…while the room instantly fell silent. Everyone appeared stunned as they stared hard at Ayano and Masachika.

"His 'chi' what?"

"Is this some kind of joke?"

"Cringe."

"Guys, wait! It was just a joke!"

But despite his desperate attempts to explain himself, neither their disgust nor the awkwardness ever went away.

"Masachika…"

"Y-yes, Alya?"

"…I know this is our school festival, and I know you like to play, but don't go overboard, okay?"

"Stop looking at me like you feel sorry for me!"

Masachika's yowl echoed throughout Class A's classroom…and then there was silence.

I haven't argued this passionately since the debate.

"I said I'm sorry. Come on, cheer up."

"I'm perfectly fine."

After being branded a "cringelord" by the students of Class A, Masachika roamed the hallway alongside Alisa in a bid to smooth things over with her. He understood why she was upset, though. After all, Alisa must have put on quite a show, since everyone had been cheering. She had failed once before, but this time, she finally caught a balloon after most likely missing countless times with her fishing string, so the taste of sweet revenge must have been incredible…until she turned around and realized that the two people who she came with weren't even watching her grudge match and were enjoying themselves without her. Even Masachika would feel unbearably lonely and left out if Takeshi and Hikaru did that to him.

"<You're supposed to be my partner…>"

"…Stop mumbling in Russian. You're scaring me."

Hearing her say that was unbearable for a whole new reason.

"Like…I know this just sounds like an excuse, but I was really planning on watching you yo-yo fish. But you saw the crowd. Everyone was surrounding you and blocking the way. You're too popular…," rambled Masachika, prompting Alisa to fidget with her hair and glance at him.

"…Says the guy who everyone depends on."

"Huh? What are you talking about?"

"When it was your shift, you naturally took control, and our classmates did whatever you said."

"…Oh."

She made a good point. Masachika provided a lot of direction to his classmates as a member of the school festival committee, whether he realized it or not. Nevertheless, even if opinions of him had changed, most of his peers probably thought he was some stupid, lazy nerd up until the end of the first semester. Of course, it wasn't to the point that people would make fun of him to his face, but many viewed him as being beneath them, which probably also had to do with the fact that he came from a middle-class family.

Regardless, Masachika personally didn't really care what his fellow students thought about him. If anything, he felt that being a little despised would actually help smooth the relationship between him and his peers. There were sayings like, "*The nail that sticks out gets hammered down*" and "*He who knows the most often says the least*" for a reason. Making himself stand out would get others' attention, but if they thought little of him, then they would let their guard down, which would allow him to gain their trust. Ultimately, he could easily reveal his value after gaining their trust. Furthermore, once someone saw his value, they would change how they acted around him, and if they didn't, then all he had to do was butter them up a little until he was the one in control. However, for the most part, Masachika didn't want anyone to expect anything from him.

"Yeah…I guess you have a point."

He couldn't recall himself proving he had value, but he did feel like his class had started to see him in a more positive light. The cause of this change…wasn't even something that he needed to think about. Everything changed after he joined the student council.

"It must have been the speech you made during the closing ceremony."

"Huh? Oh… Yeah, probably," agreed Masachika after pondering it for a moment. Looking back, he realized he'd told the entire school that he was the student council vice president in middle school behind the scenes—a sort of shadow vice president. Yuki was an extraordinarily capable partner, which was why he decided to do everything he could to support her from behind the scenes while staying out of sight whenever Yuki took the stage. That was why most students had no idea he was even the vice president in middle school until he announced it himself at the closing ceremony. Even his classmates were surprised when they heard the news.

"I guess it probably helped boost everyone's opinion of me a little? Then once the second semester started, maybe I gained some of our class's respect while working for the school festival committee? I'm starting to feel like I'm bragging..."

"That's what I think happened. They depend way more on you than they ever did on me."

"Nah, I mean... They're probably just dumping all the boring jobs on me, since they know I'll do it," joked Masachika, concerned that she might start feeling like she wasn't good enough to be his partner again. "But yeah... I guess you can't hide talent when you've got it," he said, grinning smugly while combing his bangs back with his fingers.

"<You should have tried hiding it a little longer...,>" whispered Alisa in Russian. Then she pouted and looked the other way.

"Uh... Are you still mad?"

"No. I was only worried that you might forget our promise."

"Our promise?"

Masachika tilted his head in genuine bewilderment...and was met with her piercing glare. Flustered, he promptly traced his memories until it hit him: the conversation they'd had on the staircase by the music room.

"O-ohhh, that? You mean how we promised we'd check out the school festival together? ...Wait. Isn't that what we're doing right now?"

"This... This doesn't count. You didn't even invite me."

"...? Is that important?"

"Very. Besides, the promise wasn't that we'd check out the festival together. It was that you'd show me a good time."

In other words, she wasn't having fun right now. In fact, she was in a bad mood because of Masachika, so it wasn't even up for debate.

"<Plus, it wasn't just the two of us, either.>"

Oh, right... Good point.

"<And you should actually ask me, too.>"

I'm sorry.

"<Be more romantic about it.>"

Now you're just making things difficult.

It sounded like Alisa wanted him to formally ask her out on a date, and judging by her behavior, she wanted to maintain the high ground where she was a princess and had all the power. It was as if she were saying, "I suppose I could allow you to show me a good time at the festival if you swallow your pride and invite me," and if that were the case, then Masachika could kind of understand what she meant when she said this didn't count.

"I'm sorry… I'll make it up to you tomorrow, okay?"

"…Okay," she replied curtly, before looking away with a pout, clearly upset that he was trying to claim that *this* was him keeping his promise.

Uh… What now? I mean, obviously, I'm in the wrong here, but still…

If anything, I should be grateful that she gave me the chance to make it up to her, he thought, while watching Alisa briskly walk ahead.

However, when he noticed a student up ahead holding up their phone, Masachika swiftly slid in front of Alisa and stretched out his robe with his right hand to conceal her body.

"Not so fast. I completely understand why you would want to take a picture of this beautiful elf, but you must get permission first," warned Masachika somewhat jokingly. The male student grimaced before swiftly running away, but Masachika's relief only lasted for a few seconds.

"Really? We can get a picture as long as we ask first?"

A handful of female students nearby crowded around them with smartphones at the ready, as if they'd taken what he'd said seriously. Masachika froze, but it didn't stop there. Other students, who happened to be passing by, stopped in their tracks as if they realized this was their chance.

"No, uh… It was more like a figure of speech, so—"

"Alisa! Look over here!"

"Elven Princess! May I take your picture?"

"Excuse me. If you don't mind, I'd love to take a picture with you…"

Numerous extroverts slowly closed in on Alisa while paying no heed to Masachika.

Hey?! They're being really pushy! What should I do? Should I be more forgiving, since we're in the middle of an election campaign? Surely these girls aren't going to be taking any lewd pictures, either... Wait. If I let one of them take a picture, then every single person on school grounds is going to want one.

Masachika decided to see what Alisa wanted to do first, so he turned around, only to find her already looking up at him with a troubled gaze.

Oh, uh... Yep. She's in no mood to smile for a picture right now. I need to be firm and politely tell these girls to leave her alone.

But right as he faced forward to politely refuse...

"Ladies, being pushy isn't an attractive trait."

Everyone, including Masachika, looked in the direction of the dignified, silencing voice, and their minds instantly went blank, for standing before them was a band of female knights—courage and virtue personified. Standing at the fore was a radiantly beautiful girl with honey-blond hair tied into two spiral-curled pigtails. She was the captain of the girls' kendo club and the vice president of the disciplinary committee, Sumire Kiryuuin.

"Sumire...!"

"How fierce...!"

Even the girls who wanted to take a picture with Alisa were captivated by Sumire's gallant charm. She leisurely approached them, then locked eyes with Masachika. Understanding that she was there to help, he lowered the hand holding his robe open. After a smug snort of satisfaction, Sumire shifted her gaze back toward the female students and suggested:

"You should be chivalrous when approaching a lady; don't surround her. Observe..."

Sumire elegantly pushed back her cape, then took a knee and placed her right hand over her chest while holding out her left hand to Alisa.

"O beautiful elven princess, would you do me the honor of allowing me to capture this moment for eternity?"

"...O-okay."

The knight's decorum was that of a fairy-tale prince that all girls dreamed of. Even Alisa unconsciously gave her approval.

""""*Squeeeal!!*""""

The girls' squeals reverberated through the hallway to the point that the windows almost started to shake... In fact, they actually did shake. Sumire then casually stood back up in the midst of their excitement, as if to protect Alisa.

"Do you understand, ladies? A lack of manners has no place in Seirei Academy," she reprimanded softly. "However, I don't expect any of you to be able to instantly be as graceful as I am, so I suppose I could teach you all how it's done," continued Sumire as she cast a sidelong glance at the closest girl.

"You, try what I showed you, and I'll help."

"O-okay... Um... W-would you do me the honor...?"

"You do not have to force yourself to recite it word for word. Use your own words but be chivalrous."

"Um...! Would you mind if I took a picture of you?"

"Be my guest."

After an elegant chuckle, Sumire posed and smiled perfectly for the camera while simultaneously waving her free hand behind her back, prompting Masachika to take Alisa and rush off. Of course, he didn't forget to whisper a few words of gratitude before leaving, either.

"Thank you, Violet."

"It's Sumire!"

It appeared that even during a time like this, she still wasn't going to let him get away with that. Masachika smirked a bit as he watched her pose for pictures while directing traffic.

"Wow, she has real talent for handling stuff like that. It's like she knows exactly how to enchant others. She can be a little theatrical with her approach like her cousin Yuushou, though," he muttered in admiration, although perhaps the only reason why he always found Yuushou's noble behavior somehow nasty was because he was a guy.

"Anyway, are you okay, Alya? I guess that's just the price you have to pay for being so popular."

"Yes, I'm fine... Thanks for sticking up for me," she said softly, while averting her gaze.

"Don't worry about it. If anything, I probably made things worse, so I'm really sorry about that." He shrugged.

"Don't blame yourself. Besides, I had no idea what to do, so I have no right to blame you for anything."

"Well, this isn't going to be the last time something like that happens, so maybe we both have to work on how we handle these situations."

"...Yeah."

Not much was said after that. While it seemed like Alisa was feeling better, there seemed to be a little tension in the air, which Masachika was trying to figure out how to clear. His gaze began to wander for answers when he suddenly locked on a nearby classroom.

"Oh, this must be the magician bar that Masha and Chisaki were talking about. Want to check it out?"

"Huh? ...Sure, I guess."

"All right, then. Excuse me. Can we get a table for two?"

"Come on in, and take a seat wherever you'd like."

When the student at the entrance escorted them inside, Masachika immediately squinted, surprised by how much dimmer it was than he expected. Jazz was softly playing in the background, which complemented the relaxed mood of the place. Long tables were lined up, creating a U-shape with the opening facing the entrance, and each table had a different close-up magic performance.

"Oh, Alya! Kuze! Thanks for coming. ♪"

They turned in the direction of the familiar voice to find Maria waving them over.

"Whoa! Masha... You look really...mature, I guess you could say."

"Really? Thanks. Wow! Alya, you look so cute, too!"

Her usual cheerful smile almost made Masachika smile, but it was her bartender attire—a shirt and vest—combined with the relaxed atmosphere that made her charming in a more mature way than usual. Although Maria had always been older than Masachika, she really seemed like the sweet, mature, big sister type right now, which made his heart race.

Oh, gosh... This isn't good... If an older woman like this pressured me to drink, I'd probably drink until I dropped.

That was the first thought that crossed his mind as he made his way over to Maria's table. A large tablecloth hid its short legs, perhaps to prevent the customers from seeing anything below the magician's waist. The tables also seemed to be positioned in a way that prevented customers from approaching the magicians from behind.

"Oops. I kind of sat before even asking you if you were okay with this table, Alya."

"It's fine… I'm not sure we're actually going to be able to see any magic at this table, though."

"Heyyy. ♪ Rude. ♪ Your big sister here has more than a few tricks up her sleeve. I practiced a lot, you know?"

Maria placed a hand on her hip with a pout, but her lips almost immediately curled into a bubbly smile while she handed them a menu.

"What will it be? This goes without saying, but there is no alcohol in any of these drinks, so you don't have to worry."

The menu was full of what appeared to be countless mocktails, which were consistent with the magician bar's concept. However, although Masachika had a faint idea of what some of these drinks were, Alisa seemed to be absolutely clueless. She was frozen in front of the menu as if she were staring at a bunch of gibberish. Nevertheless, her pride most likely wouldn't allow her to even ask her sister what anything was, so she only continued to glare at the menu in silence.

"I'll have the Cinderella," she finally said.

"Oh, I'll have the same thing…"

"Two Cinderellas coming right up. ♪ *Giggle.* The prince isn't going to know what to do when he sees this. ♪"

Even Maria must have realized that Alisa was too proud to ask for help, but she pretended like she didn't notice, took their menus, and squatted, but after some rattling and clinking, she stood back up with a cocktail shaker and glasses in her hands.

"Please give me a moment while I prepare your Cinderellas. ♪ I'm no fairy godmother, but I'll try my best." She mentioned this, strangely, while pulling the shaker in half before pouring bottled water into the lower half.

"Hmm? Hold on."

But despite Alisa's confusion, Maria connected the two halves of the cocktail shaker, shook it a few times, took off the lid, then began pouring…a yellow liquid into a glass.

"Huh? Ah!" uttered Alisa in genuine wonder before immediately closing her mouth in embarrassment. Nevertheless, her surprise didn't go unnoticed, and a smile curled Maria's lips as she placed the glass before Alisa.

"Ta-daa. One Cinderella for the lady."

"Wow!"

Masachika began to clap, followed by Alisa, albeit somewhat reluctantly. Of course, Masachika saw right through the trick, since he was a nerd and understood that one day he might be kidnapped and forced to play a game where his life was on the line, so he'd memorized every single cheap trick and sleight-of-hand move that he could in order to prepare.

The secret to this trick was simple. There were independent containers already in the top half and bottom half of the cocktail shaker, and the top half's container already had all the necessary ingredients inside of it to make a Cinderella. Of course, Masachika wasn't the kind of person who would obnoxiously point that out, though, since it would only be polite to pretend to be surprised even if you really weren't.

"Are you ready for my next trick?"

Maria proceeded to take out a place mat and a deck of cards. She then spread the mat over the table and put the deck of cards on top of it with a very natural movement, showing just how much she must have practiced.

"All right, I am going to separate the deck into two piles. Kuze, I want you to tell me to stop whenever you'd like, okay?"

"Sure."

Masachika continued to pretend like he was a clueless audience member and followed orders.

Like Alya, I was a little worried at first…but she's going to be fine. But, well, I guess it makes sense. Masha always acts bubbly when she's around Alya, but she's actually a really hard worker.

He was relieved for the time being, but that was only due to his ignorance, for he had no idea that there was a relatively distinct rule pertaining to whether Maria was a big sister or a bubbly sister. It was, however, actually a rather simple rule. The more Maria felt like she needed to get it together and take something seriously, the more of a big sister she became. This change would occur when she met someone who she needed to be wary of or when she was with someone who was utterly helpless on their own. On the flip side, the more she could trust the person she was with, the less pressure she felt to pull herself together, which allowed her mind to wander freely, making her into a bubbly sister—aka an idiot.

Now, who were the two people she was currently with? Alisa and Masachika—the two people she trusted and loved the most. Thanks to these two, her level of joy was through the roof, bringing her to cloud nine. A big, fat, happy cloud. If one were to measure her current IQ, it would be 50 when rounding up. As a result…

What the…? Shouldn't she have done a double lift there?

Although Masachika felt like something was off, Maria continued as if she didn't have a care in the world.

"I am placing the card that Alya picked into my pocket, but with a little magic… Three, two, one!"

Maria's fingers might as well have been two wet hot dogs as she attempted to snap over the stack of cards. She then grabbed the very top card and began to flip it over…before placing it back facedown.

"Hmm?"

"……"

She was supposed to flip the card over, and yet they were once again staring at the back of a card, for some reason… It was the last thing a magician would ever want the audience to see.

"Sorry, Masha, but do you think I could get another glass of this?"

"Oh, sure. Coming right up."

Unable to come up with any words of comfort or surprise, Masachika decided to just pretend like he hadn't seen anything. Not even Alisa seemed to know what to say as she took another sip of her drink. Even though Maria was her sister, she didn't seem like she was even comfortable joking about it.

"A-anyway, my next trick involves a cup and a ball!"

Thanks to their kind gesture, Maria promptly tried to move on to different props for her next tricks…but everything else she tried that day ended in disaster. Not a single trick went as she announced it would, and the audience saw everything they weren't supposed to see, to boot. Every time Masachika and Alisa saw a mistake, they would take a drink, and before long, they were each on their fourth Cinderella.

"Mmm… I'm really sorry. It looks like today's just not my day."

"Just like every day," Alisa stated.

"No, uh… I think you did really well. It's just really hard to perform in front of family, isn't it?" Masachika said sympathetically.

Like this, every failure was met with a cold remark from Alisa, so Masachika chimed in with a few words of encouragement until eventually, the door to the classroom slid open. Maria curiously turned toward the entrance, and her face immediately lit up.

"Oh! Chisaki! Come over here!"

"Hmm? What's wrong, Masha?"

Standing at the door was Chisaki, wearing bartender attire and a violet crystal earring dangling from one ear. Although she was wearing pants, she looked really good in them because she was tall, and her sharp facial features only further complemented her mature look.

"Whoa! You look badass."

"Ha-ha! Thanks."

Even the way she smiled back at the genuine compliment made her seem confident and mature, almost making Masachika gasp in admiration. On the other hand, his body temperature also dropped three degrees, but he pretended not to notice.

"I'm so sorry. ♪ I keep messing up all the tricks, and I feel really guilty, so do you think you could show them a trick or two?"

"Huh? Oh, sure…"

After curiously blinking a few times, Chisaki stuffed a hand into her vest pocket while trading places with Maria.

"Ahem! All right, then. You want to see a trick? Then how about this? Here is a single coin."

She took an arcade token out of her vest pocket and placed it on the table.

"As you can see, it's just any ordinary coin. Feel free to pick it up and see for yourself."

After clinking the token on the table a few times, Chisaki handed it to Masachika, who softly rolled it around in his hand for a second before passing it to Alisa. Most of the time, there was nothing special about the coin if the magician handed it to the audience. If anything, the coin was only handed to the audience to buy them some time to start the actual trick, such as replacing said coin with a trick coin, and that was why Masachika was more interested in what Chisaki's hands were doing than he was in the token.

Well, she doesn't look like she's holding anything, and if she's going to do a trick with a single coin, then maybe it's going to be all technique and no gimmicks?

Numerous thoughts flew through his mind until Alisa finished checking the coin and passed it back to Chisaki.

"Now, pay close attention, for I am about to split this coin in half," announced Chisaki with a grin oozing with confidence.

"You're going to split it in half?"

"Hi-yah!"

"Whoa!"

"...?!"

The magician's hand sliced right through the coin like paper, creating two semicircles with their edges bending in the opposite direction.

"Ta-daa. I have split the coin in two."

"Yeah, you did. Wow."

"Huh? How...? Huh?"

The two fragments of metal clinked in the palm of Chisaki's hand.

"Next, I'm going to squeeze both halves of the coin together," she revealed, squeezing both halves of the coin in her right hand and raising her fist to eye height while starting a countdown with her left hand.

"Ready? Three, two, one, haaah!"

She tightly clenched her fist with what sounded closer to a battle cry than a magic word, then slowly opened her right hand to reveal...

"Ta-daa! The two halves of the coin have magically turned into a pachinko ball!"

"Wow."

"A pachinko ball…?"

Although clapping, Alisa tilted her head in confusion, which even Masachika could empathize with. After all, the surface of the pachinko ball had the same pattern on it that the token did. Nevertheless, nobody pointed this out, since that was the polite thing to do, and it definitely had nothing to do with them being afraid of her.

"So? What do you think? Pretty cool trick, right?"

"You could be a world champion."

"I think I just witnessed a miracle…"

Masachika nodded firmly back at Alisa, making Chisaki bashfully scratch her blushing cheek, although it wasn't clear whether or not she knew why they were so impressed.

"Really? I'm so glad you liked it. I'm going to have to thank my master later for teaching me how to do that."

"Who's your master??"

"Uh… She's actually my grandmother."

"An elderly woman sage…? Wait. No. Maybe a being from an elder race?"

"I'm really happy you two had fun. Anyway, it sounds like Masha messed up a lot, so feel free to pay whatever you think is fair."

"That actually sounds like a threat after what we just witnessed."

"Wait. What?"

"Nothing."

After paying their genuinely puzzled schoolmate the menu prices for the drinks, Alisa and Masachika retired from the classroom.

"…So much for seeing a magic show, huh?"

"Yeah… Neither of them really showed us any magic."

Whatever you would call what they witnessed at the end was probably more impressive than magic, though.

"How did she do that with the token, though? Maybe it was some sort of soft metal?"

"I don't know. I'm starting to wonder if that was even a trick."

"It definitely wasn't as obvious as all the tricks Masha did.

Sigh… I feel like I've had tons of magic tricks ruined for me in just a single day…"

"Ha-ha. Yeah."

"*Sigh*… How does she do it? I hear that a lot of students really count on her as a member of the student council, too…"

"…"

Masachika smiled back at her skeptical gaze. Alisa must have really believed that her sister was some bubbly, carefree airhead. Ultimately, that was actually how she always acted whenever Alisa was around, so it was no surprise she would get that impression.

She's probably never seen just how strong and reliable her sister can really be.

Although it was kind of a shame, Maria herself wanted Alisa to see her as this "unreliable sister," so Masachika didn't say a word, no matter how much he wanted to.

"Anyway, it's about time we get back to work. Want to go get changed?"

"Oh… Yeah, sure."

"I'm guessing we should stop by the craft clubroom to give the costume back?" asked Masachika, checking out Alisa's high-quality elf costume. Alisa promptly agreed, so they decided to head there together first.

"Oooh, Masachika. Welcome."

"Oh, hey."

He waved to the female acquaintance at the door. She was a beautiful, petite girl with long black hair that was tied back into a ponytail. Put simply, she was the kind of girl you would want to introduce to your parents. Back when Masachika was the vice president of the student council in middle school, she was the captain of the craft club and his classmate as well, so they had a very give-and-take relationship. Furthermore, she was what some would describe as a beautiful, sweet nerd, which made her quite popular with certain boys. However, to Masachika, she was Professor Side Slit—a name she'd earned after some words of wisdom she'd once offered long ago. Again, she was not a professor but Masachika's classmate.

"It doesn't look like you came to check out our exhibition."

"Yeah, we're here to get Alya changed back into her clothes."

"Roger. I'll call the girls who made that costume. Oh, feel free to check out our exhibition in the meantime, okay?"

The instant they stepped into the room, they were surrounded by full-sized mannequins and mannequin torsos dressed in everything from the usual wedding dress to gothic Lolita attire, a dancer costume, a tuxedo, and even a military uniform. The room was crammed with handmade clothing asserting everyone's own tastes and preferences.

"Uh… Wow. I feel like I'm in a cosplay shop."

"That's essentially what it is. Everyone just made whatever they wanted," replied the Professor.

"Whoa! This is some elaborate lace! This looks extremely well done…"

"This dress looks like something a pro made, too…"

The unbelievable degree of perfection captivated Masachika and Alisa, almost making them forget the entire reason they came. They continued to check out all the outfits on display for a while after that until Masachika suddenly glanced at Professor Side Slit and asked:

"Hey, seeing that Alya is wearing an elf costume you guys made, does that mean that you're renting out all the costumes on display here?"

"Huh? Oh, uh… We usually don't rent out any of our costumes, but if the person who made it says it's okay, then…?"

"In other words, as long as you look like a model, you're good."

"Yeah, basically. But you also have to be able to fit in the outfit, too. Of course, some minor adjustments can be made on the spot, though."

"Interesting… Hey, can you do me a little favor?"

They began to whisper back and forth, but when Alisa approached them looking skeptical, Masachika suddenly ended their conversation.

"…? Is something the matter?" asked Alisa.

"No. I was just telling her about how incredible your costume was and how everyone was trying to take your picture."

"Yes, yes. I totally get why they would want a picture, though."

Masachika inwardly thanked Professor Side Slit for playing along while he firmly nodded. Even though Alisa pressed her lips together into a thin line, she didn't seem to doubt them at all.

"It's not like this is anything new…but I never know how to respond whenever someone I don't really know asks me for a picture."

"Huh. Do people often ask you for a picture?"

"Sometimes. I always tell them 'no,' though."

"Man, that's rough. Sounds like being beautiful comes with a price," replied Masachika sympathetically. Alisa's gaze fell, and she began to fidget with her hair and whispered:

"<I wouldn't mind if you wanted to take my picture, though.>"

Seriously? thought Masachika, taken aback. Obviously, he would love to have a picture of her right now if given the option. After all, an elf this realistic needed to be caught on film. But even then, he still felt a bit hesitant to ask her for a picture after just shooing away so many others who wanted one…

Mmm…! What should I do? I know she'll let me take a picture if I ask, but that doesn't make it any less embarrassing! B-but if a moment of embarrassment was all it would cost to get a picture of Alya, then…!

After a few seconds of brain-frying consideration, Masachika had finally reached his answer.

"Alya."

"…?"

"I know this is a little strange of me to ask after all that…but do you think I could get a picture before you change? You know, something to remember today by," Masachika asked nonchalantly, being as casual about it as he could. Alisa's eyebrows instantly jumped up, before her eyes devilishly narrowed with amusement.

"Oh? Do you really want to take a picture of me that badly?"

"…I mean, as a nerd, I feel like it's my duty to capture an elf this realistic on film."

"…Uh-huh."

Although his response seemed to rub some of the amusement right off her face, she flicked her hair back and replied:

"Sure. You have my permission."

"Awesome. Thanks. Then—"

Masachika suddenly felt his shoulder being tapped a few times, so he looked back to find Professor Side Slit grinning at him while pointing toward the room next door.

"You're free to use the room where we usually store the costumes, if you want," she suggested.

"R-really? Thanks."

"Perfect."

When Professor Side Slit walked them to the room next door, the first thing that caught their attention was the dressers lined up on each side. Although most of the room was slightly dusty, the area by the window in the back was extremely well kept and free of clutter.

"You can use that area over there. The amount of sunlight you get is perfect for taking pictures," she assured them while pointing at the back.

"Yeah, it sure looks like it."

But only after having Alisa stand in the back did he realize just how nice a shot it was going to be. The clubroom building's architecture was Western-inspired, so it also worked relatively well as a background for an elf. Plus, there was something magical about having Alisa stand against the sun peeking in through the window.

"All right, I should head back to work," Professor Side Slit said.

"Oh, okay. Thanks."

"Don't mention it," replied Professor Side Slit like a badass as she exited the room.

"Okay, then… Ready?"

Masachika took out his smartphone.

"Huh?! But I need to think of a pose…"

"You're fine just like that for now."

"Really?"

There was no telling how she would look unless he tried, so Masachika opened the camera app, peered into the screen, and began to adjust the exposure, increasing brightness…

"Whoa…"

Standing before him was an elf straight out of a fantasy world, and staring at her through the camera lens only made her seem less real.

"All right, you ready?"

"R-ready."

Their hearts were pounding nervously while he tapped the button, but when he saw the picture on his phone, he instinctively gasped in admiration.

"...So beautiful..."

"What? D-did the picture really come out that good?"

"Yeah..."

"R-really? Then do you want to take a few more?"

"I would love that," he replied in a straightforward manner, forgetting he was ever even embarrassed. Immediately, Alisa averted her gaze, albeit rather cheerfully.

"<Ready to admire and cherish me?>"

No.

"<I suppose I wouldn't mind if you rubbed my head.>"

...Not happening. Are you still letting that joke I told Yuki bother you? he thought. Fed up, he narrowed his gaze and just continued pressing the shutter button, taking one picture after another. Each time Alisa changed her pose and he took another picture, he would find something new that captivated him until he became completely immersed in his role. It was only after he'd taken around thirty or so pictures when...

"Hmm?"

...he suddenly felt like something was off and promptly checked the pictures he'd just taken.

"...?!"

Masachika's eyes opened as wide as a fish's, for Alisa's white skirt displayed on the screen...was undeniably see-through, creating a silhouette of her lower body. He had no idea why he hadn't realized this sooner. Regardless, the bright sunlight coming in through the window seemed to have been working in perfect harmony with the camera settings to create what could only be described as a miracle. Of course, her underpants weren't transparent or anything. Obviously. But...the outline of Alisa's beautiful legs under the white skirt was extremely lewd.

"What's wrong?"

"Oh, uh..."

But Masachika's struggles only truly began after he reflexively denied that anything was wrong. Alisa had no idea that he had taken such a miraculous photograph. In addition, it wasn't like you could see anything too risqué, like her underwear. Nevertheless, the gentlemanly thing to do would be to delete the picture. On the other hand, as a single man, deleting a miracle from existence like this would feel like a major loss for all of mankind. It would be truly unfortunate.

What's it going to be? Should I tell her the truth? But if I do, then she's definitely going to delete it. It's not like I meant to take this picture. In fact, I wouldn't be able to take another picture like this even if I tried!

Although the entire scenario was all over within three seconds, he struggled and struggled and struggled. Maria, the angel, even appeared to him in a vision, but before she could get a word out, the devilish Yuki kicked her to the curb. And thus, he claimed:

"It's nothing. Nothing at all. I was just surprised by how the pictures came out."

I didn't see a thing. Yep. It was all in my head. The lighting just made a few weird shadows. That's it. Duh.

He did everything in his power to lie to himself while he went back to taking pictures as if nothing had happened...until Alisa narrowed her gaze.

"Show me."

"Huh?"

"Show me the picture you just took," she insisted, before swiping the phone out of his frozen hand in the blink of an eye.

"Ah—"

By the time he even thought of stopping her, she had already clicked on the picture to enlarge it—

"Masachika."

"Yes."

"What is this?" asked Alisa with a frigid glare. Masachika closed his eyes, unlocking his hidden powers of negotiation to their full potential. The next five minutes that followed were filled with a man's quibbles thinly veiled as artistic theory, in which he vehemently argued that this was art and not smut, until he somehow forced Alisa into agreeing with him. And in the end, he somehow managed to win the right to keep this miraculous picture under the condition that he would keep it stored somewhere secure, where no one else would see it. However…

"<I knew you had a leg fetish, you creep…>"

…Alisa might have thought slightly less of him now.

CHAPTER 4 Honestly, it was tempting.

What if you got home and you were greeted at the door by your classically beautiful childhood friend, who was sitting on her knees, perfectly positioned in a traditional bow, with three fingers from each hand touching the floor? What if you lived alone, but you were welcomed home by a cute maid when you walked in through the door? Either way, a healthy, nerdy male would be thrilled, and Masachika was no exception.

"Welcome home, Master."

"H-hey…"

Therefore, at a glance, this appeared to be any nerd's dream come true. Almost immediately after opening the front door, he was greeted with a graceful bow by a beautiful maid, who also happened to be his childhood friend. Her long, shiny black hair hung over her maid outfit like a veil. She was the ideal Japanese woman. However, all that charm went out the window when she decided not to bow like a normal person.

"…What are you doing?"

Her forehead was rubbing against the floor with her palms flat on each side, far from anything traditional. Just how long had she been waiting like this? Even Masachika was weirded out.

"While it may have been a competition between two rivals, I must apologize for the countless—"

"Stop. Do you seriously think I want to listen to you explain yourself, with your forehead pressed against the floor? Lift your head up, at least."

"No, I must apologize first—"

"I can't take my shoes off with your head in the way. Isn't it a maid's duty to welcome their master home, first?"

Masachika decided to question her manners as a maid in order to force her to lift her stubborn head…but his childhood friend's response went above and beyond what he could have ever imagined.

"Please imagine that my body is but a doormat for you to make use of."

"Let's keep our fetishes to ourselves, okay? You shouldn't treat people like doormats anyway."

"Are you suggesting I should be some other kind of mat instead?"

"No," he promptly replied with a straight face. After letting out a deep sigh, he squatted, purposely tried to put on the coldest glare he could, and called out to her with a serious voice.

"Ayano."

"…!"

She hesitantly lifted her head, as if she could tell by his tone that he was upset. Masachika then peered deeply into her eyes and quietly asked:

"What kind of maid gives orders to her master?"

"…!"

"Get up."

"Yes, Master!"

Once Ayano sprang to her feet, Masachika was finally able to take off his shoes and step out of the entryway.

"If you're trying to apologize about the trivia show, then don't. We were up against each other, and we played by the rules. Now, if you went easy on me for some reason or another, I would be angry."

"I—I would never…"

"Right? So don't apologize."

He lightly patted his maid on the shoulder while she took his bag for him.

"Hey, uh… About your invisible chi bla—"

"Never bring that up again."

After promptly shutting her down before she could reopen the old wound and pour salt into it, he swiftly escaped to the bathroom sink, where he washed his hands and gargled water. Once finished, he proceeded to head back to his room, but Ayano was by the bathroom door, holding out a basket with a damp towel in it.

"Please use this to wipe off your sweat."

"Oh, thanks."

He then went to his room, took off his school uniform, and began wiping his body with the damp towel. It was right as he had finished changing into his loungewear that there was a knock at the door.

"Come in."

"Pardon my intrusion."

The maid bowed before stepping inside to swiftly collect the basket containing the damp towel and Masachika's dirty clothes.

"Oh, you don't have to do that..."

"I was already on my way to the laundry room."

"Really? Thanks."

"Your praise is more than I deserve," she replied, casually checking the pocket of his dirty collared shirt to make sure she wouldn't accidentally wash anything important. A few seconds went by until her right hand suddenly froze before pulling out a single piece of paper...or what appeared to be paper. However, it was actually the picture he took with Nonoa at the maid café earlier that day.

"Oh, that's—"

The instant Masachika realized what it was, he instinctively tried to explain himself. Before he could even finish his sentence, however, Ayano had flipped the picture around to the front side, and immediately, her eyes opened wide and her pupils dilated.

"Whoa...?!?!"

Her expression was blank, and it was hard to tell if she could even see what was in her hand, what with her unfocused gaze. The only thing that was clear was that Ayano was so shocked by what she saw that her pupils had enlarged to twice their normal size. The eerie sight sent an alarming chill down Masachika's spine.

Wait... Is this like a wife finding the business card for some sort of hostess bar in her husband's clothes?

It reminded him of something he probably saw in a soap opera, so he tried to remain as calm as possible while he explained himself.

"Ohhh, that? Yeah, Class D and Class F were doing this café

together. I was only planning on stopping by for a little lunch, but my stupid good luck struck again, and I had to take this picture."

It was strange. He was telling the truth, and yet it felt like some sort of pathetic excuse, and the more he talked, the more pathetic he sounded, so he just stopped talking instead. Regardless, Ayano didn't even seem to react. It was hard to tell if she was even listening to his explanation.

"...Okay," she mumbled, her pupils still dilated.

"Come on, stop that. I'm sorry. Really. Hearing someone just say 'okay' with their eyes like that is even scarier that hearing them repeat 'Why?' because you *know* they're not okay!"

"No, it is okay... You simply weren't satisfied with my services," she replied in an emotionless, matter-of-fact tone, not even glancing at his panicked expression.

"No, seriously. Listen to me. I wasn't cheating on you with some other maid, and it has nothing to do with your services, either..."

Ayano slowly shifted her gaze in Masachika's direction. At the very least, he was relieved to see that she had calmed down enough to listen to him, so he decided to explain the difference between maid cafés and real maids, such as herself, and of how she shouldn't get the two mixed up.

"...And that's why they're not even close to being the same thing. Got it?"

"Yes, I understand."

"Really? Good."

Seeing her slowly nod back at him filled him with relief...for but a mere second.

"I made my master feel so guilty that he even tried to cheer me up... I have failed as a maid!"

"Are you even listening to me?!"

But in spite of his pathetic cries, Ayano curtsied, and with that odd look in her eyes and a detached tone, she pledged:

"Tonight, I will do everything in my power to please you and leave you satisfied."

Having a cute maid tell you she was going to service you was like a nerd's dream come true and would make any guy's heart race...but

Masachika got goose bumps and the hairs on the back of his neck stood straight up.

◇

"..."

"..."

"...Oh, a new video's been uploaded."

"..."

I can't concentrate like this!!

Despite having access to the entire World Wide Web on his computer, he was far more focused on the person behind him than what was on the screen. Hearing her claim that she was going to "please" him and leave him "satisfied" terrified him at first, but Ayano fortunately hadn't done anything that he would consider crossing the line...yet. She stood silently in the corner of the room...and she had been doing this the entire time. Just standing.

It was impressive yet unsurprising that he couldn't feel her presence, let alone feel her looking at him, but there was no way he could relax while knowing she was there. And, as if things couldn't get any worse, if he turned around, all he would see were these dark black eyes staring back at him. What was this? Some kind of horror movie?

I—I seriously can't relax like this...! Is this how it always is for Yuki? I can't believe she's fine with this...

He trembled with fear just imagining how strong her nerves must be, but he almost immediately had a change of heart.

Now that I think about it, I used to be completely fine with it, too. I guess you just have to get used to it. They grew up together, after all.

Ever since moving out of the Suou residence, Masachika quickly adapted to living alone. Besides, even if they were childhood friends, Masachika and Ayano were still two members of the opposite sex going through puberty. Even though that didn't bother him most of the time, he couldn't completely let himself get comfortable like he did around Yuki.

I don't mind it when Yuki's hanging out in my room... It doesn't help that Ayano's only here to work and has no interest in doing anything together, either...

Masachika didn't have the shamelessness one would need to casually read comic books on the bed while their childhood friend just waited in the corner all day. Therefore, his only other option was to get her to take a break, but...

"Hey, uh... Ayano?"

"Yes, Master?"

"Just standing there without anything to do must be boring, right? I'm not really doing much, so you're free to go off and do whatever makes you happy, you know?"

"This makes me happy."

"Oh... Okay..."

She had been like this ever since he had gotten home, so there was no way he was going to be able to change her mind now.

"Then let's talk about this whole 'Master' thing..."

"...What about it?"

"Like, uh... It just makes me a little uncomfortable," he hesitantly replied, making Ayano's eyes widen.

"But...you made all those other girls call you 'Master.'"

"What? Is that really something to be upset over?" asked Masachika with a straight face, but she didn't reply... But when he strained his ears, he actually did hear her mumbling something to herself under her breath. She was too far for him to actually hear what she was whispering, but there was something undeniably terrifying about an expressionless, beautiful doll-like girl with black eyes mumbling to herself in a dark corner. It looked almost as if she were chanting a curse, prompting Masachika to quietly face forward once more.

Sigh... I'm never going to be able to relax.

That was the only thing he could think of as he casually rotated his shoulder...until all of a sudden, he felt a presence right behind him, sending an alarming chill down his spine.

"Master."

"Y-yeah?"

The voice was coming from so close behind him that he awkwardly turned his head in her direction while his right shoulder was still mid-rotation. Unsurprisingly, he saw Ayano staring right back down at him with pitch-black eyes and a strangely intimidating presence.

"Shall I give you a massage?" she quietly asked.

"...A massage?"

"Yes, your shoulders seem stiff, and you have been extremely busy lately, so I thought you could use a massage."

"O-ohhh... Right."

She was offering a shoulder massage to loosen up her master's exhausted shoulders. Normally, this was something he should be grateful for and accept, but...

Yeah, something feels dirty about this.

The fact that Ayano said she was going to leave him "satisfied" earlier was worrying his nerdy side. Alarms were going off in his head, telling him that this wasn't going to be just any ordinary massage.

"Well, uh... Hmm... I guess..."

"I give Lady Yuki a massage every day, which is always very well received."

Masachika reconsidered her offer, since this might be the only way he could satisfy her urges to please. Besides, there was no way she would massage Yuki in any sort of lewd way...

"Shall we get started? Do you think you could lie down on the bed for me?"

My incoming smut alarm is going wild.

The sudden thought almost slipped off his tongue.

"You're just going to massage my shoulders, right? I'm fine sitting here..."

"I think we should loosen up all of your tight muscles."

"O-oh? All of them, huh?"

"Yes. You are all knotted up. However, I guarantee you'll feel a lot better once I help you rub one out."

"Okay. You're doing that on purpose, aren't you?"

"...? Doing what on purpose?"

Masachika stared hard at the maid, and he could easily imagine a question mark over her head, but her blank expression made her impossible to read. Even her eyes, which were the only expressive things about her, were now somehow empty, making it impossible to guess what she was thinking.

Again, she's scaring me. Ayano, why are your eyes pitch-black? What emotion makes your eyes that dark?

The thought of what could happen if he refused made the hair on the back of his neck stand up, so although wary, he lay facedown on the bed.

"Pardon me," she promptly apologized while straddling his back, making his entire body tense up.

I-it's fine. I don't care if she weirdly presses her body against mine or touches me anywhere funny, either! I don't care even a little!

He fired himself up for whatever horrors were to come, but in the end…it actually turned out to be a regular, wholesome massage. Ayano didn't even touch him more than was necessary.

"Phew… That felt great."

"I am glad to hear that."

"Thanks. I really appreciate it. Oh, and sorry for being a degenerate nerd."

"…?"

Despite her bewilderment, Masachika refused to explain any further, since he knew that nothing good would come from telling her that he actually believed she was going to offer to relieve his stiff… lower body, too.

"Now that you're feeling better, I'm going to start preparing dinner."

"Oh… Thanks…"

"Not at all. I will call for you when it's ready."

Masachika lay on the bed lazily while watching Ayano, from the corner of his eye, silently leave the room. His massaged shoulders and lower back still possessed a comforting warmth, robbing him of any will to move, and before long, he gradually gave in to the blissful warmth as it spread throughout his body, weighing down his eyelids…

"…ster. Master."

"Hmm?"

He opened his eyes to two pitch-black voids peering right into his soul as his shoulders were being softly shaken.

"...Aya...no...?"

"Yes, Master. It's me, your Ayano."

"...Sorry. I must have dozed off."

"You must have been exhausted. Are you ready for dinner? Or would you prefer to take a bath first? Or—?!"

"Dinner," he said, cutting her off.

"...Very well."

An ominous premonition motivated Masachika to spring out of bed and sent him straight for the living room, where he found the table already set with various dishes lined up.

"You seemed very tired, so I decided to make chilled pork tonight."

"Oh, awesome. Today was pretty hot for October, too, so this is perfect... I'm sure cosplaying as a wizard didn't help with the heat, either..."

There was just one thing bothering him.

"...Why is there only enough for one person?" he asked, after noticing there was only a plate for him.

"A maid mustn't eat at the same table as her master," she replied without missing a beat.

"Come on, eat with me. We always eat together."

"I am not your usual maid tonight."

"I don't know what that means, but it sounds cool, at least."

"...It would take far too long to boil more pork, so please do not worry about me and enjoy," she advised while pulling out a chair for Masachika, giving him little choice but to sit. She then promptly headed back into the kitchen. "How much rice do you want?"

"The usual amount."

"As you wish."

After gracefully and gently scooping rice into a bowl, Ayano speedily returned to the living room, placed the rice on the table, and even poured him a glass of water. But after that, she remained standing diagonally behind him, as if that was where she belonged.

"...Thanks again."

"Enjoy."

The main dish was chilled pork over a generous portion of vegetables sprinkled with ponzu vinegar—all of which he included with his first bite. The crunchy vegetables and chilled pork were really brought together with the ponzu vinegar, but it was the steamy white rice that created the perfect collaboration in his mouth.

"...This is really good."

"Thank you very much."

It was, without a doubt, a delicious meal, and yet he couldn't completely relax with her standing behind him. Suddenly, a hand towel and some seasoning seemingly appeared out of nowhere with exquisite timing. And he never needed to ask for a water refill or more rice. Furthermore, right after he finished eating, the maid artfully carried away his dirty dishes. The service couldn't have been more perfect...and yet Masachika couldn't focus on his meal.

Mmm... I'm sure this was normal back when I lived at the Suou household...but I guess I'm too much of a peasant nowadays to be comfortable with it.

Right after coming to that conclusion, she suddenly called out to him.

"Master, would you like me to clean your ears for you?"

"C-clean my ears?"

"Yes. Would you like that?" asked Ayano, despite already taking a seat by his side without even waiting for an answer.

"Here," she said while patting her lap.

Uh... I feel like I'm kind of being forced to do this?

Seeing the darkness in her peering black eyes made it clear that refusing was not an option.

"All right... Thanks...," he replied while timidly laying his head in her lap. The soft sensation was accompanied by a wonderful gentle smell tickling his nostrils.

Err... Having my ears cleaned by a girl wearing a maid outfit makes me feel like I've wandered into some sort of sketchy shop...

Right as the thought made his entire body tense up, Ayano announced she was going to begin, as the ear pick slowly entered Masachika's ear.

Oh... But this actually feels kind of nice...

It had been years since the last time someone had cleaned his ears for him, and it felt far better than he could have imagined. Her delicate fingers brushed against his head and cheeks while he felt a slightly ticklish yet pleasant sensation inside his ear. Although a slight chill almost crept up his spine at first, the sensation gradually became more pleasurable until he never wanted it to stop.

Ah... That feels so good... I feel so safe...

Masachika was slowly mesmerized by the warmth of Ayano's body touching his cheek and the pleasant feeling of having his ear cleaned...when all of a sudden, her affectionate touch vanished.

"All done. Could you flip over for me so I can clean your other ear now?"

"Huh? Oh..."

Although a bit disappointed it was over, he nonchalantly flipped over and realized that all he could see now was her maid uniform. However, this was also the moment he came to a certain realization.

Hold on. I'm in a pretty interesting position here...

While it may have been hard to tell, due to the nature of her outfit, he wouldn't need a detective to deduce that the tip of his nose was buried in her lower stomach region. Nevertheless, the instant he realized how dangerous a position he was in was, Ayano began cleaning his other ear, and the fairly ticklish, exceptionally pleasant sensation took over again, sapping him of his strength.

Ah...! Eh... Whatever...

Masachika gradually began to space out. He figured if it really bothered him, he could just close his eyes, and he ended up completely surrendering himself to Ayano. His cheek and the tip of his nose were buried in her warmth as he almost started to feel like she was gently holding his head in her arms. It was a moment of pure happiness.

"...That felt so good," he instinctively muttered the instant he made it back to his room. Masachika took advantage of the fact that Ayano was eating dinner and allowed himself to become lost in the pleasurable sensation of having just had his ears cleaned. Time slowly went by as he relaxed...until he suddenly realized something.

Oh, right. I should probably take a bath now, while I still have the chance.

Ayano was probably washing the dishes right about now, so this would probably be his safest bet, since bath time was where he had to be most careful when Ayano was in Super Live-to-Serve Mode (phrase coined by Masachika). After all, he knew that there was an extremely high chance that she would offer to wash his back the moment he got in the tub.

The bath is probably hot and ready, too, so I can be quick and finish before she's done washing the dishes.

Once Masachika made up his mind, he grabbed a change of clothes, hid them behind his back, then left the room while pretending like he was going to the use the toilet. After placing his change of clothes into the laundry basket, he turned around to close the door behind him, just in case, only to find Ayano right in the doorway.

"Whoa?!"

"Allow me to wash your back for you."

"I knew it!" exploded Masachika, recoiling in surprise despite the unbelievably predictable outcome. "I can't let you do that, though! We can't! Think about it for a second!"

"I don't see any issues. I am ready when you are."

Ayano didn't even raise an eyebrow to his harsh rejection while she began undressing from her maid uniform right there.

"What the...?! Stop—!"

But her maid uniform hit the floor before he could even utter another word...only to reveal the swimsuit she had worn when they went to the beach...and a weapon. A swimsuit, thigh-high stockings, a headband, and a weapon.

Mmm... Only a true degenerate could appreciate this.

Ayano proceeded to remove her weapon and take off her thigh-highs before stepping into the bathroom ahead of him.

"Hey, wait—!"

The door closed before he could stop her, and he froze.

"Uh... Am I just supposed to mosey on inside like this isn't a big deal?"

Judging by Ayano's behavior today, there was probably no way she was going to back down, no matter what he said. She was most likely going to wait in the bathroom for him all night if she had to.

U-uh... Well, uh... She is wearing a bathing suit...so I guess it's okay? What was that bathing suit doing at my house anyway? Was it in Yuki's closet or something?

But other than that one mystery, the fact that she was wearing a swimsuit made it seem as though even Ayano differentiated between swimwear and underwear. Put simply, maybe it was all in Masachika's head, he was worrying over nothing, and Ayano wasn't planning on doing anything indecent to him. Even though she may have exposed her completely nude body to him once during summer break, she was probably working hard to make sure that never happened again. In other words, maybe it was safe to trust her and let her do whatever she wanted...

Plus, to be completely honest, her massage and ear cleaning felt so good that I'm actually kind of interested to see how this whole washing my back thing goes, too.

For as long as he could remember, not a single person had ever washed his back for him. Moreover, he couldn't help but wonder if it would be just as pleasant as her other services. Of course, that didn't come without a little hint of guilt, but his curiosity got the best of him. He hesitated for only a few moments before undressing, then wrapped a towel tightly around his waist and stepped into the bathroom.

"Only wash my back, okay? Once you're done with that, you're outta here," he demanded as calmly as he could to the maid squatting behind the bath stool.

"As you wish... Would you like me to wash your hair as well?"

"Hmm? Oh... Yeah, sure."

Masachika lowered his rear onto the bath stool while doing everything in his power not to look in Ayano's direction. Immediately, she squirted shampoo onto her hands, waited for the water to warm up, then began to wash his hair. It all started with the shampoo...

Whoa... Seriously? This feels so good...

It felt like having your head shampooed before a cut at the salon… except better. Ayano was applying just the right amount of force with her delicate fingers, running her fingers through his hair and stimulating his scalp, which felt heavenly.

"How does that feel? Too hard? Too soft?"

"Just right."

He closed his eyes to focus on the sensation alone.

Does Yuki get to experience this every day…? Because I'd be genuinely jealous if she did. Lucky punk. But she has a lot of hair, now that I think about it. Must be rough for Ayano…

The euphoric experience went by in a flash, and once again, Ayano didn't do a single thing he would consider indecent, which probably shouldn't have come as a surprise anymore. After she finished washing Masachika's hair and back, she promptly withdrew from the bathroom. There was no "Would you also like me to wash your—?" afterward, either.

…Looks like I got worked up over nothing.

The awkwardness and embarrassment only hit him after he finished his bath and returned to his room. When Ayano said she was going to leave him satisfied, his nerdy mind had gone straight into the gutter. While he was still concerned about her void-like eyes and her calling him "Master," she was probably taking care of him just like she usually took care of Yuki. In other words, she saw him more like a master and less like an individual of the opposite sex. That wasn't to say that she didn't see him as a man at all, since she did consider his feelings and had a bathing suit ready to go. At any rate, all Ayano wanted to do was serve him the best she could, since she was proud of her work as a maid, and yet this rotten mind of Masachika's couldn't help but expect something was going to happen…

"Yep. I wish I were dead. ☆"

The impish Yuki in his mind whispered:

"Be honest. You were kind of hoping she would do something, right? You little perv."

After she kicked his corpse into the air, the angel Maria quickly interjected:

"Don't blame him! He's a boy! It's natural!"

But her kind words felt like rubbing lemon on an open sore, which made him reflect even more on what he had done.

"Master, can I come in?"

Suddenly, there was a knock at the door, making Masachika straighten and fix his posture in a fluster.

"Yeah, sure."

"I apologize for interrupting, but I brought you some warm milk."

"Oh, thanks. You've really outdone yourself today."

After a single sip, the faint sweetness of milk and honey spread throughout his mouth, making him smile. It was as if the milk even warmed his heart, which unconsciously prompted him to thank her.

"Thanks, Ayano."

"It's nothing."

"I'm not just talking about this... Thank you for always taking care of Yuki, too."

"...?"

Masachika continued to gaze at the milk's surface, not even having to look back at Ayano to know she was confused.

"You put everything into taking care of me today...and it made me realize how much you must care for Yuki, too. I bet you work so hard to look after her every single day...so I just wanted to say thank you."

Masachika's smile marginally twisted into a frown.

"It was my duty to take care of her, and yet...I failed her as a brother."

"You didn't—"

"I did. The reason why I did doesn't matter, because the fact of the matter is that I pushed all of that nonsense onto Yuki and left her to fend for herself. And now I'm being compelled by some feeling that even I don't understand to help Alya, not Yuki, become the student council president...so I probably don't even have the right to thank you," he confessed with a sweet yet pained smile as he looked up at Ayano.

"But still...thank you. You're always there for her, and you always put her first, and that honestly makes me so happy. So...

please continue being there for her and being the person she can trust the most," he added, speaking from the bottom of his heart as he gazed straight into her eyes. It was as if a light had finally illuminated the darkness in Ayano's wide-open eyes...and she *smiled*.

"You flatter me too much, Master Masachika."

The powerfully emotional reply had his smile widening into a grin, and a relaxed air filled the space between them as Masachika took another sip of milk.

"This is really good, by the way. Does Yuki like this, too?"

"Yes, it is one of her favorites."

"It is...? Now that I think about it, I don't really hear you ever talk about Yuki unless I ask you to."

"I can tell you countless stories if you wish."

"All right, that might actually be kind of nice."

They shared stories about Yuki after that. But around the time Masachika finished his warm milk, Ayano looked up at the clock, then stood up off the bed.

"It's about time for bed."

"Yeah, you're right... Tomorrow's going to be a busy day, after all. Plus, this drink you made me really warmed me up nicely, so I guess I could go to bed a little early tonight."

"Really? I could make you another cup of warm milk if you wish."

"I'm fine. Thanks, though."

After taking Masachika's empty cup, Ayano briefly paused, as if she had just thought of something.

"Master Masachika."

"Hmm?"

"Would you like to use my boobs as a pillow?"

"You've got to be kidding me!! Way to ruin the mood."

"Lady Yuki loves to sleep on my chest."

"Curse that stupid little sister of mine!"

After Masachika's roar erased whatever good mood there was left, his smartphone vibrated with a single message from Yuki displayed on the screen:

Hey, uh... Sorry.

...Incidentally, he ended up turning down the boobies pillow. He was extremely tempted, but he still managed to decline, thanks to his iron will.

CHAPTER 5 In a way, I actually do feel better.

"Are ya sure? What about your festival committee work?"

"Yeah, I won't have to worry about that for a while, thanks to our talented upperclassmen."

"Ha-ha! It makes sense that everything's going smoothly, since the current student council president is working alongside last year's president."

It was the second day of the Autumn Heights Festival, and Masachika had invited Takeshi and Hikaru to walk around while he took a break from his festival committee responsibilities.

"Plus, the current president's and vice president's main job right now is to deal with the First Light Committee. In other words, everything was set up to run smoothly without them, so nobody's going to be missing me."

"Oh, right. The First Light Committee… I totally forgot they were coming today."

"Do you have any idea who exactly is coming from the committee?"

"No clue. Touya and Chisaki are handling all that, and honestly, I didn't care enough to even ask."

"For real? 'Cause I know tons of students who are using this as a chance to get close to them."

Takeshi observed the other students' attractions while adding:

"I mean, check out how a lot of people decorated the entrance to their attractions. They seem desperate for attention."

"Well, I'm just an ordinary guy who happens to be the son of a diplomat," said Masachika, shrugging.

"I don't know, man. Being the son of a diplomat seems like a pretty big deal to me... Plus, he's a high-ranking bureaucrat, too, right?"

"It's nothing special at this school, at least. Like, there are even rumors that having at least one parent with a career like that is the bare minimum you'd need to even pass this school's entrance interview."

"Yes... I've definitely heard people say that they filter candidates based on their family's social standing and parents' jobs."

"And *this*," joked Takeshi while repeatedly rubbing his thumb over the tip of his index and middle finger—a gesture symbolizing money—making his friends laugh bitterly.

"Yeah, no doubt. Anyway, who cares about all that? What's important right now is that I currently don't have any obligations."

"Good point. Oh, hey. They're selling rice cracker sandwiches with takoyaki inside. That sounds pretty good... What do you guys think?"

"I'm good."

"Me too. Don't worry about us, though. Go grab yourself one."

"All right, I'll be right back," replied Hikaru before heading over to the food stall. They absentmindedly watched as he went to line up, when Takeshi suddenly grinned smugly and mumbled:

"So? How'd things go yesterday?"

"Yesterday? ...You mean the trivia show?"

"No! I'm talking about what happened after that. You and Alya went on a little date, right?"

"Ohhh. I don't know if I'd call that a date, but—hold on. You saw us? Why didn't you say hello?"

"Well, uh... You know me," said Takeshi ambiguously while he glanced at Hikaru.

So that's what happened. You tried to say hello, but Hikaru stopped you, huh?

Masachika's lips curled wryly, since he was positive that he was right.

"You don't need to worry about bothering me, you know?"

"Yeah, but y'all looked like ya were having a really good time, so

I didn't want to interrupt. Anyway, how was it? You're running mates, so, like...ya must be getting really close, right?"

It was a hard question to answer. Although Masachika knew how Alisa felt about him, he didn't really have any intention of trying to take their relationship to the next level. One reason was obviously because mixing business and romance could ruin her campaign. It didn't help that Alisa herself didn't seem to realize that her feelings toward him were romantic, either. Put simply, they were getting closer, but their relationship had remained stagnant.

"...Well, we are getting closer, but that's about it. We're not dating, if that's what you're getting at."

"Oh..."

"What? Were you panicking because you thought I'd get a girlfriend before you?"

"What?! No! I just—!"

"Excuse me. Sorry to bother you, but..."

Takeshi looked to his side in the direction of the voice as if he couldn't believe a girl would ever be talking to him. Masachika shifted his gaze in the same direction to find that she was a girl around their age who didn't seem to go to their school. She was surprisingly cute, with short hair dyed a lighter color, and she was looking up at Takeshi through her eyelashes while she hesitantly asked:

"We don't go to this school, so we were looking for someone to show us around... Do you think you could help a few of us girls from Temple Academy?"

"Huh? U-us?"

"Yes, if that's okay with you." The girl grinned captivatingly. The name of the school she mentioned was a relatively famous all-girls school in the area, and standing slightly in the distance were two cute girls, who seemed to be her friends from that school as well.

So that's what's going on here.

All it took was seeing one of the girls glancing at Hikaru for Masachika to figure it out. These three were most likely after Hikaru, but they were worried that they would offend Masachika and Takeshi if they approached the best-looking guy, so they decided to take care of the obstacles in their way while their target was gone.

"O-oh, for real? Heh..."

Takeshi grinned from ear to ear while scratching his head, clearly oblivious to their true intentions. Lovestruck, he goofily checked out each of the three girls one by one, lacking any subtlety, then turned to Masachika, as if all the newfound popularity were a burden. However, after that, he faced the girl and slapped his hands together before his face.

"I'm really sorry, because you have no idea how happy you just made me, and it's an honor you would even ask, but we all have girlfriends, and we don't want them to kill us in a jealous rage later, so we just can't. I'm really sorry!"

"Huh? Oh... Well, I totally understand..."

The girl seemed taken by surprise as she blinked with a blank expression for a few moments before returning to her friends in bewilderment. After watching them discuss something before wandering off, Masachika turned to his friend, who still had his hands clasped together before his face.

"Since when did you get a girlfriend?"

"Come on, man. Give me a break. I couldn't think of any other way to let them down easy."

"Well, I think you made the right decision...but are you sure you didn't want to show them around?"

"D-damn it all! Of course I wanted to show them around! That was my only chance of ever having a harem, and now it's gone!"

"Uh..."

Masachika was confused for more than one reason, but there was no way he could tell his friend that. After that, Takeshi continued to hold his head while writhing in agony until he eventually sighed and went limp.

"But Hikaru wouldn't be comfortable hanging out with three girls he doesn't know, and, well...you didn't seem too excited about the idea, either, right?"

"Yeah, I guess..."

"Right? So I'm fine with this. Besides, I probably wouldn't have been able to show them a good time, even if I did agree to show them around," he stressed, each breath tainted with a hint of regret, but it was because of this that Masachika realized once again what a great person Takeshi was.

I mean, I already knew he was a really good guy, but still... I just hope he's rewarded for it one day.

It was a mystery as to why a guy this considerate still didn't have a girlfriend, and it made Masachika really feel how unfair the world truly was. Only a few moments went by before Hikaru returned with his rice cracker sandwich stuffed with takoyaki.

"Sorry to keep you guys waiting... Uh... What happened to Takeshi?"

"...He's just cursing his poor luck."

"...? What?"

A thud suddenly echoed nearby, followed by the surprised gasp of a flustered girl. When Masachika glanced in the direction of the noise, he found a girl with a plastic basket anxiously watching bouncy balls spilling out of it. She must have bumped into something that caused a few balls to spill out. Some hit the legs of random people walking by, while others hit the ground and began to bounce away in every direction.

"That sucks."

Masachika hesitated for a few moments, unable to decide if he should go help.

She's kind of far from where I'm standing, though, so even if I go try to help her now... Besides, she probably doesn't even care that she lost a few, so helping her pick them up might even bother her. So—

"Hold this for me."

"...!"

Hikaru dropped his food into Masachika's hands, then rushed to the girl's aid without even a second of hesitation. After grabbing each ball in sight, he headed over to nearby stalls and checked underneath them, readily crawling on all fours to retrieve any balls he could find. He didn't even seem to care that he was getting his hands and knees dirty. By the time Masachika and Takeshi caught up with him, he had already basically finished picking up every last bouncy ball on his own.

"Th-thank you so much. I really mean that."

"It's no problem. Take care."

Hikaru almost seemed troubled as he waved good-bye to the apologetic, bowing girl.

"You see that, Takeshi? That's what makes you popular with the ladies," Masachika advised sagely.

"Tsk! There's no way I can compete with that..."

"What? I'm not doing this to be popular..."

"We know. We're talking about how you went to help without a second thought. Impressive stuff, to say the least."

Hikaru seemed once again troubled as Masachika showered him with unreserved praise. Hikaru was always like this. While most people would worry about helping someone who might not want to be helped, or about embarrassing themselves, Hikaru wouldn't hesitate to extend a helping hand, even if it meant helping a girl—when he was not particularly fond of girls. Unlike most people, he actually believed in helping others in times of need. He was too kind a person for this world.

Sigh... They're too nice. Both of them.

They were friends Masachika could be proud of, and he couldn't have asked for more. He could truly admit that from the bottom of his heart...and that was exactly why he wasn't going to let anyone hurt them. There were some things that he couldn't allow to just be forgiven and forgotten.

"...Well, it looks like I should get going."

"Oh, all right. See you at rehearsal, then."

"Enjoy work."

"Thanks."

After the three checked out the festival for forty or so minutes, Masachika had to say good-bye. He began heading toward the clubroom building, but he didn't step inside. Instead, he went around to the back, where there were no exhibits or stalls, which meant the only reason to be there was if you were lost. However, standing under a large tree that couldn't be seen, even if you looked out the window, was someone waiting for him. Hanging their head low was a girl wearing her hat pulled down low, covering her eyes.

"Nao, hey," greeted Masachika in a flat voice as he approached her. It was an indifferent greeting, unlike something you would say to someone you were on friendly terms with, like, "Sorry to keep you waiting," or "Sorry for asking you to meet me here like this." The girl glared back at him without any desire to play nice either.

"...What do you want?" asked the girl, Nao Shiratori, coldly. She was a former student at Seirei Academy who transferred to a new school right before the second semester, and she'd been the lead singer in the band Luminous with Takeshi and Hikaru up until only a month ago. She was also the one responsible for the band breaking up when she decided to unleash hell on her way out.

"What were you even thinking, using something like this to ask me to meet you here?"

Her unfriendly attitude remained while she pulled a single envelope from her pocket. It was the letter that Masachika had given her former homeroom teacher to pass on to her. The fact of the matter was that Masachika had been searching for Nao ever since she left, because there was something about how she broke up the band that had been bothering him. Unfortunately, however, when she changed schools, she also changed her phone number and deleted her social media accounts, which made it impossible to get in touch with her at all. He couldn't even find out what had happened to her through any of his connections. It was as if she had disappeared into thin air.

Therefore, he came up with a plan and went to the only person he knew who could possibly get in touch with her: Nao's former homeroom teacher. After Masachika passionately convinced the teacher that he wanted to give Nao a letter after her sudden disappearance, the teacher respected his wishes and delivered said letter. Given that, however, the letter was neither a love letter nor a farewell letter. In fact, the letter was no longer than a single sentence and an invitation to the Autumn Heights Festival.

"I mean, seriously? 'If you don't come, I'm going to tell everyone in Luminous the truth'? What's that supposed to mean?"

She glared at him more after reading the letter, but her anger was met with a cold stare and a shrug.

"You know better than anyone what that means. That's why you came, right?"

"..."

They locked eyes as if they were trying to read the other for a while after that. From what Masachika had heard from Takeshi, the band broke up because Nao told the bassist—Ryuuichi Kasugano—who she was dating at the time, that she was basically settling for him and was actually in love with Hikaru. The news obviously shattered Ryuuichi's heart, and their keyboardist, who was also Nao's childhood friend, Riho Minase, was so sickened by the news that both of them ended up leaving the band. Of course, Masachika didn't see any of this firsthand, so he didn't know how accurate any of the details were...but it was because he was an outsider that he knew this was a blatant lie.

"You're not in love with Hikaru."

"...!"

Nao's lips twisted, and her brow puckered, which only made Masachika even more sure he was right. She claimed to be in love with Hikaru after Riho revealed that Nao always had a crush on someone in Luminous. When Masachika spoke to Riho after the band had broken up, she told him that Nao was the last of the five members to join the band, and when she asked Nao why she decided to join, Nao apparently said it was because she had a crush on one of the members.

Although Riho didn't seem to notice, Masachika immediately figured it out. Nao was trying to keep Riho in check. If she simply wanted to join the band for fun, then she could have just said that she wanted to be in a band with Riho, but the fact that she didn't do that and claimed she had a crush on someone made it sound as if she was trying to prevent Riho from dating someone, and what happened after that seemed to point to that someone being Ryuuichi. At any rate, common sense would suggest that childhood friends falling in love with the same person was nothing out of the ordinary. However...

According to Ryuuichi...that was far from the truth.

Apparently, Nao didn't really seem to like him much at all

during the beginning of the relationship. Was she just shy? But even then, being this passive still seemed strange for someone who was willing to do whatever she needed to keep Riho away from him. In other words, it wasn't Ryuuichi she was trying to keep all to herself…

"You're in love with—"

"Stop," Nao barked sternly, cutting him off, albeit to no avail.

"No, I'm not going to stop."

He flat-out ignored her demand, then took a step closer and conclusively declared:

"You don't have feelings for Hikaru or Ryuuichi. You're in love with Riho."

"…!!"

Her eyes went wide and her rage was clear, but Masachika continued to boldly deduce:

"You started dating Ryuuichi because you knew that Riho had feelings for him, and you joined Luminous because you didn't want to lose her. Am I wrong?"

Nao opened her mouth to reply to his confident accusation, but she couldn't seem to find the right words, opening and closing her mouth multiple times before lowering her gaze. Silence followed for a while after that until her shoulders began to shake, as if she couldn't hold it in any longer.

"…You're right," she growled eventually. It was as if those words had destroyed the dam that had been keeping her emotions from bursting out. "Are you happy?! Yes, I'm in love with Riho! And I've been in love with her for years! I've been protecting her ever since we were kids! She was always my favorite person in the world, and I was always hers! And yet…! And yet…!"

Her voice trembled through her clenched teeth as she furiously glared at her feet. She then kicked the toe of her shoe into the ground, her chest trembling while she screamed:

"And yet she fell in love with Ryuuichi! She said she was afraid of boys! So why…? Why—?!"

"…And that's why you started going out with Ryuuichi even though you didn't really like him?"

"Yes! I'd rather do that than let someone take her away—than let her be defiled by some guy!

This was the twisted...yet pure love of a girl for her female childhood friend. After she roared like a rampaging beast, her lips twisted into a frown as she fought back tears. Was it sadness? Regret?

"But after I started dating Ryuuichi, he ended up being a really great guy... He was so sweet, despite me being this way. He loved me despite it all...so I understood why Riho fell in love with him, too..."

A tear escaped her right eye and rolled down her cheek. But after she wiped her tear away, she continued through her sobbing:

"Riho never changes, either. She is always so sweet. She even told me that she would be cheering us on, with the biggest smile on her face...even though she was the one that liked him first... Both Ryuuichi and Riho are the nicest people in the world, and yet I'm nothing more than a liar. All I did was hurt them...! And I'm the only one to blame! But it doesn't matter anymore...!"

Masachika closed his eyes as he listened to her painfully recall everything that had happened while covering her face with both hands. There was no way for him to know how unbearable it must have been to continue living a lie and deceiving those who cared about you most. At first, it was nothing more than a tiny fib that Nao used so that nobody would steal the love of her life away from her, but the more she tried to keep up the lie, the more lies she had to tell. It wasn't long until her life was but a web of lies slowly trapping her loving, good-natured bandmates. Behind every one of her smiles was pain and regret. She must have been so disappointed in herself, until that disappointment transformed into self-hatred.

And when that secret of hers was about to get out and expose her for who she really was, she decided to lie one last time. She claimed that she was in love with Hikaru so that nobody would ever find out her greatest secret of all: She was in love with Riho.

I guess I can't really blame her for why she did it, though...

Nao wanted to protect her love for Riho more than anything else. It was a secret she was willing to take to the grave, and she was even willing to offer herself to a boy she didn't love to do so. Therefore, Masachika didn't have the heart to reprimand her.

They often say that people's true nature is revealed at times of greatest adversity, but Masachika didn't find this to be true. At times of greatest adversity, it wasn't their true nature but their instincts that were revealed. These were fundamental instincts for self-preservation that all living creatures had, which were twisted by reason and logic, and there probably weren't that many people who could actually prioritize others over themselves when it came to instinct. That was why Masachika couldn't truly blame Nao for lying when she had her back up against a wall. But even then…

"What about the four people you left behind?"

"…!"

But even then, he couldn't just allow all of this to be swept under the rug.

"You ran away, so you might be fine, but the others still haven't gotten over what happened."

"…"

That was probably the last thing Nao wanted to hear. Masachika knew that, and yet he still forced her to face reality.

"Ryuuichi and Riho stopped coming to the music club after school, and they haven't talked to Hikaru once since all of that happened. Hikaru's trying not to think about them, either, but to be honest, it's hard to watch. They used to be so close, and now they're acting like they don't even know each other."

"…?! But…"

"I heard Takeshi has been trying to talk to Ryuuichi and Riho lately, but they've apparently been avoiding him. Although he's still acting like his usual self when he's around others, he's honestly pretty exhausted. I mean, you know how he always puts his friends first."

"…"

Nao hung her head low in silence for a few moments before softly muttering:

"How's Riho?"

Figured Riho would be her first priority, thought Masachika before he bluntly told her the truth.

"You know the kind of person she is, too. She never had that many friends to begin with, so now that she's not practicing with the band, she's completely alone. She looks depressed every day in class, she never talks to anyone, and she goes straight home once school's over."

"...!"

Nao bit her lip, still looking at the ground.

"Don't tell me you thought that Riho and Ryuuichi would get together once you were out of the picture?" asked Masachika.

"...!!"

"You know Ryuuichi. He isn't the kind of guy who'd make Riho his rebound, and Riho—"

"I know! Okay?!"

Nao quickly lifted her head back up with a furious glare.

"What is your problem?! You don't know us! This has nothing to do with you! Who do you think you are?!"

Those words were like a bucket of ice water being poured onto Masachika, making him reflect on his actions until it suddenly hit him.

Wait. Why am I trying to make her feel bad?

He told himself that he didn't have the heart to blame her, but before he knew it, he was saying all the wrong things. Even though he was only planning on telling her the truth, somewhere during it all, he more or less started to reprimand her in a roundabout way, and the fact that he only noticed that now horrified him.

What am I doing? This isn't what I wanted to say to her...

Masachika lowered his gaze, reset his brain, then began to search for the words he actually wanted to say to her.

"...This really is none of my business. I'm not a member of Luminous, and I don't have any right to tell you what to do."

"..."

"But you know what? I don't think you should just leave things how they are now. This isn't good for any of you."

"...! Ngh...!"

Nao quickly looked away while gritting her teeth.

"Are you really okay with how things ended? Are you okay with them never knowing it was all a misunderstanding?"

"..."

"As someone who once didn't get a proper good-bye, let me tell you this: You'll start to forget about all of the good times you had together. Every happy memory will be spoiled by how you said good-bye."

Up until just a short while ago, Masachika had sealed away his memories of Mah as if they were all negative, and he deeply regretted that because he now knew that it was all just a misunderstanding.

Once again, I guess I'm in no position to lecture anyone about this.

After Masachika had calmed down, he was overcome with disappointment in himself. He turned on his heel, and while knowing this was none of his business, he added:

"Like I said, I wasn't a member of your band or even a part of your group, so I don't know what kind of people you are or what kind of relationships you had, so I'm not telling you that you have to do anything... But if you don't fix things, Luminous is just going to turn into a bad memory for all of you, especially Ryuuichi and Riho."

Masachika didn't even look back as he walked away. He headed straight to the clubroom building after that and started to walk up the stairs, higher and higher in an attempt to get away from it all. Before long, he even walked over the chains blocking the last set of stairs and made his way to the landing, where he placed his back against the wall, then slid down to his rear.

"*Sigh...*"

A deep sigh escaped him.

"...What was I being so critical for?"

But he already knew the answer to that. He was mad at her for hurting Takeshi and Hikaru. Of course, he truly believed that Luminous shouldn't break up due to a misunderstanding, and that was also why he felt that he needed to convince Nao to talk to them one last time. He didn't regret that.

What bothered him was the fact that he was harsher to Nao than he needed to be and ended up hurting her. Masachika, who wasn't even a part of their group, took out his anger on her when maybe that should have been Takeshi's or Hikaru's job, since they were the ones who actually got hurt.

"...I was trying to be calm."

But he wasn't calm. She had hurt two of his best friends, and ever since then, the fury inside of him smoldered until it burst into flames that fueled his aggression.

I essentially sent her a threatening letter, then exposed her for her lies, even though she told me to stop... Was that really necessary? Or did I actually just want to hurt her to give her a taste of her own medicine for what she did to Takeshi and Hikaru?

The way she glared at Masachika and the words she said suddenly came back to haunt him, making him clench his jaw. The regret and feelings of self-loathing were overwhelming, for those feelings were all he had right now.

"'Who do you think you are?' Heh. You can say that again. Who do I think I am, telling others how to fix their relationships?"

Somebody had to do it...would have been a heroic thing to say, but that wasn't the kind of person Masachika was. If he didn't do anything, then memories of what happened would have faded along with the flow of time until they were no more. Masachika's ego was what made him dig up a buried memory of the past and expose what was inside it. It wasn't as if anyone had asked him to do it. He just thought this would be the right thing to do. That was it...but now he was starting to realize that maybe he shouldn't have meddled.

Maybe those five band members would have eventually worked out their issues on their own...just like how fate brought Masachika and Maria back together and allowed them to straighten out a misunderstanding from years ago. If the members of Luminous really did have an unbreakable bond, then...

Yeah, that's the issue here! Nao might just be a stranger to me, but she's Takeshi's and Hikaru's friend!

Realizing that he had hurt a friend of a friend made him even more depressed.

Sigh... Dammit. I hate myself so much that I want to die... I need to apologize to Nao later.

His mind had drifted into a spiral of negativity, making him clutch his head before dropping onto his side on the ground. The regret began eating at his soul while he continued to curl into a ball—

"Kuze?"

...A voice, which he shouldn't be hearing, echoed from the bottom of the staircase, making Masachika sit straight up in a fluster. There, his eyes met Maria's, peeking up the stairs from the landing below, and his heart leaped out of his chest.

"Wh-what the...? What are you doing here, Masha?"

"I just happened to be walking by when I saw you, and you seemed really upset...so I followed you," she revealed with a worried note as she walked up the stairs, took a seat next to him, and turned toward him with a worried gaze.

"Are you okay? Did something happen?"

Masachika returned her genuine concern with silence. But even then, Maria didn't rush him, gently wrapping her hand around his clenched fist in his lap, and the comforting, gentle sensation warmed his cold heart.

"I hurt someone," he softly muttered, still grimacing.

"Oh? Why?"

"Because she hurt my friends... No, that's not it." He shook his head. "I was angry that my friends got hurt, and I took out my anger on her without even talking to them. I know she had a reason for what she did, and yet...I let my anger get the best of me and hurt someone who was already hurting more than enough."

After getting all of that out in one breath, he smirked in a self-deprecating manner.

"So right now, I'm just kind of disappointed in myself. I messed up. Anyway, I'll be back to normal once I get tired of beating myself up over it, so don't worry about me," he jokingly added, but Maria's expression was completely serious while she gazed into his eyes. She then slowly got up on her knees and tightly wrapped her arms around his head.

"There, there."

She gently rubbed his head, furthering his confusion.

"...What? Wh-why are you hugging me?"

"Because you're hurt, and I want you to feel better."

"Uh...? Were you even listening to me? I'm the bad guy here. I should feel bad. I let my emotions get the best of me, and I ended up hurting someone, so…"

"So you don't deserve to be consoled?"

"…!"

Her sweet voice rendered him speechless.

"Oh, Kuze." She sighed and smiled softly, as if she could tell by his reaction that she had hit the nail on the head.

"You would feel that way, wouldn't you? But you know what? What you think you deserve doesn't matter right now!"

"…O-oh," grunted Masachika, overwhelmed by her confidence. It was as if she was saying, "What do you think about that?" as she did things her own way.

"How you feel about this isn't what's important right now! I'm doing this because I want to spoil you and give you all the affection in the world!"

"O-oh…"

There was no way he could argue with a declaration like that.

I guess if Masha wants to do this, then who am I to stop her?

Apathetic resignation filled his heart while he spaced out, but Maria continued to gently rub his head.

"You've always been this way, haven't you? It's like you don't think you deserve the affection of others."

"…"

Her sharp remark pierced him. She was right, after all. In Masachika's mind, he didn't deserve to be treated with kindness, especially after forcing his sister to deal with all that hardship alone while he was living the life of a lazy, no-good degenerate.

"Whenever I see you like this, it's heart-wrenching. It makes me so sad, and I just want to hold you in my arms and shower you with all the affection in the world."

"…Uh-huh," grunted Masachika, but Maria smiled as if she could once again see right through his act and knew he was only trying to hide his embarrassment.

"If you can't forgive yourself, then I want to forgive you. If you want to hurt yourself, then I want to protect you from yourself."

Maria softly rubbed his head as if to prove she meant what she said.

"Don't ask me why, though, okay? Because you've always meant so much to me…ever since we met at that park when we were kids… so don't pretend to be stronger than you are. You don't have to suffer alone. Because I understand you."

Yeah, she…

Maybe she did really get it. Maybe she understood how weak Masachika really was. Maybe she knew of all his flaws and mistakes. Maybe she understood everything about him and still decided to embrace him with love.

"…Yeah."

"Yep."

"Yeah…"

"…Yep."

There didn't seem to be much communication happening between them, and yet Masachika knew that she understood exactly what he wanted to say, so he closed his eyes and surrendered himself to her embrace. There was no telling how much time went by after that, but when he eventually calmed down a little, he opened his eyes and muttered:

"I feel like I've been allowing myself to be coddled by you almost my entire life."

"Hmm? Really?"

"Yeah… I've been too dependent on your kindness."

Ever since they'd reunited at the park, Masachika had been occasionally having flashbacks of all the times they spent together. In each memory, Masha was always so cheerful, affectionate, and warm… She was Sah's savior—his everything. That was what Masachika genuinely believed now.

"Oh… But this goes both ways, you know? Sah was so sweet to me and made me feel so good."

"Ha-ha! Oh, really?"

"Really. I can't even count all of the sweet things he did for me."

But Masachika was sure that he hadn't done even half of what she did for him.

I never kept my promise to her, either...

He thought back to last month, when he remembered an old promise he'd made with Mah, filling him with regret.

Maybe it's still not too late...? No, it's way too late. Besides, I'm obviously not going to be anywhere as good as I used to be.

Maria's arms around him tightened even more, as if she could feel the weight of his sadness...but Masachika couldn't help feeling embarrassed.

"Hey, uh... Maybe it's about time we... You know?"

"Hmm? Why? I'll hold you for as long as you want me to."

"This position's a little..."

You could say that the heavy load on his shoulder was really getting to him and that he had the happiest right ear in the world that was perfectly positioned to feel Maria's heartbeat.

"Ah..."

Maria's expression was somewhat troubled yet just as bashful as she let go of her embrace and gave him some space, realizing what Masachika was hinting at.

"Oh, Kuze..."

"Sorry."

"Mmm... Well, you are a boy, so I guess it just can't be helped. ♪"

She spread her arms out like a goddess, her smile brimming with compassion.

"I don't mind if it's you, Kuze. Come here."

"Wh-what? I, uh..."

"Oh, right. You don't feel like you deserve others' kindness. I guess that means I'll have to go over there myself. ♪"

"Wait—!"

He leaned back in surprise for a split second before she seized his head with both arms, and it was at that moment that Masachika knew the brute force known as motherly love.

"...Well, that was...incredible."

After being drowned in Maria's motherly love, Masachika began to head to the music room with trembling legs. The band was about to have its final rehearsal before the show…but he couldn't really even think about that right now. Any regret or feelings of self-loathing that he may have had were gone. It was so incredible that it sucked all the energy right out of him.

How is Masha so full of life anyway…?

While Masachika was utterly exhausted, Maria seemed to be overflowing with energy when they said their good-byes in front of the stairwell. Was she somehow able to relieve some stress from fulfilling her desire to shower someone with love?

Oh gosh… Don't tell me that's going to happen every time Masha notices I'm depressed? If she keeps doing that, then eventually…things could get messy.

He was instantly swept by a mysterious sense of danger as a chill shot down his spine until, out of nowhere, he suddenly made eye contact with Yuki at the end of the hallway.

"Yuki…"

"Masachika…?"

He straightened and tried to pretend like everything was all right, but Yuki knit her brow skeptically, then approached him briskly with a practiced smile.

"There you are."

"Huh?"

"We received an additional request for renting some school equipment, so I was wondering if you could help me."

"O-oh, okay."

Awed by her unbreakable smile, Masachika helplessly followed Yuki to the storehouse. Their journey was in almost complete silence until she unlocked the door, stepped inside, and made sure there was nobody else there. Immediately, she sprinted back toward Masachika, grabbed his arms, and peered closely at her brother's face as her expression inexplicably clouded with urgency.

"Masachika, are you okay?! Do you need me to use the Happiness Beam on you?!"

"No."

"I-Wuv-You Beeeam!!"

"I said no!"

After a sweet older woman showered him with love, a sweet younger girl showered him with love as well. It was a combination of kindness that really helped Masachika feel like everything was going to be okay.

Combat power is what's really important.

"Man, is it just me, or was that perfect?"

"I thought that went very well, too."

Both Takeshi and Hikaru expressed satisfaction with their final rehearsal before the show. Sayaka didn't have a single complaint this time, either. Alisa and even Nonoa, more or less, seemed pleased as well. Masachika was no different, genuinely feeling that this was their best performance yet. Furthermore, each member seemed more fired up than ever in the new outfits that Nonoa had made specifically for the show.

"That was incredible… I mean it," uttered Masachika, deeply impressed, as he clapped.

"Come on, bro. You're making it sound like that was the show. That was just practice," Takeshi chimed in bashfully.

"Ha-ha. Yeah, I know. But seriously, I'm honestly impressed what a great team you guys make."

"You're the one who brought us together, Kuze."

"Yeah, bro."

"…Oh, yeah."

"Did you seriously forget?!" joked Takeshi, making Alisa and Sayaka burst into laughter. Incidentally, Nonoa had stopped calling Masachika by his first name, since according to her, it didn't feel right.

"All right, guys! I know it's a little early, but now that we got our manager's seal of approval, let's head backstage!"

"Hold up, Takeshi. You're forgetting something important."

"Huh?"

"Seriously? You still haven't decided on who the band's leader is going to be, right?" explained Masachika, fairly surprised that Takeshi seemed genuinely confused, but the moment he finished his sentence, he noticed Alisa tense from the corner of his eye. Takeshi, on the other hand, seemed oblivious and was sluggish to react, to boot.

"O-ohhh, that. Right."

"How could you forget something so important?"

"I wouldn't say I forgot. Just..." He looked at Alisa. "In my head, Alya was already the leader, to be honest..."

"...?!"

As Alisa's eyes widened in surprise, Hikaru chimed in to agree with Takeshi as well.

"I feel the same way. If anyone's the leader here, it's Alya."

"...?! Hikaru...?"

After Alisa shot Hikaru a look of utter shock, he gently smiled back at her and added:

"Masachika was right when he said we make a great team...and I honestly believe that you're one of the biggest reasons it all worked out, Alya. You have no idea how happy it made me seeing you approach everyone to make sure we all got to know each other. Plus, when you came up with our band name..."

Hikaru paused and bashfully scratched his cheek.

"While everyone else was prioritizing things they like, you were the only one who came up with a name that spoke to every one of us as a group, and I honestly feel like that influenced the direction our band took. That's why...ever since that moment, you were the only one fit to lead, in my eyes."

Alisa pressed her lips together, as if she were holding back powerful emotions, and her eyelids fluttered.

"Hikaru?! Come on, bro! Why do ya have to be Mr. Cool, saying all the right things here?! You're making me look like an idiot!"

"Read the room, idiot."

"Nobody has to make you look like an idiot."

"Hey?!"

Both Masachika and Hikaru promptly chimed in with their

swift counters to shut Takeshi down, since right when the mood couldn't have been more perfect, he started complaining and ruined everything. Even Alisa seemed deflated.

"Anyway, that's two votes for Alya. What about you two?"

Masachika quickly turned to Sayaka and Nonoa to regain control of the conversation.

"It would be in poor taste to vote against her after all that," said Sayaka, shrugging, with a blank expression.

"Oh, Sayaaa. You can be honest with us."

"Excuse me, Nonoa?"

"Oh, Sayaaa. You can be honest with us."

"I didn't ask you to repeat yourself!"

Everyone in the room chuckled at their heartwarming exchange.

"What about you, Nonoa?"

"Why not? Let's do this, Leader," she immediately replied while waving at Alisa. The spotlight was on Alisa as she began to tremble, but after closing her eyes and relaxing her expression for a few moments, she grinned confidently and clenched her fist.

"Okay, everyone. This is Fortitude's first live show. Let's do this! Is everybody ready?!"

Alisa raised her fist into the air while everyone, even Masachika…

"Yeahhh!"

"Y-Yeah!"

"Yeah?"

"Yeah…"

"Sure…"

"Guys, would it kill some of you to show some enthusiasm? And what was with the delay?" interjected Masachika, which was immediately followed by Alisa's clenched fist slowly lowering as her shoulders gradually hunched.

"…!"

"See?! Look what you guys did! You embarrassed her! She put a lot of heart into that! She did something she has never done before, and now look! Stop bullying our leader!"

"Masachika."

"Hmm?"

"Please shut up."
"Yes, ma'am."

"Whoa… Look at the crowd. Dammit. I'm getting nervous."

"Ha-ha-ha. Right? I think the crowd's going to be bigger than this by the time we start, though. We seem to have gathered a lot of attention."

"Yeah, man… A lot of people actually stopped me to talk about the band yesterday."

Twenty minutes before showtime, everyone moved backstage. A slight shiver of excitement ran down Takeshi's spine while he took a peek at the stage from one of the wings, but he soon turned to Masachika.

"Oh, yeah. We ran into Kiryuuin yesterday, which got me wondering… Did something happen between you two?"

"Kiryuuin? Which one? The guy? And what do you mean 'Did something happen?' That's kind of vague."

"Yeah, the guy. And I don't know, either, man. He just kept asking over and over if ya were gonna be onstage playing with us…"

"…? What? Me?"

"Yeah."

Masachika tilted his head in confusion, but after thinking about it for a few moments, he vaguely recalled Yuushou asking him something similar the other day. He had no idea why, though.

"I told him ya were the manager, so ya weren't going to be onstage with us, and he, like, rolled his eyes and walked away all annoyed. Any idea why?"

"…No clue."

"Oof," another voice grunted suddenly, which immediately attracted the attention of both Masachika and Takeshi, where they found Nonoa with her eyes half-open.

"…? What's wrong?"

"That poor little runner-up…," she muttered, as if she were talking to herself, making Masachika frown.

"Poor little runner-up"? What the...? Something about this seems vaguely familiar...

Feeling fragments of the past coming to the surface of his mind, Masachika lowered his gaze, in search of the memory that would connect the dots, but Takeshi suddenly spoke and broke his train of thought.

"Oh, hey. It's probably about time I go get Kanau."

"All right, be safe."

"You better be back before we go on."

"Yeah, I'll be back soon."

Once Takeshi rushed off, Nonoa spoke up as well.

"A'ight, I'm gonna go grab Leo and Lea, then."

"Who?"

"My little brother and sister. B-R-B."

"Sorry, I think I'm going to go to the bathroom before we start..."

"Seriously?" Masachika shrugged as each member started to disappear one after another.

"...I guess waiting backstage for so long is just making everyone needlessly agitated."

When he turned around, he coincidentally made eye contact with Sayaka, who immediately glanced at Alisa, then looked up and off to the side before suddenly turning on her heel.

"I think I'm going to go say hello to Leo and Lea, too."

"Come on, you don't have to do that."

"Do what? I'll be back in ten minutes."

"Hey—!"

Before he could even get another word out, Sayaka was gone, leaving only Alisa and Masachika backstage. There was something awkward about being alone with Alisa, especially since he was still rather embarrassed after being caught backstage alone with her just yesterday by someone who thought he was proposing to her.

"So, uh... I thought this team had a real sense of unity at first, but look at us now. Everyone's gone. What do you think, Leader?"

But his lighthearted joke was met with silence, so being the moderately concerned manager that he was, he took a closer look at her, and his eyes opened wide.

"A-Alya?"

Her eyebrows were drooping, and the muscles around her eyes seemed tense. It was as if she were about to burst into tears at any moment. But when Masachika worriedly called out her name, she immediately lowered her gaze in genuine surprise while trying to hide her face. However, only when he saw her shoulders faintly trembling did his confusion finally reach its peak.

...?! I-is she crying? Wh-what should I do? Should I gently hug her? Wait, wait, wait. Only really good-looking guys can get away with stuff like that. Besides, I don't even know why she's upset, so maybe I should stand in the way so that nobody sees her crying?

The intense conflict resolved itself in his head in a mere second. He decided to go with a compromise and lend Alisa his shoulder instead, since it wasn't as intimate as a hug. He approached Alisa and awkwardly placed her head on his shoulder, then started to rub her head as gently as he could, just like how Maria rubbed his.

"What's wrong? Did being picked as the leader really make you that happy?"

When he put the only reason that he could come up with into words, he felt Alisa nodding into his shoulder.

"Am I going to be able to live up to their expectations...?"

Her trembling voice expressed a seed of doubt that stunned Masachika, and almost immediately, he was overcome with regret for how shortsighted he had been. At the end of the day, he alone was the one who gave her the task to surpass Sayaka and become the leader. That was the drive that drove Alisa to push herself as hard as she could to live up to his expectations, and yet all Masachika had done was get jealous. He didn't even consider how much of an emotional toll this all must have taken on her.

I'm such an idiot...! Just because she makes everything look easy, that doesn't mean that she's not hurting on the inside! She has been so scared, and I'm an idiot for not even noticing that until now! Alya has never really asserted herself in the student council. She more or less

has kept to herself, and yet she worked so hard to communicate and get to know four people who she wasn't even friends with. I should have been there for her!

The psychological burden of being asked to simultaneously get along with four new people for someone who had never gone out of her way to make a friend in her life was something Masachika hadn't even considered. It didn't help that he claimed he would be there for her like he always was, then not help at all, since he wrongly assumed that she was doing fine on her own, and to top it all off, he got jealous…

"You've exceeded all of my expectations as a partner… I really admire you. I'm sorry I wasn't there for you as much as I should have been. I'm really sorry…" Masachika apologized in a voice tainted with regret. Alisa shook her head, but Masachika still seemed to be pained by a sliver of guilt, and he passionately added:

"You really are amazing… You worked as a team, and you even found out how to be a leader—two things you weren't used to doing. You have been working so hard."

He lightly patted her on the back until she eventually spoke up.

"I always thought I was the hardest worker and that I was the best, but I was wrong."

It was an unexpected confession, but Masachika didn't say a word. He only listened.

"I finally realized that it was nothing more than a fantasy during the closing ceremony speeches."

Hearing her self-deprecating monologue immediately reminded him of her speech, where she acknowledged how inexperienced she truly was.

"While I'm working hard on some things, others are working hard on completely different things. There is not a single person that I'm better than at everything. Take my singing, for example. I might be able to sing well, but I can't play a single instrument…"

Her voice relaxed before she quietly added:

"I don't have the skill set that Sayaka has to see the whole picture and give precise instructions to others. I don't have the flexibility to adapt, like Nonoa. I don't have the radiance that Takeshi has to light up the mood when things get dark. I don't have the heart to be as considerate of others, like Hikaru. It's no surprise, though. I never put in the effort to improve any of my relationships."

Alisa had concluded that she had neglected forming any sort of meaningful relationship with others because she had continued to work alone all these years in order to avoid conflict, and Masachika was both touched and inspired by how stubbornly honest and harsh she was being with herself.

"So when I decided I was going to do whatever it took to be recognized as a leader...I knew my only chance was to approach them head-on. I wasn't going to play games. I told myself that I had to work harder than anyone else so that I could lead them."

"Yeah... You worked really hard. I mean it."

Masachika's heart was still festering with regret as he began awkwardly rubbing Alisa's head again.

I should have done this a long time ago, he thought. *I should have listened to her and been there for her. "Do they even need me here?" What was I thinking? Alya needed me. I'm her partner before I'm their band manager, dammit. If the band seemed like it was going well, then my first priority should have been Alya...*

Regret and self-reflection filled his mind.

"I'm glad it all worked out for you," he warmly told Alisa.

"...Me too."

After she nodded, she buried her face into Masachika's shoulder and whispered:

"<It feels so good to be appreciated...!>"

He couldn't completely comprehend exactly what she meant by that. She appeared to be relieved that they recognized her as a leader, but that didn't seem to be the full story. However, before he could clear up any doubts there may have been, an unwelcome visitor suddenly appeared backstage.

"...?! Huh?!"

The scream belonged to the same boy who, by curious coincidence, had seen them alone backstage yesterday as well. But this time what he saw was Alisa trying to hold back her tears while burying her face into Masachika's chest while he gently stroked her head. The male student smirked at the misleading sight and asked:

"So, uh… I take it she liked the engagement ring?"

"…Sure, let's go with that. Do you think you could give us some privacy now?"

"Oh, of course. Enjoy…"

After making sure the student returned to the stage wing, Alisa stepped away from Masachika with a slightly uncomfortable expression.

"…Are you feeling better?"

Alisa touched her eyes.

"I think my eyes might be a little red."

"A little, but you'll be fine. The audience won't be able to tell, and your bandmates won't say anything about it, either."

"You're probably right."

After she agreed, Masachika quickly changed the subject with a bright note in his voice.

"All right, then. I know it already kind of feels like we did it and the show's over, but it's time—"

An explosive *pop* suddenly echoed from the stage.

Earlier that day.

Around the time the band was practicing one last time before the show, Touya and Chisaki were busy greeting the VIP guests of the Autumn Heights Festival: members of the First Light Committee. Incidentally, all the work that needed to be done by the school festival committee was being handled by other members so they could focus on this important task.

"Welcome to our school festival. I am the current student council president, Touya Kenzaki."

"And I am the vice president, Chisaki Sarashina."

Gathered in the student council room, which was tidied up for the guests, were not merely former presidents and vice presidents of the student council but also the biggest heavyweights in the corporate and political world. Even the CEO of Taniyama Heavy Industries, Sayaka's father, was among them. And…

"You must be Gensei Suou, yes? We are proud to have Yuki with us as a member of the student council."

"You don't say?"

...even Gensei, Masachika's and Yuki's grandfather, was there.

"Now, how about I show you all around? This way, please."

After finishing their nerve-racking introduction, Touya promptly began to guide the tycoons around the school festival. Once they stepped out into the hallway, every student who saw the members of the First Light Committee (aka FLC) were overcome with surprise as they quickly moved out of the way, clearing a path for them. Of course, these students would love to say hello to these political figures and big-shot CEOs, who they would usually only see on TV or in magazines, but even the smallest greeting was forbidden. There was an unwritten rule that members of the FLC mustn't be bothered during their time at the school festival. The only ones permitted to entertain them were the student council president and vice president, and the only exception to the rule was when a student needed to reply to something a member of the FLC said to them. Obviously, crowding around them or trying to take their pictures was out of the question. Even visitors at the school festival who were not students enrolled at this school had been asked not to bother them.

Therefore, everything was going smoothly even though their bodyguards weren't present. They didn't even have to limit the number of people allowed at the festival, either.

"Oh my... I do not remember a greenhouse being there when I was a student."

"An alumnus actually donated it to our school eight years ago for the gardening club and flower arrangement club."

"Interesting. Are you saying that the flower arrangement club is growing flowers inside there?"

"Yes, they are."

"Someone donated an entire greenhouse. Impressive... I forget who it was, but didn't someone donate a boxing ring a while back for the boxing club, too?"

"That would be Mr. Tamura, the CEO of Forestin. I hear he is a huge fan of boxing."

"Ah, yes... Him..."

Touya smoothly answered the alumnus's question while gazing at the greenhouse out the window, but while he may have seemed confident, his heart was hammering against his chest as he wondered what they were going to ask next. Put simply, he was so nervous that he was about to vomit.

After all, Touya never really had nerves of steel. In fact, up until around a year and a half ago, he was more timid than anything. One could even claim he was mentally weak. He didn't have any confidence, and he had this insecurity that everyone around him was looking down on him and making fun of him. His groundless fears came from the inside, and he had built a wall around himself to protect his heart from the outside, and it would have stayed that way if the bold, lively warrior, Chisaki, hadn't mercilessly knocked that barrier down. Touya was instantly attracted to her unapologetic attitude of sticking to what she believed, and it motivated him to change himself. And now...she was right there by his side, supporting him.

"...?"

Chisaki blinked curiously back at Touya's gaze, but it was this face of hers, which knew no fear, that gave him the courage to push forward and stand tall.

"Would you like to see the greenhouse up close?"

"I would if we have time."

"Is everyone else okay with that?"

After receiving the other alumni's approval, Touya tightened his core and leg muscles while he confidently started to walk ahead. He was going to be a school representative that his peers were proud of and a boyfriend that Chisaki wouldn't be ashamed of.

Once he had a taste of confidence, his tunnel vision naturally widened until it was no more, allowing him to clearly see the faces of each student staring his way, and their awestruck gazes moved his heart. Who could have imagined that someone once mocked by his peers was now respected and being watched in admiration by students in every direction. Even Chisaki, who used to be afraid of men, now looked up to him with a strong and ever-growing sense of trust. When Touya realized that he had earned all of this through his hard work, he felt something warm swelling in his chest.

"Touya? What's wrong?" whispered Chisaki, as if she noticed something different about his expression.

"I'm fine…," replied Touya, genuinely smiling to let her know that everything was okay.

"Can you feel that? Their gazes…"

There was no denying that people viewed them differently this year. But despite his lack of words, Chisaki glanced quietly at her surroundings and nodded as if she knew her other half like the back of her hand. As Touya's lips curled slowly into a loving smile, Chisaki faced forward and replied with a detached tone:

"I felt two bloodthirsty stares."

"Yeah, no. I don't know anything about that."

"Twenty meters ahead in front of the stairwell: the man in a blue shirt and the man wearing the black hat."

"Wait, wait, wait. What?"

Touya followed Chisaki's gaze, despite still not processing what she was saying. There, he found two people exactly as she described, and they were gradually getting closer.

"Wh-what do you think we should do?"

He trusted Chisaki's judgment even more than his own during situations like this, and he was very much aware of this, so he wasted no time asking her to make a decision.

"You wait here, Touya. I'm going to—"

Chisaki began to make a move before she even finished talking, but the two men were one step ahead of her.

"…!"

They started running straight for them, prompting Touya to brace himself for whatever was to come.

"You two! Stop right there—!"

The instant that final word left his lips, the sprinting man in blue stuffed his hand into his bag before pulling out something metallic with a black luster, startling the student council president.

What…? Brass knuckles? A gun?! You've got to be kidding me?!

The reality went beyond anything he could have ever imagined, making him completely freeze. His brain refused to interpret the reality right before his eyes. His body wouldn't listen to a single command, even as the man pointed the muzzle of his gun at someone behind Touya. And when the stranger put his finger on the trigger—Chisaki kicked the pistol right out of his hand. Her left leg sliced through the air like a powerful gale, accurately hitting the weapon away, before she followed up with a relentless right kick straight into the man's groin.

"Gah?!"

There was no telling how hard she kicked him, but the man crumpled and simultaneously flew into the air. Incidentally, this would be the first time Touya had ever seen an aerial combo in real life. As the man leaned forward, he left his chin wide open for Chisaki's fierce uppercut, knocking him even higher into the air while unfolding his body until it was perfectly straight. He had become nothing more than the ideal sandbag, forsaken by gravity itself. His pathetically helpless body was thereupon introduced to five powerful blows via Chisaki's fists. At least it appeared to be five blows to Touya's eyes, but it could have been even more, for all he knew.

"Rrr...bt..."

The man grunted like a frog that had been squished, before hitting the ground in the hallway. Meanwhile, the other man seemed to have been struck dumb with astonishment. Only when Chisaki set her sight on him did he begin to panic, while holding his smartphone in the air.

"W-wait! It was just a prank! It was just a prank, bro!"

"Uh-huh. Well, let me show you a reverse prank," she proposed with a blank expression before performing the exact same aerial combo while unenthusiastically saying, "Hilarious, right?" Within the span of a mere two seconds, two men were piled on the floor. It all happened so quickly and unexpectedly that the surrounding students couldn't even process what had happened and froze. However, after a few moments went by, a male student suddenly looked at the first man to drop and speculated:

"Hold on. Isn't that Guilish?"

"Huh? That infamous internet prankster?"

"That's him? Wasn't he arrested for trying to prank some random guy on the street and injuring him?"

"Yo, this pistol's a toy."

"Did this guy legit try to pull off a fake assassination as a prank? Is he stupid?"

The first student's comment triggered the other students to start moving around and talk while also giving Touya a moment to mentally regroup as well. He thereupon turned and bowed deeply to the members of the First Light Committee.

"I am terribly sorry for this. It appears a couple of people unfit for our academy have sneaked into our school festival. I am fully prepared to be punished, but would you mind if the vice president left first?"

After Touya's humble apology, the oldest member of the FLC spoke on behalf of his peers.

"There appears to be some mismanagement at the gate…but, well, do what you need to do."

"Thank you very much!" shouted Touya while he lifted his head back up. He then approached Chisaki and hastily whispered:

"Sorry, Chisaki, but do you think you could deal with these two bums for me? We have to figure out who invited them. I'll handle the First Light Committee in the meantime."

"Got it. I'll take them to the disciplinary committee room for questioning."

"…Don't overdo it, okay?" advised Touya just in case, since she had already demonstrated self-defense to an almost excessive degree, but surprisingly, Chisaki firmly nodded back without even putting up a fight.

"Don't worry. I'm just going to separate the burnable trash from the non-burnable trash."

"I'm not sure that's a good idea. What does that even mean?"

"Huh? It means that I'm going to first peel their flesh from their bones—"

"Ow, no! I hope that's just a figure of speech! Either way, don't do that!"

But despite his horror, Touya still left them in Chisaki's hands...

"———! ———!"

...when all of a sudden, a violent, furious voice began echoing down the hallway.

◇

Around that same time, Takeshi was wandering around the schoolyard with his phone in hand while searching for his little brother.

"Uh...? He should be around here somewhere... How am I going to find him with all these people here?"

His nine-year-old little brother was still very short, especially when compared to most of the crowd, who were high school students or older, so it was starting to feel like searching for a needle in a haystack. But even then, Takeshi didn't give up as he desperately searched for his little brother...until he noticed the backside of a familiar individual wearing a baseball cap so low, it had to have been obscuring her eyes. His gaze was drawn to her, but only when she unexpectedly turned to the side did he gasp in surprise.

"...?! Nao?"

It was his supposed friend who'd suddenly disappeared a month ago. She turned around when she heard her name being called, and their eyes met.

"Takeshi..."

"Why...?"

They exchanged confused, awkward gazes within the crowd, but eventually, Nao opened her mouth to be the first one to break the silence...when all of a sudden, there was an explosion somewhere in the distance.

◇

What? This can't be happening...!

Sayaka stood in front of the source of the explosion with her teeth clenched while she ruminated on a conversation she'd had the week before.

"Sayaka, what is the most important trait for a member of the disciplinary committee to have?"

That was the question that Sumire had asked her during the disciplinary committee meeting before the school festival. Sayaka had rapidly racked her brain to find the answer that her peer desired, since she originally wanted to be a member of the disciplinary committee for extremely self-serving reasons. The first reason was simple: It would look good on her school record. The other reason was that it would help her get dirt on her fellow peers, which she could exploit. Both reasons were needed for her to elevate her standing at school. Furthermore, it would help her build a network of contacts that could be beneficial for her down the road as well.

Sayaka was known as a serious person and a model student, but this wasn't a burden to her, since she figured that this was how someone needed to behave if they were going to lead. It wasn't like she especially loved rules or despised those who broke them, so she wasn't going to force anyone else to behave the way she did. In fact, she didn't care about others enough to even worry about how they behaved.

Nevertheless, Sayaka wasn't foolish enough to honestly admit that right now.

"Hmm..."

She bought time while searching for the best answer in her mind.

"Perhaps a will to always make sure there is a balance between school rules and student wishes?"

How'd you like that? Sayaka had thought while proudly making finger guns in her head. However...

"No, Sayaka."

Her answer was immediately shot down, making her eyebrow twitch. Sumire stared off into space as if she were peering into a world that not even she had reached yet.

"The most important trait for a member of the disciplinary committee to have is..."

She paused for a second before continuing in a voice rife with envy and conviction.

"Combat power."

What the hell is she talking about? Sayaka had wondered from the bottom of her heart, but once again, she wasn't so foolish as to honestly put that thought into words.

"Oh... Well, if that's the case, then I suppose I don't meet the requirement..."

Even then, she still couldn't help but reply sarcastically, but Sumire elegantly smiled back all the same.

"You needn't solve everything on your own. If there is ever an emergency and you require combat power that you lack, then you would be right to call for someone who possesses the strength you need. If you can protect the weak that way, then that is the only thing that matters."

She had posed haughtily, pressing the back of her hand against her cheek while she cackled.

I think you watch too much anime, Sayaka had thought, but she simultaneously felt a sense of closeness with Sumire. However, never in her wildest dreams did she imagine that an emergency such as this would come. After Sayaka left backstage, she started to wander around the schoolyard under the guise of finding Nonoa...when some guy suddenly lit a firecracker right in front of her.

"Eek!"

"Whoa?! What the hell?!"

As the crowd began to scream in panic, the man kicked the smoking firecracker on the ground into the crowd. Unsurprisingly, everyone nearby ran away while screaming bloody murder.

Wh-who is that guy?! Did he sneak in?!

The agent of chaos himself seemed to be strangely expressionless. There was something utterly bizarre about him, and it wasn't only his unkempt mustache and stretched, worn sleeves.

"If there is ever an emergency and you require fighting power that you lack, then you would be right to call for someone who possesses the strength you need."

Facing an emergency reminded her of Sumire's advice, but before she could act, a child, who had to have been in elementary school, was shoved to the ground by another student trying to run away.

"Ah!" cried the boy, clutching his knees. After Sayaka made the split-second decision to lift him up, she immediately took out her phone.

"Are you okay?!"

"Ah. Y-yes. Thank you, lady."

Sayaka called Sumire right away while making sure the boy was okay.

"Hey, it's me! Sayaka! I'm in the schoolyard by the—"

But even as she explained the situation, the man slowly turned toward the outdoor stage, then began to march straight for it with his unchanging, eerie blank expression.

"Wh-what the...?!"

The sudden explosion didn't end with a single pop but continued, eliciting an earsplitting noise that clashed with the students' screams.

"...!"

Masachika rushed toward the stage wing to see what the thunderous noise was, immediately followed by Alisa. While still acknowledging her from the corner of his eye, he shifted his gaze toward the stage, where he saw something spewing smoke, accompanied by aggressive blasts as members of the dance club ran this way and that.

"Firecrackers...?!"

But even uncovering the source of the racket didn't make Masachika any less confused, and before he could even process what was going on, another firecracker was thrown onstage while another simultaneously went off in the seating section.

"Hey! Get off the stage! Now!"

He yelled to the dance members onstage, but the firecracker must have been thrown in the middle of their performance, since two or three students seemed to have fallen down and couldn't get up.

Tsk! I need something that can protect us from these giant firecrackers...

As Masachika's eyes darted around in search of something he could use as a shield in order to take the fallen students to safety, Alisa sprinted right past him with a microphone in her hand.

"Hey?!"

She rushed onstage and surveyed the seating section until she discovered the man responsible for this chaos. The middle-aged man, who was dressed in worn-out clothes and standing behind the seating section, pulled out another firework from his shoulder bag, lit the fuse, then cocked his arm back.

"Stop right there!" she immediately shouted as her microphone-enhanced voice powerfully echoed through the speaker, making the man freeze along with the audience members he was aiming at. Their eyes reflexively shot toward the stage, where a breathtakingly beautiful young girl boldly stood as her silver locks flowed in the wind.

"Whoa…"

"Princess Alya…"

Both those who knew her and those who did not were equally captivated by her. A few seconds of silence followed until a sudden blast broke them out of their trance. The man, who had unconsciously stopped, seemed to have forgotten that he'd lit the firecracker already, allowing it to blow up in his own hand. He immediately dropped it in a fluster, then set his eyes on Alisa onstage, with an unhinged stare.

"Please do not panic and safely evacuate to—"

Alisa ignored him for the time being to evacuate the audience, but that worked out perfectly for the stranger, as he threw yet another firecracker right at her.

"Ah…!" someone shouted, his voice trembling with panic as the firecracker rapidly approached Alisa. The audience watched, their hearts drumming against their chests…when a young man unexpectedly rushed onstage from the wing and kicked the firecracker away in midair. It was like something you would see in an action movie, which warranted faint gasps from the audience. Meanwhile—

Ouch! …Wait. That actually didn't hurt! That was a close one, though! There's no way I'm going to be able to pull that off again!

Despite how brilliant that move he just pulled off was, Masachika was drenched in a cold sweat. One minute, he was giving other staff members directions, and the next, he was rushing onstage to protect Alisa from an incoming firecracker. Once he realized that using his hands would be dangerous, he quickly switched to his feet, but it was mostly luck that saved them.

"Are you okay, Alya?"

"Y-yeah."

"Good."

He made sure Alisa was safe immediately after making sure the firecracker landed somewhere safely offstage.

If I'm prioritizing Alya's safety, then I should have used my hands...

While reflecting on his poor judgment, he stood in front of Alisa to protect her as he considered his next move.

Should I go over there myself and grab the guy? Wait. I can't leave Alya behind...

His eyes wandered in search of a good solution until he noticed a gorgeously dressed group cutting through the crowd and heading his way. Leading the group was a female student with her signature honey-blond hair tied into two spiral-curled pigtails.

"...!"

Immediately, Masachika grabbed Alisa's hand holding the microphone and shouted:

"I need everyone standing in front of the takoyaki stall to please clear the path! Everyone at the entrance, move out of the way, too!"

The panic-stricken crowd immediately followed orders, creating a two-meter-wide path for the beautiful woman in men's clothing to sprint down as quickly as she could. Her honey-blond spiral-curled pigtails danced in the wind as three girls, dressed masculinely, followed in an orderly manner.

The middle-aged man seemed sort of startled by their sudden arrival, but then he threw the three firecrackers he was holding at the leader of the pack—Sumire. However, Sumire showed no fear as she calmly raised her cape in front of her face and ran straight through the fireworks without slowing down for even a moment. The instant she reached the man, she unsheathed her katana and swung in a single stroke. Although he quickly turned on his heel to escape, it was too late, for the blade had already connected with his back. Despite being a mere replica, it was sturdy enough to probably break a few bones if you swung hard enough. Plus, it was being swung by a master swordsman who easily put male adults to shame with a bamboo sword, despite being a teenage girl. Put simply, it went exactly how anyone guessed it would.

The man's back arched until he was the shape of a shrimp, and as the lit firecrackers slipped from his hands, two female students shot past Sumire from each side to slice their fuses, extinguishing the fire like they were performing some sort of parlor trick.

The last to arrive and most petite of the girls then drilled her sheathed rapier straight into the man's right side.

"Guh?!"

The hit to his liver brought the man to the ground, where he was immediately restrained by the female students.

"Whoa…"

"Th-that was so badass…"

"Sumire…! Ah…!"

The crowd instinctively erupted with applause, as if they had just witnessed a historical play in real time. As the crowd continued to roar, Sumire took the stage, where she was greeted by Masachika with a bow.

"Thanks, Sumire."

"Not at all. I should be thanking you. We were only able to make it here as quickly as we did because of you, after all."

She's tough, thought Masachika while Sumire brushed her spiral-curled pigtails back like it was nothing.

"Will the disciplinary committee be able to handle the rest?"

"I wish I could say we have everything under control, but we have run into a few issues," replied Sumire, glancing at the restrained man.

"'Issues'?"

"Apparently, that man isn't the only uninvited guest who sneaked into our school's festival."

""What?""

"The student council president and my lady seem to have run into two scoundrels as well."

"What?!"

"Is the president okay?" said Alisa, sounding worried, but Sumire proudly puffed out her chest and replied:

"Of course he is. My lady was there with him, after all."

"Uh…?"

"She's talking about Chisaki."

"Huh? O-oh."

Alisa blinked in wonder for a few moments, for this was a world she was very unfamiliar with.

"There were a few more incidents around school as well… It appears a few different unwelcome groups have somehow infiltrated the festival."

"But how…?"

Masachika immediately shook his head before thinking about it any further, since speculation could wait. What he needed to focus on right now was dealing with the situation at hand.

"All right. I should get back to work after finishing up a few things here."

"Oh, then I'll come—"

"You stay here, Alya."

"Huh?"

Masachika looked back at Alisa, whose eyes were wide, and confidently replied:

"I need you to keep the audience calm. After that, talk to the students on staff here, prepare for your performance, and sing your heart out."

"What? But…"

Are we really going to be performing after all that? Besides, I'm a member of the student council. Shouldn't I be helping? That was what the clear hesitation in Alisa's eyes was saying while Masachika peered right into them with a piercing gaze.

"As the manager of Fortitude, I have a duty to make sure the performance goes smoothly. Besides, I told you already. I'll get rid of anyone who holds you back or slows you down," he reminded her, his voice full of determination. The vow he'd made to Alisa yesterday erased all the doubt in her eyes, revealing a radiant glow.

"So trust me…and wait for me. I'll make sure this performance happens," he said.

Alisa clasped her hands together before her chest with a smile brimming with a sense of trust.

"I believe in you."

"Good."

"...Be careful."

"I will."

Masachika confidently smiled back at her before turning around to speak with Sumire.

"All right, so... Do you think the disciplinary committee could lend us a few members to act as security here?"

"But of course. Hiiragi!"

"At your service."

Whoosh!

Sumire snapped her fingers, suddenly revealing a female student in glasses standing behind her... Was she a ninja or something?

"Help Alisa Kujou here calm the masses."

"As you wish."

Even though the female student dressed in male attire theatrically bowed to the point that it was almost comedic, she turned out to be the vice president of the girls' kendo club. In other words, the students would be safe with her around.

"I really appreciate this. Anyway, I'll see you guys later."

"Okay."

After thanking Sumire once more, Masachika made eye contact with Alisa one last time before hopping offstage and heading off to sort out this mess.

CHAPTER 7 Violence is always the answer.

"Takeshi!"

Masachika's first mission was to send all of the band members back to Alisa's side, so he ran over to where he'd last seen Takeshi from his vantage point onstage.

"Hey! Takeshi!"

"O-oh, hey…"

Takeshi's eyebrows were knit with concern, and he was slow to reply, even though Masachika was nearby, so Masachika followed his friend's line of sight…and froze.

"Nao…"

"…"

Nao said nothing and averted her gaze as if she didn't know what to say. Masachika hesitated for only a second before facing his mystified friend and protested:

"Takeshi, you can deal with Nao later. We need you back at the stage."

"Huh? But…"

"She's not going to run away, so you can talk to her later! Right now, I need you to focus on the show! You made a promise with your brother, right?"

Takeshi's shoulders twitched, and he immediately began to look around in a fluster.

"O-oh, yeah! Kanau! Where is he?!"

"Hey…?! Nao!"

Masachika was caught off guard after seeing his friend suddenly dash off, but after running only a few steps after him, he stopped and turned to face Nao, startling her. However, right as she returned the gaze, he swiftly lowered his head and bowed.

"I apologize about earlier! I was out of line!"

"Huh—?"

"Sorry, I'll explain later!" he hastily added before chasing after Takeshi. Fortunately for him, Takeshi was wandering around the area in search of his brother, so he managed to almost immediately catch up with him...right as Takeshi found Kanau as well.

"Kanau!"

"Ah! Takeshi!"

"Are you okay?! Are you hurt?!"

"I-I'm fine. This lady protected me..."

The boy glanced at the girl who was holding his hand: Sayaka. Immediately, Takeshi grabbed Sayaka's free hand and bowed deeply.

"Sayaka! Thank you so much!"

"I—I just happened to be around when he needed help. That's all..."

"I mean it! Thank you, thank you, thank you!"

Takeshi's intense gratitude almost made Sayaka start to tremble, so she decided to readjust her glasses to give her a moment to hide her surprise...when she realized that both of her hands were being held, and she froze. Although seeing her obviously flustered was a rare treat that took Masachika by surprise, he had no choice but to face Takeshi and reiterate:

"I'm sorry to interrupt your touching moment, but do you think you could head back to the stage for me? You can take your brother with you."

"Huh? But..."

"The show hasn't been canceled. We're going to do this, so I need you to trust me and get ready. I'll go grab Hikaru and Nonoa in the meantime."

After Takeshi and Sayaka exchanged glances, they nodded firmly and went straight back to the stage with Kanau. While he watched them from afar, Masachika took out his phone and began to speculate about where the other two could be.

"Hikaru's...probably in the bathroom. The one in the schoolhouse."

He called Hikaru's phone while he sprinted toward the schoolhouse.

◇

"*Bff*... I still feel sick... I always get nauseated when I'm nervous..."

After finishing up in the bathroom, Hikaru was walking down the hallway toward the schoolyard, but as he stepped outside, he heard a couple arguing over something. When he looked in the direction of the noise, he noticed a kind of flashy girl surrounded by a crowd of guys. The intense nature of the interaction made it clear that these boys weren't just trying to get her number or anything else innocent. Besides, the fact that it was four guys surrounding one girl was already terrifying enough. Each one of them had gaudily dyed hair as well: some blond and some even green. They were dressed way too casually—borderline sloppily. They appeared to be run-of-the-mill delinquents, which wasn't something often seen in this neighborhood, let alone at Seirei Academy.

What in the world? What are people like that doing at our school?

It didn't seem feasible that they were just some student's mischievous friends. Plus, all invitations included the student's name, so they would be responsible for any guest that caused trouble. In other words, it was hard to believe that someone would risk inviting a group of troublemakers, then let them loose to freely roam the school.

What am I doing? There's no time to be speculating right now.

There seemed to be other students here and there who noticed something was wrong, but not one of them was lifting a finger to help the girl. Furthermore, Hikaru himself didn't have any fighting experience, much less had he even spoken to a delinquent before, but that didn't mean he could turn a blind eye.

"Hmm?"

He ignored his phone suddenly vibrating in his pocket and began to approach the ruffians.

"I told you already! I promised my sister I was coming, so I need to go! She's waiting for me!"

"And that's why I'm sayin' you should just tell her to meet you here."

"Yeah, that way, you'll both be *coming*."

The guys surrounding the clearly aggravated girl cackled vulgarly while gradually herding her toward a more private location.

"Hey, uh… Excuse me," murmured Hikaru with every bit of courage he could muster, but the ruffians gave him no more than a single glance before going back to completely ignoring his existence.

"Hey! Excuse me!"

"Tsk!"

Hikaru grabbed one of them by the shoulder after realizing that talking wasn't going to get him anywhere, and the delinquent immediately turned around with a wicked glare, making Hikaru's breath catch.

"As a member of the school festival committee, I am going to have to ask you to leave her alone. She is clearly uncomfortable."

Although bluffing, he spoke with confidence, but the guy he was talking to wasn't someone rational.

"Yeah, yeah. Whatever, man."

After knocking Hikaru's hand off him, he grabbed the girl by the arm as if he was done pretending to be "nice."

"Ouch! Let go!"

"Hey! Every one of you was invited here. If you cause any trouble, then whoever invited you is going to be punished for it!"

The delinquents froze for a few seconds when they heard the threat, before bursting into laughter.

"Oooh! He is, is he?"

"Just so ya know, the guy who invited us specifically asked us to do this."

"What…?" The grin instantly disappeared from the delinquent's face. "…?! Gah…!"

It happened in the blink of an eye. Hikaru's legs went limp as he collapsed to the ground, clutching his stomach. The unbearable pain didn't register until a second later, when it felt like his intestines had been turned inside out. He groaned in agony, feeling as if he were going to vomit his innards.

"Pffft! Ha-ha-ha! Pathetic! Maybe put on a little muscle before you try to act cool next time!"

"Daaamn. They don't got gyms in that mansion ya live in, Prince Charming?"

"Wh-what is wrong with you people?!"

Hikaru could hear the girl screaming at them while they mocked him, but he couldn't even focus on what she was saying, since he was experiencing the most pain he had ever felt in his life, tears clouding his vision as he stared at the ground. However...

"Ah! Sis! Leo!"

...at the very least, he knew someone was finally coming to help...

Oh, thank goodness...

It was a faint sense of relief amid a world of pain, but relief, nonetheless.

Nonoa was four years old when she realized there was a distinct difference between her and those around her. It all came to her during lunchtime in kindergarten. There was a rumor going around that there was a huge frog in the small pond at the corner of the playground, so a dozen or so children in the same class had gathered there in anticipation. Lo and behold, perched on top of a dead tree protruding from the water at roughly the center of the pond was a frog bigger than any of them had ever seen before, so of course, a few rambunctious boys started throwing rocks at it.

A teacher almost immediately came rushing over in a fluster. The children were often told not to play near the pond, since it was dangerous, so that was most likely why she was in such a hurry. However, when she saw how persistent the boys were being as they continued to throw rocks at the frog as it tried to swim away, her expression immediately changed.

"Stop that this instant! What did that frog do to deserve this?!"

The boys, who were throwing rocks, instantly froze. The kids watching lowered their gazes with a twinge of embarrassment as well. Only Nonoa genuinely wondered what the teacher could have been talking about. After all, there was no way the teacher knew what that frog deserved, so how could she lie with a straight face? Adults were always telling kids that lying was bad, so why…?

"Sorry!"

"We'll stop!"

Why were her peers fine with the answer the teacher gave? It went beyond strange. It was eerie. The lying teacher and deceived children were equally disgusting to Nonoa, who couldn't help but feel as if they weren't even from the same planet as she was.

She knew that they weren't supposed to be near the pond, since you could drown. She knew that you weren't supposed to hit your friends, since they would hit you back. But she couldn't figure out why you weren't supposed to throw rocks at frogs. It wasn't like the frog could throw rocks back at them. In fact, no matter how long she scratched her head over it, she couldn't come up with a single scenario where an ordinary frog could hurt a human being. It wasn't like they could turn into human beings, like in fairy tales, with a little magic, and the teacher didn't tell them to stop because frogs were dangerous. Put simply…

Oh. Everyone's just stupid.

That was the only explanation. The teacher probably didn't actually know why you shouldn't throw rocks at frogs. She was just lying and trying to trick everyone, and it worked. The other kids were fooled. But both the teacher, who thought she could deceive, and the deceived children were all idiots. That was all there was to it, and the moment Nonoa noticed that, she realized that she couldn't trust teachers. They were liars, after all.

"Promise me you all will never do that again."

""""Yes, ma'am.""""

But she understood that pointing that out wouldn't lead to anything but trouble. Plus, her mother often told her to listen to her teachers, and that was why…

"Yes, ma'am."

...she obediently agreed, just like her peers, but her distrust for her teachers only continued to grow after that day. When she actually started paying attention, she realized that teachers told countless lies and contradicted themselves as well. This was what a child could pick up on, so in actuality, they were probably lying even more than she realized. There was no way she could trust anything any of them said anymore after that.

"Hey, Daddy? Mommy? Why do teachers lie?" asked Nonoa one day at home. Her peers and teachers were making her skin crawl, and she couldn't take it anymore. After her parents' eyes opened wide in astonishment, they asked her what had happened, so she explained as best as she could for a child her age. She explained how her teacher wouldn't tell the truth—how she would just say whatever came to mind and tried to force everyone to believe her. But after she put her heart into explaining how she felt, her father nodded with a serious expression and rubbed her head.

"Nonoa... You're far more mature than your classmates. You're such a clever little girl."

"...I'm clever?"

"Yep. That's why you can tell when adults are lying."

Clever. It was a word she was not expecting to hear, for she had always believed that she was just weird, and that was why her father's unforeseen praise was like a brilliant light in the darkness to her.

"Lying... So does everyone lie?"

"Hmm... That's a difficult question to answer, but..."

Her father had fallen silent for a few moments, so her mother chimed in:

"Nono, I'm going to let you in on a little secret. In this world, whatever everyone believes is true becomes the truth."

"What? Even lies?"

"Even lies. If everyone says that a lie is the truth, then that's what it becomes."

"...That makes me sick," Nonoa had muttered and frowned, worrying her parents. The truth of the matter was that her parents still hadn't realized how unique their daughter truly was. They hadn't realized that she was born without a sense of empathy and couldn't

feel remorse. They believed that she was clever for her age, so she could tell when adults weren't telling the truth, but they were wrong. The reality was that Nonoa didn't understand emotionally charged arguments. She never let anyone's opinions influence her emotions, so she figured that her teacher was merely hiding her true nature. Nevertheless, it was this misunderstanding that miraculously allowed her parents to say just the right thing.

"Nonoa, you can feel proud that you're smarter than others...but it's still very important that you make sure to get along with them. Because creating friction between you and those you interact with will only lead to resentment and fighting, and that wouldn't be fun, right?"

"Exactly. And if you're still not happy about what your teacher says, you can come to me or your father and talk to us. Because we'll talk to your teacher if we have to."

Her parents' words really resonated with her because it was clear that they genuinely felt they were doing what was best for her. It was at this moment that Nonoa's parents became the only two adults she could trust, so she decided to do whatever they told her to do so that she could avoid conflict with the intellectually deprived. This ironclad rule was the only law keeping Nonoa in check and protecting her.

But right now, Nonoa was questioning that law of hers while a smugly grinning man approached her. Behind the ruffian was another man grabbing her sister Lea by the arm. Hikaru was clutching his stomach while curled up on the ground, and her brother Leo had also been beaten up for trying to save his sister. It was the first time Nonoa had felt her heart race in a long time.

Ah, this is nice...

Her heart was beating. Her body was on fire. She always felt like she had an overhead view of the world as though she were separate from her body, but this was different. It was as if she was finally returning to her body. She was experiencing the ecstasy of finally becoming human.

Wish I could enjoy this sensation a little longer...but I need to do something about that.

Nonoa racked her brain, glaring at the obstacle heading her way.

She wondered what she should do while recalling numerous rules her parents gave her:

"Be nice to your siblings."

"Cherish your friends."

"Do not, unprovoked, put your hands on others."

"Do not do anything dangerous."

"If you feel like you're in danger, run. If you can't do that, call for help."

"If anyone is making you uncomfortable—"

She considered each rule, trying to decide the best course of action…until she finally found her answer.

"Yooou. You've gotta be kiddin' me. This one's pretty damn cute, too—"

"Helllp! Somebody, help!!"

"…?!"

Nonoa began to scream her lungs out as the vulgarly leering man stood right in front of her. The sudden shriek startled the man, paralyzing him with fear…or so it appeared, but the real reason he was unable to move was because the girl in front of him didn't show any signs of being scared. She was calling for help, despite seemingly being unafraid, and once she had finished screaming, her eyes resembled glass beads—as lifeless as if she were responding only how she was programmed to act. The bizarre robotic nature coupled with her beauty and refined features made it all the more eerie.

"…!"

The man instinctively took a step back from the mysterious life-form, but it was already too late. After keeping her promise with her parents, Nonoa looked up at the man with a blank expression and decided it was time to eliminate the obstacle in her way.

Guess I'll gouge his eyes out first.

It was an extremely logical solution that she wasted no time implementing, thrusting two fingers toward his eyes.

"Whoa?!"

The man reflexively lurched back, turning his face to the side, so while she didn't manage to take his eyes, she managed to perfectly convey what she was willing to do.

Th-the hell? What was that?!

But he already knew the answer to that. He just didn't want to admit it. She was trying to gouge his eyes out. While it was a technique obviously forbidden in martial arts, there was an unwritten rule in street fights that you couldn't go for the eyes, and yet Nonoa still aimed for that weak point. There was even a hint of surprise and disappointment in her eyes, as if she couldn't believe she missed, like the reaction a soccer player might have when they'd missed a shot.

"Eek!" the man shrieked instinctively, for he was overcome with a spine-chilling fear like he had never felt before. Even this man, who was used to violence, had never experienced something like this before. There was no murderous intent, anger, or amusement in Nonoa's eyes. It seemed to be nothing more than a sudden act of brutal violence, and the fact that she seemed to be entirely unfazed by it frightened the man.

"A-ahhhhhh!!"

Therefore, his body reacted with violence for the sake of survival. The creature in front of him, who took the form of a young girl, had to be eliminated as soon as possible, for it did not belong in this world. The man was driven by madness as he swung his fist... and completely missed as his target suddenly moved back, leaving him wide open—

"Bffaaah?!"

—for another fist to hit him square in the nose, knocking him unconscious.

"Oh, Kuze. 'Sup?"

"Come on, at least try to dodge," said Masachika, sighing and holding Nonoa close to his chest after having pulled her away and throwing his punch. Even though he had his arm wrapped around her shoulder, he didn't seem to be embarrassed. While Nonoa's expression was as blank as always, there seemed to be something vaguely resembling emotion flickering in the back of her eyes, but before even another second went by, she suddenly cracked a brilliant smile, then buried her facc in Masachika's shoulder.

"Th-thank youuu. ♡ I was so scared...!"

Blech.

Every muscle on Masachika's face tensed to hide how disgusted he was by her theatrical performance of pretending to be an innocent, scared little girl. However, the only person who realized it was an act was Masachika, so the other students, who happened to be nearby, all looked at Nonoa with relieved, loving gazes. Incidentally, her "wonderful friends" seemed to have heard her cry and came rushing over to save her as well.

"Tsk! The hell do you punks want?!"

"Excuse me? Who do you think you are? And what did you do to Nonoa?"

"You're dead. I'm going to kill you."

Two large male students suddenly showed up to Nonoa's rescue and began to corner the remaining delinquents. Masachika watched in dread with his arm still around Nonoa's shoulder. Although he didn't really know much about these two guys, he knew that they worshipped the ground Nonoa walked on and acted as her henchmen who would "handle things" for her without having to get the law involved. On the surface, they were merely fans who adored Nonoa from afar, but in reality, they were fanatics who would make any obstacle that got in her way disappear.

I guess I can let them deal with those guys… In fact, I should probably be more worried that they'll overdo it.

The second Masachika came to that conclusion, he ran over to Hikaru, who had finally managed to sit up.

"Hikaru! You okay?"

"Y-yeah… I'm fine now."

Hikaru slowly tried to stand while clutching his stomach…but his legs seemed a little numb, making him stagger.

"I gotcha."

Masachika immediately grabbed Hikaru's right arm to keep him from falling…while someone simultaneously grabbed his left arm… then tightly wrapped her arms around it.

"Thank you so much for saving me!"

"O-oh, uh…"

The young girl, who the delinquents were bothering, snuggled up to his left arm with sparkles in her eyes.

"Wait. Are you Nonoa's…?"

"Yes! I'm Lea Miyamae, Nonoa's little sister! Oh, and that's my brother Leo," revealed the girl while halfheartedly pointing at a somewhat arrogant-looking boy who was sulking nearby with bruised and swollen cheeks.

"Hey, are you okay? Did those guys do that to you?"

"Hmph. This is nothing."

Leo looked away from Masachika as if the older boy's concern annoyed him. Immediately, Lea briefly glanced at him with a look that said "What a brat" before grinning as she gazed up through her eyelashes into Hikaru's eyes.

"What's your name?"

"Huh? Oh… Hikaru Kiyomiya."

"Hikaru Kiyomiya… What a wonderful name! Do you mind if I call you by your first name?"

She tilted her head curiously in an almost calculating manner. She was unbelievably cute—which should come as no surprise, since she was Nonoa's little sister. However…

"Ha… Ha-ha…"

…Hikaru honestly couldn't stand girls like her, so he forced himself to smile while giving an evasive reply, but Lea didn't seem to be bothered in the least.

"All right, I'll start calling you Hikaru, then. Thank you so much for saving me, Hikaru."

"I actually didn't do anything…"

"You were the only one who came to my rescue! Who knows what would have happened to me if you didn't show up…"

Lea placed a hand over her mouth and looked away as tears began to well in her eyes—a gesture that would trigger most people's desire to protect the person crying, but Hikaru's reaction proved to be rather lukewarm.

"At any rate, I'm glad nothing happened to you…Well, I suppose something did happen, so I apologize if that came off as insensitive…"

"*Giggle.* You're so sweet, Hikaru. I'm more worried about you, though… Is your stomach okay?"

"Yeah, I'm fine."

Masachika sharpened his gaze.

"Were you punched or kicked in the stomach?"

"Punched, I think."

"By who?"

"Uh… By the guy knocked out right there."

Hikaru glanced at a man lying faceup nearby.

"Oh?" muttered Masachika and he slowly walked over toward the man, but Hikaru sensed danger and immediately grabbed him by the wrist.

"Hey! What do you think you're doing?"

"Give me a second. I'm going to give him a few smacks, wake him up, and have him get on all fours to apologize to you."

"No, stop. You've already done more than enough. Blood is already gushing out of his nose, too… And I think you broke his front teeth? Uh…"

"All of that was in self-defense, so it doesn't count."

"It counts! Really! You've done enough!"

Hikaru tightened his grip around Masachika's wrist, stopping him again. Masachika glared at the unconscious man and snorted with contempt before facing Hikaru.

"Fine. Let me walk you to the school infirmary, then."

"What? No, I'm fine."

"You're not. You could have a broken bone or a ruptured organ."

"He's right! Come on, I'll go with you," Lea said.

"Oh god. Anything but that" was what Hikaru obviously wanted to say, but Masachika didn't have any more time to spare. There could still be ruffians like these guys somewhere else, so he needed to keep moving.

"Sorry. Lea, was it? Do you think you could take care of Hikaru for me?"

"Hey, wai—!"

"Of course! Come on, Leo. Let's go."

"No, I'm fine…," replied Leo with a sour pout.

"You're so not fine. Like, you totally cut the inside of your lip pretty badly, right?" stated Nonoa in a matter-of-fact manner.

"Stop treating me like a kid!"

Leo smacked Nonoa's hand away before she could touch his swollen cheek.

"...? I'm not. I'm treating you like a little brother."

"What's the difference?!"

Masachika approached Nonoa's side, then whispered into her ear:

"I need you two backstage once Hikaru's done getting fixed up. Do you mind if we let your two big friends here handle the rest?"

"Sure," she responded softly.

But even a halfhearted reply like that felt reassuring after everything that had happened.

"I'm counting on you."

After expressing his gratitude, Masachika immediately took off, with the sole desire to keep his promise to Alisa.

Around that time, another group of hooligans showed up at the maid café run by the freshmen in Class D and Class F.

"Eeek!"

"Yo, yo, yo! Did ya hear that? She literally just screamed 'eek!' Even their screams are cute."

"S-stop... L-leave me alone..."

"Come on, be a good maid, and let me touch that little butt of yours. What do ya got to lose?"

Although a few goons were misbehaving and acting like they were at a hostess bar, the female students were far too afraid to say anything. What made the situation worse was the fact that the core members of the staff, Sayaka and Nonoa, were away preparing for their performance. Ultimately, Seirei Academy was a school for the wealthy, so most students grew up in a sheltered environment where they never had to deal with ruffians, especially ones like this that appeared violent. In fact, they seemed to be flaunting how uncivilized they were, which was something these students had never had to deal with before, either.

"Heh. I thought hangin' out at a rich kids' school would be boring, but this is kinda fun."

"Hell yeah. Now, these are ladies, unlike that trash we got back at our school."

"Thank you for inviting us, Gonda!"

"Yeah, ya better be grateful," said a thin-eyebrowed man even larger than the other guys. He was this group's leader, Gonda, and he had absolutely no connection to Seirei Academy. In fact, he went to a public high school eight stations away and was well-known in the neighborhood for being a hooligan. All he knew about Seirei Academy was that it was basically a school where smart, rich kids went. In other words, why would he have brought his crew to the Autumn Heights Festival? It was all because of an anonymous envelope he'd received two weeks ago.

Inside the envelope were ten invitation tickets, along with a single letter. The letter was a request that he make a mess of the festival, and it included specifics, such as what time he could sneak inside without getting stopped by security, what route to escape by after he caused a scene, and how he was going to be paid for his work. Although skeptical at first, he checked the station locker specified in the letter and found money inside that served as a sort of deposit for his services and thus erased any doubts he may have had.

"Are ya sure you're fine payin' for us?!"

"Damn right, I'm fine. I got a little extra cash from one of my side hustles the other day."

"What a gentleman! That's Gonda for ya!"

Be that as it may, he wasn't planning on foolishly following orders to a T and going on a rampage. The letter may have said that he wouldn't be charged for whatever he decided to do, but he wasn't stupid enough to believe that. Therefore, Gonda wasn't going to do anything that would get the police involved. Instead, he was going to use this advance payment to enjoy himself, and if he ended up getting paid a reward for his services, then that would just be a bonus.

The crowd here ain't bad, though...

All the people nervously glancing in their direction seemed to be proper young ladies from well-off families. Their skin was nice, they wore little makeup, and they all had beautiful black hair that had probably never been dyed before. Despite being girls in high school, they were fundamentally different from the girls in Gonda's high school. They obviously lived in completely separate worlds from students like Gonda, who couldn't afford to go to cram school, much less a private school.

And now they were getting attention from these refined ladies who they usually wouldn't even be able to speak to as equals under normal circumstances. For Gonda, there was no better feeling than this. It was a different feeling from being the boss of a bunch of underclassmen, as it filled both his desire to rule and his desire for absolute power.

"Excuse me! How long do you guys plan on hanging around here?!"

But it wasn't long before someone decided to put a damper on the mood. Her dyed hair and excessive makeup as she placed her hands on her hips set her apart from the other girls, and she was glaring at the group of ruffians. This girl was one of Nonoa's so-called fangirls, although there was no way any of these delinquents would know that. "I'm not going to allow such savage behavior during the queen's absence," she seemed to be saying with her eyes, bracing herself to stand her ground while narrowing her gaze.

"I hear you've been sexually harassing my girls! I don't even want your money! Just leave!"

"Excuse me?"

One of the guys raised an eyebrow and stood from his seat, when—

"Hey."

—Gonda shot him a piercing glare, making him sit right back down.

"Sorry about our poor behavior," he apologized with a shady sneer as he faced the female student.

"We didn't know that touching a few asses counted as sexual harassment here. We'll order something and be good, so could ya cut us some slack?"

The female student blinked in bewilderment a few times as

though his unexpected, ridiculous proposal took the wind right out of her sails, but after a few moments went by, she frowned and turned him down.

"I don't want to hear excuses. You're making people uncomfortable, so we want you to leave."

"Yo, seriously? I said we'll pay. Besides, who are we even bothering? Look," replied Gonda, surveying the empty classroom. Every other customer had already left...for glaringly obvious reasons, of course.

"Other customers are afraid to come inside because of you guys!"

"That's rough. How 'bout this? We'll pay for your lost business, too."

"Looks like I'll be having a sodaaa!"

"Oh, I'll have a beer."

"What is wrong with you? They obviously don't serve beer here, numbnuts."

The goons guffawed, allowing Gonda to easily evade the female student's demands as they slowly wore her down mentally... Suddenly, the door to the classroom flung open.

"That's enough!" announced the voice of their hero.

A radiantly beautiful lady with honey-blond spiral-curled pigtails appeared with impeccable timing.

""""Sumire!""""

As the maids squealed in joy at her charismatic entrance, Sumire boldly glared down at the dumbfounded hooligans and confidently insisted:

"Talking is not going to solve a thing. It appears a bit of gentle violence is needed!"

"'Gentle violence'?"

The words of a meathead must have seemed ill-suited coming from a gentlewoman's mouth, because each one of the delinquent's eyes filled with confusion. Regardless, Sumire boldly stood before them with her unsheathed replica sword while wearing an elegantly vicious grin.

"Restrain them. ☆"

Five members of the disciplinary committee suddenly charged into the classroom as if that were the signal.

"H-hey, wait?! We're not looking for a fight! We—gah?!"

"Th-this wasn't what I—*mmmff*?!"

"Weapons are for cowards—*bffuh*?!"

Not even a minute went by before they were overwhelmed and restrained, without a single soul even willing to hear them out.

"Maria! We received a call about more people causing trouble!"

"Where?"

"Um... By the gym... Three guys are apparently trying to pick up two girls, and they're being really aggressive."

"We got a call just like that a few minutes ago. President, let's have security go check it out."

"Hmm? Excuse me, but I think someone already took care of that. A few guests, who just happened to be around, apparently apprehended the troublemakers..."

"'Guests'? Did anybody get hurt?"

"Not from what I heard. I still haven't been able to get any details, but when they checked their tickets, they seemed to be related to Chisaki Sarashina..."

"Oh, Chisaki's family..."

The school festival committee's headquarters was set up in the main conference room where Maria worked with the president and the vice president to get a grasp on and to remedy the situation. Calls were coming in one after another about troublesome visitors, violence, and the like, so every single member was flushed and stressed, since nobody could have ever predicted that this was going to happen. But despite everything, they managed to deal with it all, thanks to the calm direction of these three individuals.

"President! There's apparently a man trying to force his way onstage in the gym!"

"Relax. There are already a few teachers at the gym. More importantly, are we still waiting for them to close the gate? Is the school PA system ready to go?"

"The gate has been closed! Inoue is currently explaining things to the guests at the gate as well."

"Perfect. Then—"

"Guys!"

The door to the main conference room opened, revealing Touya and Chisaki—an unexpected visit that both shocked and relieved all.

"Touya… What happened to the First Light Committee?"

"We called for their bodyguards, who were on standby outside, and now they're all waiting in the student council room. There was no way we were going to be able to show them around with all of this going on."

"Hmm…"

The president of the school festival committee seemed concerned for a few moments, but he eventually nodded.

"All right. Touya, you stay here to help us. Chisaki—"

"I know. You want me to snap every last troublemaker in two, right?"

The president's expression twitched uncomfortably at the violent, murderous flames glowing in Chisaki's eyes.

"Don't go overboard, okay? And make sure nobody innocent gets hurt. We have a few people looking over security footage, and the paper being used for these intruders' invitation tickets seems to be different from the paper we used to make them, so if you see anyone who seems suspicious, make sure to first check their—"

"Got it. Oh, but I can't promise I won't go overboard. These people ruined the school festival we have been working so hard on… I'm not going to let them get away with this," she interjected, her voice seething with anger as she stormed from the room without even waiting for a reply. The committee president's eyes pursued her with both relief and worry that she might overdo it…when a single male student, who was wearing glasses, suddenly stood up.

"I'll go help."

"Kaji?"

"You don't need me now that Touya's here. Plus, there has been something that I've been wanting to ask the teachers about security."

I guess it would be kind of awkward to have him work with Touya, thought the festival committee president before agreeing.

"All right. You're free to go."

"Thanks."

"President! The situation involving Year One Class D has been dealt with!"

"Really? Great."

Although multiple acts of terror were happening all at once, the school festival committee and disciplinary committee were promptly taking action, gradually bringing an end to the chaos.

"What nonsense," muttered Yuki while checking the middle-aged man's invitation ticket. Only a few moments ago, he was screaming nonsensical complaints, such as "My life is ruined, thanks to you people" and "You people destroyed my company" until Yuki restrained him. Although the names of both the guest and the one who invited him were written on the invitation, the student's name didn't ring any bells. Basically, the name was fake.

"There is no way anyone would let him in with an invitation like this."

The disciplinary committee was performing name checks at the school gate, so there was no way anyone could use a fake student's name to get inside.

"Young lady, where would you like me to take this man?"

"Oh, my apologies. Do you think you could take him to the disciplinary committee's room? Do you know where that is?"

"But of course. I used to go to this school, you know?"

"Wonderful. Thank you."

"Yeah, no problem."

After leaving the middle-aged troublemaker in a nearby adult's hands, Yuki turned to face Ayano and shrugged.

"Not only did somebody send out numerous fake invitations, but it seems someone from the inside is helping these people sneak in. I guess it could be the same person, but..."

"I see."

"...Anyway, tuck your weapons away for now. We wouldn't want anyone seeing you with those."

"Ah... My apologies."

Ayano slipped what appeared to be mechanical pencils, which she'd used to help Yuki restrain the man, somewhere up her sleeves.

"...The student council room," she suddenly muttered.

"Hmm?"

"I believe if Master Masachika were here, that would be where he would go."

"...Interesting. So they're after the First Light Committee..."

After Yuki's quiet soliloquy, they promptly began to make their way to the student council room together.

Inside the student council room sat the members of the First Light Committee, since a school-wide disturbance happened to take place the day a group of alumni came to visit. Whoever was supposed to be supervising the event was going to be both responsible and liable for this scandal, so it would be no surprise if the members of the FLC were upset...but they weren't.

"Now... I wonder how they plan on getting this mess under control?"

"More importantly, I want to know who was behind all of this. I feel like it would have to be someone who wants to sully the current student council's reputation...or perhaps their targets are the previous student council president and vice president."

If anything, the FLC seemed to be enjoying this disaster. Their eyes looking down over the schoolyard conveyed more curiosity than concern. They were like spectators observing a show from a safe distance. Of course, they would send their bodyguards to help get the situation under control if people continued to get injured, but for now, they wanted to quietly watch over the younger generation to see how they worked under pressure. After all, in their eyes, this was nothing unusual during the election season.

"The previous student council president takes the role of school festival committee president, while the current president manages the Autumn Heights Festival. So back in our day, students tried to use this opportunity to overthrow the current student council all the time."

"If anything, safely overcoming whatever the Autumn Heights Festival threw at you was what earned you the right to join the First Light Committee back in the day...but times change, I suppose."

"This is pathetic, if you ask me... Oh, my apologies. I wasn't trying to insult your granddaughter, Mr. Suou."

"No. The fact of the matter is that my granddaughter failed to prevent this from happening."

Back when they were students—back when physical punishment was still the norm in schools across the country—Seirei Academy was a wonderful social arena for students, and the elections were respectable rivalries between factions, where each student running would be representing their family. Once a place for influential alumni to gather, the First Light Committee eventually implemented a voting system around seventy years ago to concentrate power and cultivate the elite. Ever since then, the academy's students had been utilizing anything it took to win these two positions, whether it be authority, wealth, or sometimes violence. In other words, anything goes during the elections, so it wasn't all that uncommon to see students get hurt or even drop out of school.

However, that was simply a testament to how special the positions of president and vice president of the student council were. Whoever defeated their rival faction and rose to power would become a ruler of their generation, and the First Light Committee was a place for these rulers to gather. It wouldn't be an exaggeration to say that they had the power to steer the nation. In fact, there was perhaps nothing they couldn't do within Japan with their network and connections, and that was why this generation's presidential races looked like child's play in their eyes.

The development of social media and reinforcing the notion of following the rules took this generation by storm, which softened the once-fierce presidential races where nearly anything was tolerated.

Therefore, while there were still ruthless debates and speeches by the student council members, which could eliminate rivals from the presidential race, it essentially boiled down to merely winning the popular vote from their peers. That was how the current president and vice president were selected, and that was why the alumni didn't respect them. In fact, they weren't even considering welcoming them into the First Light Committee.

"There does seem to be one student who stands out a bit this year, though. I heard that this student also plans on making their rivals join the student council as well, if elected," a man announced suddenly, trying to clear the slight awkwardness in the air. Gensei's eyebrow twitched, but other than that, he hardly even reacted, and it was a completely unrelated man who ended up expressing interest.

"Oh? A willingness to work with past rivals, you say? Hmm… That is interesting. It sounds like that student understands the true nature of the presidential race."

Networking was the true nature of the race. Students could make connections that would benefit them in their future, create inner circles and political factions, and grant highly ranked positions within their faction when elected. That was how they truly ruled over the students of the academy and their generation, and this was what the presidential race really was about in their eyes.

"I'm now marginally more excited for the upcoming presidential race. There seems to be a student somewhere among us with the guts to strike during the school festival as well."

"*Chuckle.* And it appears everything is going exactly as they planned. Now, let's see how the others are going to deal with this mess."

Perhaps nobody would have batted an eye a few decades ago if something like this had happened, but there was no way this was going to go unpunished anymore. Then again, there was one way the perpetrator could get away with it all, and everyone in this room knew that was why they decided to wait. They decided to wait until someone walked through the door of the student council room.

◇

"Oh..."

"Oh, my..."

When Masachika stepped into the hallway that led to the student council room, he saw Yuki and Ayano coming from the exact opposite direction, making him freeze briefly. The other two, however, continued to approach the room, so he silently proceeded ahead as well until the rivals were facing each other in front of the student council room.

"..."

Masachika and Yuki silently exchanged gazes for a few moments before they almost simultaneously directed their gazes at the two bodyguards on each side of the door.

"Excuse me. Hey, I'm Masachika Kuze. I handle general affairs for the student council, and the student council president, Touya Kenzaki, sent me here to check up on the First Light Committee."

"He sent me, Yuki Suou—student council publicist, as well."

"Ayano Kimishima. General affairs."

After introducing themselves and showing their student IDs, Masachika spoke on behalf of the group and asked:

"Did anyone else stop by before we got here? I'm sure the First Light Committee is safe with bodyguards such as yourselves here, but I must make sure that no wrongdoers know they're here."

The bodyguards quickly exchanged glances before briefly replying:

"No, nobody else has been here."

"...Really? Thanks."

Masachika and Yuki were inwardly overcome with relief. *We made it in time*, they thought.

"Now, Masachika, what are you planning on doing next?" asked Yuki after they walked down the hallway away from the student council room.

"..."

She then gazed into her brother's eyes and let out a snort.

"Then how about we both keep watch? We will keep an eye on the way we came while you keep an eye on the way you came. That should be fair, right?"

"Yeah," Masachika agreed, then nodded before smoothly turning on his heel. Yuki and Ayano turned around as well, then began to trek back to the area from which they came. Right after Masachika turned the corner of the hallway, he leaned against the wall, then waited a few minutes until someone suddenly showed up. The much-expected encounter, however, made him smirk as he pushed off the wall and proceeded to stand in the middle of the hall.

"Yo, Kiryuuin. What brings you here?"

"...Hey, Kuze. I was just about to ask you the same question," replied Yuushou with a grin just as chilling as Masachika's joyless smile.

"...You were behind this?"

Meanwhile, another male student suddenly appeared before Yuki on the opposite side of the hallway in front of the stairs. The male student narrowed his gaze while he looked up at her from the staircase landing.

"I am truly disappointed. This is not the behavior I expected from a student council president," she said in a matter-of-fact way, making the male student grimace.

"I'm not the student council president anymore, Yuki Suou."

"Yes... But you are still the president of the disciplinary committee, Taiki Kaji."

The sixty-seventh president and sixty-eighth president of the student council in middle school locked eyes.

CHAPTER 8 If you can't beat 'em, *break* 'em.

Taiki Kaji was the son of a home appliance manufacturer's CEO and had been the student council president three years before during middle school. Sayaka, Nonoa, Yuushou, Sumire, Yuki, and Masachika ran the student council under his leadership, and if he didn't lose to Touya in the most recent presidential race, then Yuki would still be calling him President Kaji.

"You purposely left a gap in security in order to let those intruders inside, didn't you?"

Taiki lowered his gaze in response, but that was enough for Yuki.

"Why would you do such a thing?"

"...'Why?' You, of all people, should know why. Am I wrong?"

He returned Yuki's question with a question of his own.

"Kirika?" replied Yuki without even blinking.

"...Yes, exactly. I have to get Kirika back...and in order to do that...I have to become a member of the First Light Committee, no matter what it takes!" Taiki cried out emotionally and somewhat off-key. Kirika Asama was not only Taiki's partner during the presidential race but his fiancée as well. Although it was an arranged marriage for the sake of their parents' businesses, they didn't have a bad relationship at all. Taiki especially took a liking to Kirika, but after he lost to Touya in the presidential race, the door leading to the First Light Committee had seemingly shut, so the Asama family apparently backed out of the arrangement.

"They told me they didn't need a son-in-law that'd lose to a commoner, and they tossed me aside like trash! If I don't do something, then Kirika is going to be married off to some other powerful family... That's why I'm willing to do anything to stop that and why I need the First Light Committee's approval!"

His voice was intemperate and wavering, and his pupils constricted behind his glasses. He was far different from the Taiki that Yuki used to know.

"Yeah... It never made any sense... He wanted to become the student council president so he could ask the girl he likes out? How original. Kiss my ass. They have no idea how I feel about Kirika, and yet...they all voted for that commoner like he's special. They messed up. This isn't right. I am far more fit to be president than him..." Taiki continuously mumbled this while chewing on his fingernails, causing Yuki to soften her gaze as if she almost felt sorry for him.

"Who put you up to this?" she asked softly, making Taiki suddenly freeze before slowly lifting his chin. Yuki stared back at him with unclouded eyes and added frankly:

"The Taiki I knew was neither this arrogant nor selfish, so let me ask you this one more time. Who put you up to this?"

The eyes of a girl who wanted to believe someone she respected made him hesitant...but eventually he snorted with a grim grin.

"You don't know me."

After Taiki pushed her away, as if to tell her to mind her own business, Yuki narrowed her eyes and barked:

"Shut the hell up."

"...What?"

She was the model gentlewoman and a lady of the Suou family, so there was no way such crude language would escape those lips. Taiki's jaw dropped in bewilderment, as if he thought he was hearing things, but of course, he wasn't.

"'You don't know me'? Who do you think you are? Of course I don't know your dumb ass! I don't even really care to get to know you, either! You didn't have what it takes to win. That's all there is to it. Her family broke off your engagement, so you joined the dark side? That's all it took? Pathetic! You're an insult to all the villainesses who were framed, had their engagements called off, and were exiled from the country! Apologize to them this instant!"

"...?!?!"

This was the most flustered Taiki had been in years. The gentlewoman had removed her mask and was now hurling insults and demanding apologies for who knows what. He was having trouble keeping up with what was happening, but Yuki didn't seem to care in the least as she continued at full throttle.

"Listen, the only guys allowed to join the dark side are the ones who have already wooed the heroine! Because you need a heroine who will walk through the darkness with you to trigger an event that will take your relationship to the next level! When it comes to love, there is absolutely no value in joining the dark side when you're single! If you want to go fight windmills, then go do so somewhere else! I mean, you're on track to become some gross stalker obsessed with his ex at this rate."

"Wh-what?! I would never stalk anyone!"

"Then stop being a pansy and go talk to her! Her parents are the ones who broke off the engagement, so this situation might actually turn in your favor if you play your cards right! Your masculinity is being tested, so stop using that passion of yours in all the wrong ways, dammit!"

As Yuki yelled, all color gradually faded from Taiki's face…but by the time he came back to his senses, he was emotionally stable again. The only emotion he felt now was depression as he listlessly asked:

"What should I do now…?"

Yuki quickly pointed behind him.

"First! You need to go see Kirika, get on all fours, and apologize. Tell her everything you did, then tell her you just couldn't give her up and were willing to do anything to get her back. Now go. I already told her to wait behind the school building."

When she jerked her thumb to the side, Ayano, who had actually been there the entire time, suddenly took a step forward and held up Yuki's smartphone. Taiki jumped in genuine surprise, since it looked like she had just appeared out of nowhere, but after a few moments went by, he smiled, as if a load had been taken off his shoulders.

"Ha-ha… Yeah… I should have just tried talking to her about

it…," muttered Taiki before he swiftly bowed, with his usual calm expression.

"Thank you so much. I'll try talking to Kirika one more time."

"Good. Oh, hey! I honestly already think I know the answer, but Yuushou Kiryuuin's the one who put you up to all this, wasn't he?"

"Yeah… He wants to ruin the Autumn Heights Festival so that the current student council falls and loses its authority. Incidentally, he also plans on using this as an opportunity to have Sumire resolve all the disputes to improve their standing at school. He apparently got anyone he could find to ruin the festival, from delinquents and people with grudges to magazine journalists and kids who do prank videos online. I don't really know the details, though, since I was probably nothing more than a sacrificial pawn to him in the end…"

"Interesting. I suppose that means this is going to be over very soon, then. Masachika will make short work of that wannabe evil-doing 'prince,' too," Yuki mocked with a laugh, which made Taiki smile ruefully.

"You really trust Kuze, don't you?"

"Of course I do. He's the best."

Yuki placed a hand on her hip while puffing out her chest, which only made Taiki smile even more uncomfortably as he shook his head in a self-deprecating manner.

"He is, huh? Ha-ha-ha… I thought you two had a falling-out or something… You think you know it all one day; then you realize you know absolutely nothing the next."

He glanced up at Yuki one last time before descending the stairs, and the moment his footsteps faded into nothingness, Yuki immediately relaxed her shoulders.

"*Sigh*… What a pain in the ass that was. He really made things far more complicated than he needed to. I get that she's his first love, but I'm exhausted. Then again, I guess he owes me now, so it's not all bad."

"I agree. Having a former student council president who's also the current disciplinary committee president on our side could help us in the presidential race. At any rate, your excellent performance brought a tear to my eye, Lady Yuki. I'm sure it wasn't easy persuading him."

"Yeah, I don't know if I was that persuasive. I kind of just tore down his whole argument. But, well, I'm lucky he's actually a good person deep down inside," replied Yuki, waving her hand before Ayano's adoring gaze before directing her gaze down the hallway in her brother's direction.

"I'm sure it's not going to be that easy over there, though."

Over there. Hidden behind the smiles of Masachika and Yuushou were knives pointed at the other's throat.

"We have some VIP members waiting in the room up ahead, and nobody is allowed near them except for the president and vice president."

"Which you're neither, right? Being a member of the student council doesn't make you an exception, right?"

"That's right, so how about you turn around and we head back together?"

They wore fake smiles while they exchanged shallow pleasantries. Despite realizing the other's true intention, they continued to probe the other as if this were an art. However…

"Sorry, but I can't do that."

The instant Yuushou firmly rejected his offer, Masachika decided to erase his fake smile, then lifted his chin up with a serious expression while glaring down at Yuushou with contempt in his eyes.

"Wow, you're not even going to try to hide it anymore."

"Hide what?"

"You think you can do whatever you want, and it'll all be forgiven as long as a few powerful people in that room over there take a liking to you, right? You're naive. Even if the First Light Committee gave you a pass for the stunt you pulled today, do you really think the school will let you get away with this?"

But Masachika's taunt didn't break his smile.

"I have no idea what you're talking about, but the only one naive here is you. Do you really think this school will disobey the will of the First Light Committee?"

"The police are going to get involved after what happened today. The public's not going to let this whole thing get swept under the rug."

"I wouldn't be so sure about that. This school has extraterritorial rights, you could say. Besides, even if what happened today was an issue, wouldn't the hosts of the Autumn Heights Festival be responsible? Namely, the current and previous student council presidents and vice presidents?" said Yuushou with a shameless chuckle, making Masachika click his tongue. Yuushou must have been worried about being recorded, so he was making sure not to tell on himself. Furthermore, seeing how smug he was being must have meant that he didn't leave a single shred of evidence that connected him to what had happened today. Even Masachika didn't have any proof that Yuushou was behind this disturbance.

Eh. Even if I did find proof, the First Light Committee would have no problem making it disappear, since winning the presidential race is considered a just cause in their eyes.

And from what Masachika's grandfather Gensei told him as a kid, the First Light Committee didn't seem to care what students did during the presidential race, no matter how dirty things got. That was also why he knew that Yuushou was planning on paying them a visit in an attempt to get off scot-free.

"Why are you even doing this…would be a stupid question to ask, huh? Obviously, you've got to attack from the rear to ruin the current student council's reputation, since there's no way you'd be able to win a popularity contest. This is a very on-brand thing for you to do, too."

"I told you already. I have no idea what you're talking about." There was a subtle change in his expression, even though it was clear he wasn't planning on coming clean. "But… Hmm… Generally, elections are all about winning, whether you attack from the rear or not, right? Don't tell me that you truly believe these struggles for power around the world are always settled peacefully and fairly?" Yuushou ridiculed Masachika with an unapologetically ambitious grin. "Money, power, violence—this is what makes winners in the real world, and I plan on using all of these things to win. Only those who have the strength, will, and determination to do so are fit to join the First Light Committee. Conversely, the weak and scared have no place among them."

"Cute. Save the rest of your speech for the First Light Committee after you make it to the student council room, though."

"Good idea. So…I think it's time you move."

Yuushou smirked, brimming with confidence once more as he took something from his school jacket pocket. Masachika's eyebrow immediately rose, since like most people, Masachika had only seen that *something* on TV before.

"Whoa. Seriously? Bringing a stun gun to school? Is it really that dangerous out there for rich kids like you?"

"I usually don't have it on me, but I knew a lot of strangers were visiting our school today, so I brought it just in case. And hey, look what happened. A lot of bad strangers did end up showing up."

"Wow, what a coincidence," Masachika replied blandly with a shrug. Yuushou then narrowed his gaze and held out his stun gun while the smile faded from his face.

"So do you think you could move? As I mentioned a minute ago, I will not hesitate to use violence if I have to."

"Good. Because I don't plan on holding back, either," replied Masachika in a carefree manner as his demeanor instantly changed. But even though his gaze was piercing, his voice remained calm.

"Everyone in the student council worked their ass off to make this school festival happen…"

Even though there were cries that they were short on manpower, rivals set aside their differences as the student council became one.

"Takeshi and Hikaru put their hearts into preparing for their performance, despite being hurt…"

The band breaking up destroyed them, but even then, they decided to keep pushing forward with their instruments in hand.

"Alya finally mustered up the courage to face the weakness in her heart…"

The girl who never showed weakness finally opened up to Masachika backstage.

"Do you really think I'm going to let you ruin everything?" Masachika's quiet yet seething rage could be felt in each of his words, making Yuushou gulp. His palm holding the stun gun began to sweat while he took a step back with his left leg, assuming a diagonal stance. The tension rapidly grew, filling the five-meter gap between them. "By the way, do you like big boobs or huge boobs?"

"...What?"

It was an absurd, nonsensical question ill-suited for the situation, which caught Yuushou off guard, leaving an opening that Masachika immediately capitalized on. Masachika used to practice karate when he was younger; he took kendo in middle school; and he was learning judo now in high school. He'd received his black belt in karate while he had the skill set of someone with their third dan in both kendo and judo, thanks to his inherent ability to rapidly absorb everything like a sponge. That said, what he ended up doing was a good ol' fashioned *shukuchi*—aka a "godspeed"—a move loved by all nerds. His masters were 2D, and his textbooks were comic books.

"...?!"

Only when his right wrist was grabbed did Yuushou even realize that Masachika had moved. His eyes opened wide in surprise as a sharp pain shot down his wrist while his collar was simultaneously grabbed and his legs were swept from beneath him. The world violently spun before him until his back slammed against the ground, knocking the wind right out of him as he saw stars. However, before he could even process what had happened, he had already been flipped over onto his stomach as his right arm was being twisted behind his back.

"G-gah...!"

There was no way he was going to be able to get up, with a knee on his left shoulder and with his right arm twisted. The most he managed was turning his head as far as he could to glare at Masachika, who easily pulled the stun gun from his hand.

"Using money, power, and violence to win, was it? So? If using violence is okay, then what are you going to do now?" replied Masachika in a flat tone, glaring just as coldly back at Yuushou. But even though Yuushou's brow was furrowed in agony, he still smirked audaciously.

"What about you? Do you really think you're going to get away with injuring me like this? More importantly, what if someone happens to see you on top of me like this—?"

"I don't care who sees this. I'm sure I can break a few bones before they can even get close to stopping me. I told you. I'm not going to hesitate to use violence, either."

Masachika then grabbed Yuushou's right index finger and began to slowly bend it backward.

"Ah!" cried Yuushou with a soft grunt, but Masachika paid no heed to his cries and emotionlessly added:

"I'm going to break your fingers one by one until you admit that you were behind all of this. Once we're done with your right hand, we'll move on to your left. You'll probably never be able to play piano again, or at least not as well as you play now. But don't worry. Once you admit what you've done, I'll take you to see the First Light Committee. We'll show them how you used cheap tricks and still lost like the loser you are," he vowed, tightening his grip around Yuushou's index finger. It was the first time that every last bit of confidence vanished from Yuushou's face.

"D-don't! Stop! Do you really think they'd be willing to overlook something like that?!"

"Probably. Anything goes when it comes to the presidential race, right? Didn't you say something like that? Besides, I honestly don't even care what they decide."

"Wh-what?"

Masachika peered into Yuushou's skeptical eyes while a cold-blooded sneer curled his lips.

"If we're forced out of the race, then Yuki and Alya could just join forces. They'd win, and Alya would get to be the student council president while Yuki would get to join the First Light Committee. Hell, I'd even be able to make Alya the student council president without having to betray Yuki this way, to boot. It'd be a happy ending for everyone. In fact, I couldn't think of a better ending."

"Mnnn…! D-don't tell me you were planning on doing this from the start?!"

Masachika silently smiled back at his panicking schoolmate, then pressed his left knee heavily onto Yuushou's back, applying pressure on his lungs so that he wouldn't be able to scream.

"As you can see, unlike you, I have nothing to lose. In other words, you should probably start admitting what you did before it's too late."

"…! N-no! Stop! Stoppp!"

He desperately struggled, straining his voice as he tried to yell as loudly as he could, but Masachika continued to bend his finger back until—

"But, well, I guess we don't have to settle this with violence. Unlike you, I can play by the rules. I'll give you a choice."

"What…?" panted Yuushou.

"You decide. I break your fingers or we settle this at a debate while following the rules."

"A debate…?"

"If I win, then I want you to confess to the entire school that you were behind what happened here today. But if you win, then I'll look the other way and let you off the hook."

Masachika's one-sided conditions made Yuushou's lips twist in an odd smile.

"That sounds like a pretty lopsided deal to me. You're not really risking any—"

"All right, no deal, then."

"What?! Stop! W-wait! How would we even make sure the other keeps their promise?!"

"That's simple. We'll have Sumire act as our mediator and witness."

"…! That's…"

Yuushou seemed visually upset by his suggestion, and it was that reaction that told Masachika everything he needed to know about Sumire: She knew nothing of Yuushou's scheme. It also helped him discover one of Yuushou's weaknesses, bringing this all to an end.

"Don't worry. We won't tell Sumire why we're fighting each other until after the match. In other words, you have to beat me if you want to keep this a secret from her. Hmm… Hey. If these are going to be the conditions, then I guess we can give you a little bit of a handicap and do something you're good at."

"…What do you mean?"

Masachika leaned in closer to Yuushou's furrowed brow, grinned scornfully, and whispered:

"I'm saying let's settle this doing what you're best at: piano, Mr. Runner-Up."

Yuushou's eyes instantly widened and he practically growled.

"I knew it…! Suou…!"

Masachika was all too familiar with that competitive glare as he recalled a similar look that a boy used to give him long ago at piano competitions and recitals, eliciting a haughty snort.

"So that was you. My bad. I was hardly even aware of your existence back then, so I had no idea that was you until Nonoa brought it up again."

"You little…!"

"So? What's it going to be? By the way, I haven't even touched a piano in over five years, so you definitely have the advantage here. But, well, I still really doubt I'd lose to Little Runner-Up here."

Despite obviously just trying to get a rise out of him, Yuushou couldn't even pretend to be calm as he emphatically replied:

"Don't you dare underestimate me… I'll do it…! This time, you're going down…!"

"Masachika's still not back."

Takeshi looked up at the school building with a slightly worried gaze from backstage. Around forty minutes had gone by since the firecrackers incident, and things had finally started to settle down in the schoolyard, thanks to Alisa reaching out and the hard work of everyone on staff. Therefore, they decided to resume the stage performances. Furthermore, not only did they make an announcement on the school's PA system that all the intruders had been caught, but they also announced that they were going to keep the school festival open for an extra thirty minutes as well, which really helped with everyone's anxiety.

Yet in spite of all that, Masachika was still missing.

"They may have caught all of the intruders, but he might be dealing with the aftermath," suggested Hikaru, and Alisa's expression clouded over. She had exerted herself in a bid to calm the crowd, just like Masachika had asked her to, and she'd helped deal with the aftermath of the fireworks incident as well, but that was the extent of it. Deep down inside, she felt like there had to be something else she could do as a member of the student council and as Masachika's partner. She began wondering if it really was okay for her to wait around like this until her anxiety and impatience gradually transformed into agony and doubt.

"You seem restless. A leader needs to be calm and strong," Sayaka suddenly said while pushing up her glasses.

"Yeah, for real. Like, be a little more laid-back, Alisa."

"...You're a little too laid-back, Nonoa," sassed Sayaka as Nonoa only continued to take selfies in her stage outfit. Regardless, seeing these two act so normally brought smiles to Takeshi's and Hikaru's faces.

"Yeah, worrying isn't gonna help anything. Besides, I think you'd be wasting your time worrying about Masachika, of all people!"

"Ha-ha! Yes, you can say that again. Alya, we need to trust Masachika, because what we need to focus on right now is putting on the best performance we can. Let's not give those intruders what they want. We will not cower. We're 'Fortitude,' after all, right?"

Hikaru's encouragement suddenly reminded Alisa of the words Masachika left her with.

"So trust me...and wait for me. I'll make sure this performance happens."

Masachika kept his promise, so what Alisa needed to do...was crystal clear. She closed her eyes briefly before opening them to make eye contact with each of her bandmates, conveying that her doubt was no more.

"Thank you. Everyone."

All of a sudden, her phone started to vibrate, so she slipped her hand into her pocket to promptly check the message, as if this were fate, and displayed on the screen was a brief message from Masachika:

You've got this.

That message alone lit a passionate fire in Alisa's heart.

"<Thank you, too,>" she whispered with her smartphone touching her lips, quickly followed by a strong, confident grin.

"All right, everyone. Let's make sure our first performance is a great one! Is everybody ready?!"

"Y-yeahhh!"

"Yeahhh?"

"...Yeah."

"Sure."

"Are you even trying?!" joked Alisa, making the other four laugh, which made her start laughing as well.

"Now, give it up for Fortitude!" announced a member on staff suddenly, so after each band member exchanged gazes and shared a nod, they took the stage.

CHAPTER 9 I will keep my promise.

I bet everyone's having the time of their life over there...

Masachika stood in the wing of the auditorium's stage while thinking about the band's performance in the schoolyard.

"*Sigh*... This is the last time I do something like this for you, Kuze. This is reckless."

"I concur. I have a show to put on after this, you know? It doesn't help that those lawless scoundrels wasted all my rehearsal time, either..."

"I'm really sorry, guys."

The stage director's expression was overcome with exhaustion while Sumire's tone conveyed displeasure, so Masachika bowed humbly and apologetically, since even he was well aware of how reckless his request was. The stage performances in the auditorium and in the schoolyard were put on hold due to the sudden disturbance, but the auditorium fortunately didn't run into any trouble, so the performances were still on schedule. They had increased the number of teachers and security on patrol as well.

That said, they extended the festival by thirty minutes, which left the auditorium's stage with an entire thirty minutes to spare, so Masachika decided to use this time to challenge Yuushou to their match.

Under normal circumstances, it would be relatively easy to add another show with the extra thirty minutes, but the kendo club needed to use the gym for their sword-fighting play around that time as well, so adjusting the schedule ended up being a bit of a mess. But despite all their troubles, they managed to make the schedule work, perhaps thanks to the staff's trust in Masachika, since he had helped with the auditorium's stage performances to make sure everything went smoothly.

"Then again, I suppose I can't say no when Yuushou's involved... What is this about a piano match, though? There is no precedent for rivals competing on piano. It has always been a traditional debate. Furthermore, this isn't a match between the two running pairs but between someone running for student council president and someone running for vice president. This is unheard of..."

Sumire shifted her dumbfounded gaze at Yuushou, who was standing in the back, then raised an eyebrow. After placing her right hand on the hilt of her replica sword at the waist, she took a few steps toward him as he still continued to look away before loosening her sword slightly out of its sheath.

"Yuushou? Since when did you start thinking it was okay to ignore me?"

"...I'm concentrating. Just leave me alone, Sumire," he replied curtly, prompting her to furrow her brow even more. But after a brief sigh, she faced Masachika and asked:

"So? This is officially a debate, right? What are each of you putting on the line?"

Debates were held to argue opinions, and even though this was technically a piano competition, it was common knowledge that the winner would have his demand met. Nevertheless, there was no way Masachika could answer Sumire's question, given the conditions of the match.

"I'm sorry, Sumire, but I can't tell you what we each put on the line until after the match is over."

"Oh? ...Then how are we going to make sure the loser honors their agreement? Usually, each contestant during a debate would make their demand before the audience so that the audience could act as witnesses, right?"

"We don't plan on announcing our demands to the audience. Written here are the demands for whoever wins this competition. I would like for you to open the envelope of whoever wins, then make sure the demand is honored."

Naturally, Yuushou's winning envelope was empty.

After Masachika handed Sumire the two envelopes, she raised her eyebrows.

"...Very well. And? Do you need me to moderate?"

"While it's going to be set up like an exhibition match, it's still, in a way, a debate, so I asked someone from the student council to be the moderator. I appreciate the offer, though."

The instant Masachika finished his sentence, a door in the stage wing leading outside suddenly opened.

"Hey."

And the girl, who with a small voice stepped inside, was the moderator who Masachika had asked to help with the debate: Maria.

"I'm really sorry about this, Masha. I know it was sudden."

"Don't be sorry at all. ♪ Things have calmed down, so don't worry about a thing. ♪"

Her face lit up with a bubbly smile the instant she saw Masachika, and she shook her head. It was a smile that could erase all nervous tension, curling Masachika's lips.

"Thanks... I really appreciate it... Anyway, we don't have much time, so let me explain how this is going to go down."

"Okay. ♪"

After Maria nodded back, Masachika started to explain her role...when Sumire, who had been staring at the floor, suddenly lifted her chin and snapped:

"This isn't fair! I want to stand out, too!"

"...What?"

Masachika looked back, but the instant he saw how much she was pouting, he was overcome with exhaustion.

"...How about you both moderate, then?"

"Yes! That would be lovely!"

"That sounds good to me. ♪"

Sumire proudly puffed her chest out with noticeable satisfaction as Maria replied with a bubbly smile, each of their reactions dampening his enthusiasm in their own special way. Regardless, he proceeded to explain their roles.

◇

"Ayano, are you sure you don't need to be with Yuki right now? She apparently ran into some sort of trouble," Yumi Suou asked quietly. The mother of Masachika and Yuki was sitting next to Ayano. Yumi had only planned on seeing her daughter's class's attraction before heading straight home, but Ayano had ended up collecting her at the school gate and taking her to the auditorium, for some reason.

"It won't be an issue. We did run into a little trouble, but the issues have more or less been solved, thanks to the efforts of the student council. Lady Yuki is a little tied up at the moment, so I figured we could wait for her here until she finishes."

"Oh... But why the auditorium? If we have time to walk around, then..."

Yumi's eyes wandered until she gradually fell silent. Ayano knew what she wanted to say as well...and that was exactly why she replied:

"I decided it would be best for you to see this. That's why."

"...? What do you mean...?"

Right as Yumi put her curiosity into words, the brass band club's performance came to an end. Yumi and Ayano joined the applause while each student exited the stage with their instrument in hand before being almost immediately replaced by two beautiful girls.

"Hmm? Is that Maria and Sumire?"

"What are the student council secretary and disciplinary committee's vice president doing here?"

"What the...? I thought the literary club was doing a reader's theater after this?"

Students around them started to raise voices of surprise and bewilderment at the sight of the two girls onstage as well. Some were concerned that something had happened, while others, who stood up and were about to leave, sat right back down. There were even those who took out their phones and texted their friends, as if they sensed something big was about to happen. Basking in the anxious and excited gazes of the audience, Maria announced:

"Thank you all for coming today. Are you enjoying the show? First, I would like to introduce myself. I am the secretary of the student council, Maria Kujou. Next, I would like to apologize for the trouble that we have caused you. As a member of the school festival committee and of the student council, I would like to take a moment to say that I am deeply sorry for what happened today."

There was not even the smallest sign of her usual bubbly self as she earnestly bowed, but to make sure that the mood didn't get too gloomy, she lifted her head back up, lightened her tone, and added:

"Now, I know this is sudden and doesn't make up for what happened, but we have a surprise event for you all."

Maria directed her gaze to her side, where Sumire took a step forward with a microphone in hand.

"I, vice president of the disciplinary committee, Sumire Kiryuuin, will be moderating the surprise event. Today's event is a tradition at our Seirei Academy—a battle between two rivals in the presidential race—a showdown with their pride on the line."

A stir suddenly rippled throughout the crowd, as if people were starting to catch on, and right as the crowd couldn't be any more excited and surprised, Sumire firmly grinned from ear to ear and declared:

"I present to you today a debate…with a twist!"

The audience exploded with cheers. It was a surprise that neither the current students nor the alumni could have ever even imagined. People among the crowd began to enthusiastically explain what this meant to the confused visitors to the school festival, but as their excitement slowly calmed, they began to wonder who was going to be debating over what and what was so special about the debate's format.

And it was none other than Maria's job to explain the format.

"I am sure there are numerous visitors here today, so I would like to explain what makes this special. This will not be a traditional debate where one argues their opinion with words. This will be a special match between two individuals. Allow me to introduce them!"

Maria held out a hand toward the stage wing where two male students walked out.

"Masachika Kuze, a member of general affairs in the student council."

"And the captain of the piano club, Yuushou Kiryuuin."

Maria's and Sumire's introductions were once again met with explosive enthusiasm from the audience.

"*Squeeeal!* It's the prince!!"

"Prince Yuushouoo!!"

"Huh?! Kiryuuin?! He's running for president?!"

"I totally wasn't expecting to see Yuushou here! This is insane!"

"Interesting. So that's why Sumire's here..."

The numerous comments were mainly directed at Yuushou. However...

"Kuze... That's the guy who beat Sayaka Taniyama at the debate last semester."

"The unsung vice president in middle school... Wait. Why is he debating instead of our princess?"

"It's not often you see him onstage alone like this."

A small portion of the calmer audience members had their eyes curiously on Masachika.

"Masachika Kuze is partnered with the student council's accountant, Alisa Kujou. And I am running for student council vice president as Yuushou's partner," Sumire said.

"These two will be competing on...that!"

Maria held out her hand toward the brass band's grand piano, which a few members on staff had rolled back onto the stage.

"Yes, the piano. Each of these young men will take turns playing the piano, and after they are both done, you, the audience, will decide which performance you liked best."

Confusion immediately swept through the crowd like a gust of wind.

"Huh? Piano...? Yuushou Kiryuuin is going to crush him."

"What in the world? How is this even going to be fair?"

"Can Kuze even play the piano?"

"No clue... I was in his class in sixth and eighth grade, but I don't remember ever hearing anything about him playing piano..."

The unexpected turn of events lowered everyone's enthusiasm, unsurprisingly. The currently enrolled students were especially disappointed.

"Oh, great. I guess this is just some sort of sideshow act," complained a student with a bored stare. This was, however, how they expected the audience to act, so Maria and Sumire promptly proceeded to start the show.

"Now, let's start the show."

"Our first performer will be Yuushou Kiryuuin."

After the other three onstage disappeared into the wing, Yuushou prepared for his performance as the audience continued to voice their concern.

"Wait. Are they really going to be having a piano battle?"

"What does the winner even get out of this? They didn't even tell us that, right?"

"Hmm? Now that you mention it..."

Skeptical whispers were exchanged around Yumi as she stared at the stage in blank amazement.

"He still...?"

Her eyes almost unconsciously turned to Ayano, who knew exactly what she was trying to say.

"No, as far as I know, Master Masachika hasn't even touched the piano since that day," she replied, making Yumi's expression cloud over. However, Ayano made a point of not even looking back at her and quietly added:

"I thought you might want to see this."

"..."

The tension lasted for thirty or so seconds. Even Ayano, who continued to face forward, could feel that Yumi was terribly conflicted.

"..."

But eventually, Yumi settled down in her seat, which Ayano sensed without even a single glance.

I wonder, though... Who is Master Masachika going to perform for this time?

Whenever he used to play piano, he did it for someone else. However, it was never for the audience. It was for someone special. A single person. At times it was Yumi, at times it was Yuki, and at times it was Ayano... However, neither Yuki nor Alisa were here right now, and Masachika had no idea that Yumi and Ayano were here, either. Which meant...

Master Masachika... For whom are you performing?

The surrounding students began incorrectly speculating about the entire ordeal.

"Ohhh... I get it. I bet this is some kind of exhibition match that the school festival committee came up with."

"That makes sense, 'cause I've never even heard about Yuushou running for student council president."

"Yeah, that's probably it. They probably couldn't get Alisa and Yuki on the spur of the moment, so they settled for these two."

"Plus, it'd be weird for someone running for president to battle against someone running for vice president anyway."

A number of members in the audience had already come to their own conclusions, creating a slight air of disappointment among the crowd...but all of their disappointment vanished the instant Yuushou started playing.

The band's performance was going far better than any of the five members could have ever dreamed of. Perhaps having Alisa onstage before the show to calm the crowd helped attract a larger crowd than they might have had otherwise, since every seat was already filled before the show even started, and there were many people who were already standing nearby to watch the show as well, but it didn't end there. They had currently just finished their second cover song, and there was no way the place could get any more crowded. Masachika, however, was not among them.

Masachika...

The person Alisa wanted to be there the most to see her performance—to see her big moment—was nowhere in sight. No matter how much she searched for him, he was not there. It felt almost like a dark rain cloud slowly forming in her heart. But...

"Alya."

...she wasn't alone. She had friends who recognized how she felt and who were there for her.

It's going to be okay.

Alisa exchanged glances with Hikaru, who called her name and nodded back, and then she directed her gaze back to the audience. At the height of the show, she projected her voice powerfully, hoping that it would reach Masachika, and announced:

"All right, our next song is going to be our last. It's called 'Phantom.' I hope you enjoy it."

◇

"Marvelous! I have never had a student who could pick things up as quickly as you!"

"He's a prodigy. There's no doubt about that. He's probably going to grow up to be the greatest pianist in all of Japan."

Stop. I don't need your obvious lies. You're just trying to flatter me.

"I could listen to him play all day. That's the Prince of Piano for you."

"Yuushou is the epitome of the term 'child prodigy.'"

Shut up. Enough with your shallow praise. 'Prodigy'? The only reason why you people can say that is because you've never seen a real prodigy. You have no idea how it feels to hear a melody that makes a chill run down your spine. You have no idea what real talent sounds like—talent that can captivate an entire venue with but a single note. That's why you can spew such nonsense. You probably can't even imagine what true talent sounds like. Nobody knows just how miserable their thoughtless compliments make me.

"D-didn't I see him on TV?!"

"Yeah, that's the guy who got gold at the contest the other day. Yuushou Kiryuuin… He's so cool."

"Hmm? He's not playing last?"

"Nah, they put him on TV because he's good-looking. You know how TV is. Whoever won the last competition gets to be the closing act, by the way."

"For real? 'Yuushou'? More like 'Yu-should have tried harder'! That poor little runner-up."

"Pfft!

"Pfft! Quit it! He can hear you."

Those were the words of children my age at a certain piano

recital, forever to be carved into the back of my mind. "Runner-up." I wasn't a winner, and the only reason people ever complimented me was because I was good-looking. The humiliation was unbearable. My lungs strained as I felt myself panting violently through my clenched teeth.

Shut up! How dare you pigs insult me when you didn't even get close to second place?! You didn't even place! Don't you dare look down on me!

My first impulse was to grab them by their collars, but I couldn't do it…because I realized that deep down inside, they were right. I never could beat him. I was always second place when he was around. He was a true prodigy, born of talent. Masachika Suou…

"All right, Yuushou. You're up."

Once the official in charge called me to the stage, I was showered with cheers and applause simply for showing up, and when the performance was over, the entire venue was filled with praise for me. But…the instant *he* started to play, the entire mood changed. The audience, who were so eager to make noise up until a few seconds ago, were now sitting in complete silence. The tension was something you would expect to see if the performance was a professional orchestra, not a child in front of a piano.

"That was marvelous, Masachika!"

"Thank you very much."

But that was a testament to how powerful a performance he put on. And yet he didn't even react to the teacher's praise at the stage wing or to the belated applause and cheers of the audience or even to the frightened gazes of the other performers, either. He went straight back to the waiting room as though it all meant nothing to him. He didn't even glance in my direction as I glared at him, my eyes trembling with frustration and regret.

Masachika Suou's existence was an eyesore, and I cursed him from the bottom of my heart. All compliments just sounded empty because of him. Being praised by anyone who knew him felt like they were just trying to be nice and flatter me, and the opinions of those who didn't know him felt worthless to me. I practiced frantically in a bid to free myself from that curse. I practiced every day until the tips of my fingers started to bleed, preventing me from even holding chopsticks, and I started to despise the piano, which I used to love, over and over again. But even then, I couldn't quit. I continued playing the piano every day for the sole reason of defeating him one day.

And yet...he suddenly disappeared one day, as if he wasn't even interested in the piano. He put a curse on me and left me behind. No matter how many competitions or recitals I went to, he never showed up. I was left dumbfounded and dazed while awards and trophies endlessly rolled my way.

What is this?

Even becoming number one felt like garbage. All I ever wanted was to win, but their praise still felt empty. "Runner-up." That word was still haunting me, tucked away in the back of my mind.

This is stupid...

Did I really practice all those hours for this? For something as stupid as this? Why was I taking this so seriously? He knew from the very beginning—even before that—

"And last but not least, I want to ask you about your dream. What do you want to be when you grow up? A famous pianist, I assume?"

I plastered a smile on my face as the microphone was held toward my mouth.

"No, I want to take over my father's business one day. Piano is nothing more than a hobby to me."

Taking piano so seriously is stupid. A waste of time. Isn't that right, Masachika Suou?

Today is the day that I break free from my curse.

A mixture of rage and excitement swirled in Yuushou's heart as he sat before the piano. His anger was born from the humiliation, along with those sinister memories that still haunted him in his sleep. However, there was joy within the darkness, because he was finally going to be able to rid himself of what had been tormenting him over the years. Yuushou desperately tried to suppress these overpowering emotions, but there was no way he could keep his lips from twisting into a grin.

He was going to defeat Masachika Suou in front of an audience. He was going to prove that he was the best and free himself from this curse. It was finally time for him to face the piano, which he once loved, and face the praise from those around him. When he really thought about it, nothing else mattered. He had gone through a lot of trouble and used a lot of time and money in order to create a path to join the First Light Committee, but even that didn't matter right now. All he needed was this: being able to compete against Masachika Suou again on piano.

I have to crush him so that there is not even a single shred of doubt who the best is.

Therefore, he requested to go first on purpose, just like old times. He had to be aggressive and defeat the man who used to always get to play last at recitals...and he had to win with the piece that Masachika was best at.

Yuushou's lips remained curled with delight as he placed his fingers on the keys...and proceeded to perform Chopin's "Nocturne in E-flat Major, op. 9, no. 2."

A beautifully sweet melody echoed throughout the auditorium. Even the somewhat disappointed members in the audience were now captivated as they naturally sat up straight in their seats.

"Wow... He's really good," whispered Maria in admiration at the stage wing as she listened to the master of the art perform.

"You can say that again," agreed Masachika in a soft voice.

"That's all you have to say? That's who you're up against, you know?"

But Masachika shrugged back at Maria's skeptical gaze, then casually replied:

"I never thought I could beat him."

"What?"

Even Masachika knew that he was no match for Yuushou. Not playing for an entire five years put him at a huge disadvantage, for starters. Even if he instinctively remembered how to play the piece, his fingers probably wouldn't be able to keep up. He wasn't underestimating the piano or Yuushou, and he was well aware that someone who hadn't touched a piano in so long didn't stand a chance.

As long as they don't laugh at me, I'm good, I guess.

But that wasn't an issue. Masachika accomplished what he set out to do the instant Yuushou agreed to the challenge. In other words, he prevented Yuushou from contacting the First Light Committee, and thus kept this incident from being swept under the rug. Furthermore, it kept Yuushou from getting their approval, since they seemed to love it when students fought dirty during the presidential race. That was why he was willing to resort to violence and provocation to get Yuushou to lose his composure so that he would agree to this glaringly unfair match.

Because it was unfair. That was for sure. It didn't matter that Yuushou had a distinct advantage, because Masachika couldn't care less if he lost, and the audience's reaction from a few moments ago only made him even more sure that this competition didn't matter. Not only was this an unfair matchup and not even an actual debate but instead some bizarre piano competition, but they didn't even reveal what each of them was putting on the line, both of which conditions were unheard of. Therefore, that, plus what Maria and Sumire explained to the audience, made most of the listeners believe that this was just a sideshow act set up by the student council to make up for what had happened today.

In reality, both contestants actually were putting something on the line, though. If Masachika were to lose, then he would leave Yuushou alone, regardless of whether he actually had anything to do with today's incident or not. Therefore, from the audience's viewpoint, there was no reward for winning, which meant that this wasn't an official "debate" in their eyes. To them, this was nothing more than a freak show between a pianist and a nobody, so losing wouldn't tarnish Masachika's reputation one bit. Even if Yuushou were to complain later about it, all Masachika had to do was play dumb and say things like, "What? That was just a sideshow act. We didn't even bet anything." After all, it was Yuushou who needed their bet to be kept secret, since he'd never gotten a chance to get the First Light Committee's approval.

I definitely wasn't expecting him to accept my proposal that easily, though. Was losing to me all those years ago really that traumatic? Like, he's even playing the piece I used to play back then, too...

This was the first piece that Masachika learned how to play. His mother loved Chopin, so he often enjoyed playing it at recitals when they were allowed to freely choose their pieces.

But even though it's the same piece, it feels completely different when he plays it.

Masachika's mother and piano teacher often said that even the same piece would sound like a completely different composition, depending on the pianist, and they were apparently right. Yuushou's performance was textbook perfect and extremely pleasurable to listen to, but to Masachika's ears, the tempo sounded a bit rushed.

It feels almost like he's letting his competitive nature get the best of him...but, well, I guess it's actually helping make his performance much more exciting. Who do I think I am? I'm in absolutely no position to be criticizing anyone else's playing, he immediately thought afterward in a self-deprecating manner. He then directed his focus toward Maria's concerned gaze and assured her:

"It's really going to be fine. It doesn't matter if I lose."

"...As in it won't hurt your election chances?"

"Hmm?"

While Masachika blinked, not quite understanding what she was getting at, Maria gazed into his eyes with genuine concern and tugged at his sleeve.

"Even if this doesn't affect your chances in the election...I don't want you to get hurt, so if this is going to hurt you in any way, then let's call it off."

"...!"

Her suggestion caught him off guard at first but ended up bringing a soft smile to his face.

"Thank you...but I'm fine."

"Really?"

"Really. I don't care how the audience sees me or feels about my performance. Besides..."

"...?"

The thought of saying it embarrassed Masachika so much that he hesitated, but there was no way he could lie after seeing her curious, worried gaze, so he looked away and admitted:

"I plan on playing…for you today, Masha."

"…?"

"You know…? That promise I made you when we were kids. I promised that I'd play the piano for you one day."

"…!"

It was a promise that Sah had made with Mah long ago. Mah really wanted to hear him play piano, so he promised to invite her to one of his recitals, but Mah had unfortunately moved back to Russia before he could ever keep that promise. Put simply, the true reason he'd asked Maria to host this match was actually because he wanted to fulfill the promise he'd made to her over five years ago.

"…You remembered. That was so long ago."

"Sorry, uh… I honestly forgot about it up until recently."

"*Giggle.* But you still remembered in the end, so I'm happy."

"…Well, keeping promises is important."

A soft hand tightly wrapped around his, making his cheeks burn until the heat was almost unbearable. However—

"…I apologize for interrupting whatever secrets you're whispering to each other, but Yuushou's performance is almost over," Sumire pointed out with a reproachful glare.

"Oh, sorry."

"…It's fine, but… I feel bad for Yuushou." She sighed. The comment reminded him of what Nonoa had once said, which made him uncomfortable, but before even another second went by, the venue suddenly exploded with applause.

"Prince Yuushou!!"

"Prince of Piano!!"

Girls who were probably in the piano club squealed and cried as he waved good-bye to them on his way to the stage wing.

"Looks like I'm up."

"Yep… Good luck."

He smiled back at Maria while passing by Yuushou as he stepped onto the stage, but Yuushou's fleeting glance was reminiscent of old times—unapologetically competitive, which made Masachika tense uncomfortably.

You don't have to look at me like that... I don't plan on taking this seriously, not like it would matter if I did...

Masachika currently didn't have the wish or the skill to live up to Yuushou's expectations. Besides, it wasn't his job to appease him, either. All Yuushou was to Masachika was an asshole who tried to ruin the Autumn Heights Festival for everyone. Nothing more, nothing less. Unlike with Nao, he didn't have it in himself to even sympathize with the guy. In fact, he couldn't have cared any less why Yuushou did all this.

I mean, it felt kind of good to scare him earlier...but none of that matters anymore.

What was important right now was keeping his promise to Maria.

The question is...what should I play for her?

After bowing to the audience, Masachika took a seat in front of the piano and began to ponder what he should play, now of all times. He wondered what would be the best piece he could gift to Maria... when it hit him.

Technically, this isn't for Masha. It's for Mah.

The person he made a promise with was Maria but a different version of her: an innocent, pure little girl named Mah who vanished one day after a misunderstanding. Masachika thought back to the conversation he'd had with his piano teacher many years ago.

"You're honestly good enough to play anything, Masachika... This composition is a very advanced piece, you know?"

"Really? I thought that 'Revolutionary Étude' *was harder..."*

"That's also an advanced piece... Oh, hey. Did you know that Chopin actually wasn't the one who named the piece 'Revolutionary Étude'*?"*

"What? Really?"

"Really. There are actually a few solo piano works written by Chopin that were given alternative titles by other people."

"Does that mean that this piece also has another name?"

"It sure does. It's known by many in Japan by the name—"

Masachika suddenly smirked while he placed his fingers on the keys.

Yeah… Right now, I'm not Masachika Kuze. I'm Masachika Suou.

That must have been how his opponent felt as well…so for now, maybe it was okay for him to be his old self. Maybe it was okay for him to be Masachika Suou while he dedicated this piece to a girl in his memories from long ago.

Chopin's "Étude in E Major, op. 10, no. 3."

Saying thank you and good-bye to first love.

The live show ended up being a huge hit. The cheers and applause from the audience echoed like thunder while a few people even jokingly started yelling "Encore!" Alisa thereupon stood before the other four members as a prisoner of some sort of sensation she had never experienced before. Had she ever felt this adored before in her life? Had she ever felt this wanted before?

Oh… This is…

This was what it felt like to have your hard work finally pay off. Up until now, she had continued to work hard while avoiding the praise of others. She felt that she was the only one who needed to feel good about her efforts. However…

Once I just mustered up the courage to take that one step forward, I found so many people who accepted and appreciated me.

As something warm suddenly began to swell in Alisa's chest once more, she narrowed her gaze as if to hold it back while bowing deeply to the audience. Amid the ever-growing applause, Alisa then made eye contact with the other four band members before they all retired from the stage.

"Yesss!! That was so awesome!!" exclaimed Takeshi the instant he stepped down the stage wing. His body trembled as if he couldn't take it anymore while grinning from ear to ear. The other four rather excitedly nodded back at him as well.

"Yes, that really was great! Really, really great! And I mean it! That was probably the best we have ever sounded!"

"…I agree."

"Hmm? Saya? Oh my god. Are you tearing up?"

"No! I'm not…"

"Are you suuure?"

"Nono, stop! Ah…!"

Sayaka looked away uncomfortably, realizing that she had called Nonoa by a nickname that only her family and close friends used. The sight made Alisa smile even more, and she bowed to her friends.

"Everyone, thank you."

Thank you for making me your leader. Thank you for showing me something so wonderful.

There were so many different things she was grateful for as she bowed while her friends smiled back at her.

"We should be thanking you, Alya! I honestly think the biggest reason the show went so well was because of your singing! Ah! Of course, Sayaka's bass playing and Nonoa's skills on the keyboard were incredible as well!"

"Thanks for the footnote at the end… Anyway, we all worked together to make that happen. There's no need to thank anyone."

"Come on, I didn't mean for it to sound like a footnote. I—"

"Like, other than Takeh-C dissin' us, that was a lot of fun. Thanks, Alisa."

"Allow me to thank you as well, Alya. We couldn't have done it without you. Not only did you agree to be our vocalist, but you became our leader and gave us guidance as well."

"Now you're all making me feel awkward for saying there's no need to thank us."

"Nah, I'm the one in an awkward position here. I—ah! Kanauuu! Did you watch your big brother's show? I was so cool, wasn't I?"

Almost immediately after leaving the stage, Takeshi found his little brother among the crowd before running straight for him. The others warmly smiled while almost rolling their eyes, but before long, other members of the audience started to notice them, too.

"Alisa Kujou! You were incredible!"

"Nonoa, I love you!"

"Hikaru! Over here!"

Passionate voices began to push through the crowd, so Hikaru promptly stepped forward to guard the female members of the group, but heated female gazes immediately began to lock on Hikaru as well, making him tense and tremble in despair.

"Oh my god, Alisa. Look at you. How about hitting 'em with some fan service so we can peace out?"

"'Fan service'? 'Peace out'?"

But the unfamiliar phrases only confused Alisa.

"Like this," added Nonoa while she put on a radiant smile like a celebrity. You could almost see a star shoot from her eye when she winked at the crowd.

"Thank you all sooo much. ☆ I'm sooo sorry, though. We actually have somewhere we have to be, so do you think you could clear a path for us?"

The incredible fan service immediately took the passionate fans' breath away, immediately causing a ripple in the crowd as people asked those behind them to move to the side and make way until a path opened before them.

"And that's how you do it."

"Uh…? Sorry… I can't…"

Alisa smiled awkwardly, unsure how to convey that there were countless reasons why she would never be able to do that.

"Anyway, I wonder where Masachika is. Maybe he's still busy helping the school festival committee with something?" Hikaru muttered suddenly, prompting Alisa to begin surveying the area as well.

Oh, yeah, she thought. *I want to share this excitement with him—these powerful emotions. This world he brought me to… These friends he introduced me to… The stage that he prepared for me… I want to share every emotion I experienced because of him as soon as possible. Masachika…!*

She grew restless, her eyes suddenly darting in every direction… when a voice suddenly caught her attention.

"What?! A debate?!"

The discussion inevitably piqued her curiosity, and she reflexively directed her gaze in the direction of the voices, where she saw a male student holding his phone out while talking enthusiastically to the girl by his side.

"Yooo! It's actually not a debate?! They're having a piano competition in the auditorium!"

"What? Who is?"

"Yuushou Kiryuuin and Masachika Kuze! And the match has already started!"

It was the name of the young man she had been searching for, but she was immediately overcome with surprise after hearing the flood of information.

Masachika...? Debate? Piano...? Why...? What is going on?

Her eyes wandered in search of an answer...until she noticed Hikaru staring hard at something.

"...Hikaru? What's—?"

When Alisa followed his gaze, she noticed three strangers up ahead, but she knew who they were. Call it intuition. Call it a gut feeling. Regardless, she somehow knew that these were the original band members in Takeshi and Hikaru's band.

"Hikaru—"

"We've got this, Alisa. Go."

"Huh?"

Alisa turned around to find Nonoa lethargically narrowing her gaze back at her.

"You wanna see what's up with Kuze, right? So go."

"Yes, just go. Hiiragi! Can we get some help?"

Hiiragi Kurasawa, a member of the disciplinary committee who was wearing glasses and men's clothing, suddenly appeared out of nowhere, pushed up her glasses, and assured everyone:

"You need me to be Alisa Kujou's bodyguard, yes? Very well."

"Thank you."

"A'ight, let's clear a path for you, then," Nonoa stated listlessly before doing a little fan service for the crowd while asking (ordering) them to move. The crowd moved to each side as if Moses from the legends had held up his staff, creating a small path for Alisa to follow Hiiragi down.

Why is Masachika...?

The baffling question felt like a tornado spinning in her head while the anxiety and frustration swallowed her like a wave, making her unable to process what was going on. It was as if Masachika had gone somewhere really far away, so Alisa began to run as fast as she could so that she wouldn't get left behind. She ran, believing that once she saw him, this anxiety would go away. It would prove that she was only worrying over nothing, and that this bad feeling in her gut was nothing but a little restlessness.

After Alisa arrived at the auditorium smoothly, thanks to Hiiragi's guidance, she took a moment to catch her breath, then bowed in gratitude.

"Thank you so much."

"It was my pleasure. Anyway, I need to head back to the stage, so you're on your own now."

"Thanks."

Alisa faced the door to the auditorium after Hiiragi ran off.

"...All right."

She then mustered up enough courage to push open the large double doors and stepped inside, but what she found...was silence accompanied by the soft melody of a piano.

This is...

The crystal-clear notes were reminiscent of a moonlit lake. It was so tranquil that one would worry to even make the slightest of sounds. Alisa, however, slowly moved forward until she saw the young man who had created this world.

Masa...chika...

It was the one she sought, and yet it wasn't. The individual there was not the Masachika she knew. The young man she knew would never open himself up to everyone like this. Instead, he would always joke around to hide his true feelings. Never would he put his true feelings into words—into music.

Stop...

Alisa knew. She knew that this piece was dedicated to a special someone. The way the notes echoed, the way his fingers danced, the way his entire body performed: every bit of him conveyed his undeniable yearning and sorrow that he had tucked hidden away in his heart, and it made Alisa unbelievably jealous of whoever this music was for.

Stop! Make it stop!

Her voice inwardly exploded with cries like a spoiled child. She wanted to cover the ears and eyes of every person in this auditorium. She wanted to hide the true Masachika from everyone else. She didn't want him to open up to anyone but her.

He's my partner... I'm the one closest to him... I should be the one who knows him better than anyone!

Alisa couldn't make sense of the powerful, overflowing emotions as she was suddenly overcome with the urge to scream and cry for reasons that she didn't even understand herself. It was as if she didn't even know who she was as she clenched her fists tightly.

Masachika was so far away. Further than he had ever felt before. *I thought I was standing right by his side. I thought I had found my way a little closer to his heart. But he went off all by himself, yet again...*

"<My wizard...>"

But Alisa's faint whispers were erased by the piano.

I never really understood what it meant to have a sense of accomplishment. Being praised by my grandfather made me happy. Being praised by my mother made me happy. Making my little sister happy made me happy. Those were emotions I could understand, but a sense of accomplishment was foreign to me. Maybe that was why I always felt a bit empty inside. Maybe that was why this emptiness was all I had ever felt since I stopped being Masachika Suou.

The boring days of freedom went by while I lived with my grandparents on my father's side, but the emptiness remained. One day, however, I casually turned on the TV and randomly began watching a cartoon for children, which actually made me realize why I felt so empty.

"I have a dream! And I'm never going to give up, no matter what obstacles get in my way!"

The talentless protagonist of the show worked as hard as he could to make his dream come true. At first, everyone simply laughed at his foolishness, but their laughs eventually transformed into admiration until everyone was cheering him on. Although he struggled at times and suffered setbacks at others, he managed to succeed with strong passion and tireless effort.

He was a true hero whom everyone wanted to succeed, and when he did succeed, they were all there to celebrate his success. Furthermore, the happy ending for the hero and the heroine, who had been supporting him through it all, couldn't have been any better.

...Struggles, setbacks, passion, effort: I had none of these. All I had was a waste of talent that I was born with. Never were there struggles nor setbacks, and the effort was just menial work, as if I were grinding in a video game to level up. There was no way to feel a sense of accomplishment from easily succeeding like that. Who would cheer someone like me on? Who would celebrate my success with me? I was sure nobody even wanted me to succeed.

But when the emptiness gradually swelled like a black hole until I was apathetic about everything...she was there to give me hope. She appeared out of nowhere like a miracle. My heroine. If she was going to cheer me on and celebrate my success, then why would I care what anyone else thought? Her smile was my hope. Her smile alone filled the emptiness in my heart. The memories had been sealed away so long because I believed they were terrible memories that I wanted to forget, but the truth was far different from what I thought I remembered. The long-standing misunderstanding had been dispelled... and now all I felt toward her was gratitude.

And that's why...

That was why I had to fulfill my promise and end this once and for all. The story of my first love needed a conclusion so that I could continue to move forward without any regret. I was going to tell her what I should have told her that day, and I was going to do so with a smile. I was going to tell her that meeting her was a miracle full of nothing but happiness. I was going to tell her with all the gratitude and love in my heart:

Thank you for everything. Good-bye.
[Спасибо Тебе За Всё... Прощай...]

The whispers left his lips as he removed his hands from the keyboard, and when he closed his eyes, he could see her innocent smile just how he remembered it. Masachika smirked wryly at how convenient his interpretation was, but it was being able to laugh at himself that felt somewhat refreshing as well.

Once the last note finished ringing, he stood within the unchanging silence, bowed, then withdrew from the stage.

Only after Masachika disappeared into the stage wing did the audience begin to clap, but Ayano didn't join them. She was busy rubbing Yumi's back.

"Madam Suou..."

"I'm sorry... I'm so sorry...!"

Yumi buried her face in her handkerchief, sobbing convulsively while repeatedly apologizing, so Ayano just continued to rub her back—the back of a woman overcome with regret. Far behind them—standing even behind the last row of seats—were people who not even Masachika could have predicted would be here, clapping as well.

"...Who was that? There's no way a pianist of that caliber goes unheard of," exclaimed one of the men, but not a single person answered him. A few in the group glanced at Gensei to gauge how to react and noticed he was going to maintain his silence, so they remained silent as well.

"What a shame," groaned another woman, prompting others to quickly agree.

"Yes, it really is a shame."

"Losing is losing, though."

After nodding heavily in agreement, the oldest man in the group coldly handed down his verdict.

"I respect his ambition and the courage it took to raise hell at the school festival...but if he cannot deliver checkmate and falls in battle in the end, then this is as far as he goes."

The old man then turned on his heel and faced Touya, who had brought them here.

"Let's head back."

"What? Are you sure you don't want to stay to see the results?"

"No need."

"...Very well. This way, then, please."

Each member then followed after Touya as they left the auditorium behind.

"Uh... Why am I winning?" grumbled Masachika as he walked out the door leading outside from the stage wing. Right after the performance ended, they promptly had the audience vote for who they thought had won...and most people were surprisingly voting for Masachika. What was most astonishing was that it wasn't really even close. Each member of the audience raised their hand to vote for the winner while members on staff used tally counters to count the votes, exchanging glances as if to say, "We don't really need to tally the votes, do we?"

"...Masha, I hate to ask you this, but did you hire plants to pretend to be audience members?" asked Masachika, 30 percent seriously, but Maria immediately pouted in protest.

"I would never. How rude."

"I know, but, like... You saw that, right?"

He laughed bitterly as he could feel his heart gradually grow cold, for Masachika had won, making him much more aware of the emptiness inside.

Sigh... Life on easy mode sucks.

Although Masachika grimaced at his despicable victory, Maria wore a gentler smile as she stepped in front of him and wrapped her arms around him.

"O-oh...?"

"Thank you for keeping your promise... That was a wonderful performance. I almost wanted to cry."

"...Really? I'm glad you liked it."

Maria's words seemed to fill the hole in his heart a little bit. While he still didn't feel any sense of accomplishment, her praise comforted him just like in old times. He surrendered his body to her while being smothered in her kindness and the memories of what once was. He gave in to her embrace…and gave in some more…and…

Uh… How long does she plan on hugging me for?

It was a long hug…and it gradually felt like it was becoming more passionate. In fact, she was starting to stand on the balls of her feet while rubbing up against his body, slowly reaching his cheek.

O-oh, gosh! This is kind of bad. This is kind of bad! We aren't kids anymore! She's softer all over now! Like, there's a lot different about her!

An alarm went off in his head, warning him that he was reaching the point of no return, so he reached out to gently push her away… when she suddenly let go of him herself. Maria's lips innocently curled while she gazed at Masachika's relieved, yet also a little disappointed, expression.

"You're so cute, Sah. ♡"

"I, uh…"

"*Giggle.* Yep. I'm still in love with you."

"Ah—"

Her casual admission was genuine, and that was why Masachika's eyebrows reflexively slanted downward. However, seeing how he reacted put a touch of sorrow into her smile.

"I'm sorry. I wasn't trying to make you uncomfortable. I just had to say it."

"No…"

But he was unable to tell her that it made him really happy to hear her say that.

I like Masha as a person…but she isn't that girl anymore.

He couldn't feel the same way about Maria as he felt about Mah. But…

I already found closure and said my good-bye. So maybe one day…

Complicated emotions twisted his heart as he gazed at Maria, which made her eyebrows lower even more in despair.

"If—"

But right before another word was spoken…

"Masachika!!"

…a sharp voice called out Masachika's name.

"Huh...? Alya?"

He shifted his focus toward the voice to find Alisa still dressed in her stage clothes, wearing a panicked expression for some reason.

"What's wrong...? Did something happen?" he asked, as though he was alarmed by her behavior, but Alisa clenched her teeth, swallowing her words.

"...Go talk to her."

"Uh... But..."

"It's okay. Go," Maria said, gently smiling and patting him on the shoulder. After a brief bow, Masachika ran over to Alisa's side while glancing back a few times, but Maria continued to wave and smile.

"<If only we had actually promised to see each other again that day, then... Then again, maybe it's a good thing I was interrupted, for I said too much.>"

There was a hint of sorrow in her voice as she watched until she could see him no more.

"Not only did you resort to nasty tricks, but you lost at what you're best at as well. I cannot even look at you," Sumire muttered while reading the letter Masachika had handed her. She stood by the grand piano after it had been rolled back into the stage wing while Yuushou gazed at the piano in a daze, with a hand on the keys.

"Therefore, I must ask: Why do you look so happy?" she asked with a worried tone, but a few moments went by before he finally replied:

"Sumire... I actually do love playing piano."

"Oh my. You are just now figuring that out?"

Yuushou snorted at her unceremonious, unsurprised reaction, since this was a rather important admission, in his eyes.

I'm really no match for you, Sumire.

He had been telling himself a lie all these years. He claimed that piano was nothing more than a hobby and convinced himself that it was nothing to take seriously. But that was merely an excuse so that he wouldn't have to admit how he really felt. His true

feelings were sealed away, pushing him to find something else to fill the void in place of the piano…and he somehow convinced himself that taking over his father's business was his goal in life, but that was all over now. He couldn't keep up the lie any longer.

This was the first time that he took the piano seriously in what felt like years. He gave it everything he had, and he lost. There was no denying it anymore. There was no way he could hold back this overflowing passion that he felt when he played piano.

Even the smallest note Masachika played was unlike anything Yuushou had ever produced—to the point that it was hard to believe that they were even using the same piano. Masachika's performance was otherworldly. He made the piano cry. He made it scream. If this were a battle of technique, then Yuushou was confident that he wouldn't have lost, but he somehow instinctively knew that he had lost. There was just something about Masachika's performance that made him feel that way.

Yuushou had not yet figured out what that something was, but he knew that he could find it one day if he kept searching. His only regret now was that he wasn't able to put every bit of himself into his match against Masachika.

I'm sorry for not taking you as seriously as I should have all these years.

His fingers softly caressed the piano while he promised to dedicate himself completely to the instrument from now on. Although he didn't know if he would ever get to compete against Masachika like this again, he was going to make sure that he wouldn't have any regrets next time if an opportunity were to arise.

"Sumire."

"…?"

"I… I'm going to go to college to study music."

"Do it."

"…?!"

Her quick, simple reply immediately attracted Yuushou's gaze, where he found her clearly fed up, glaring back at him.

"Obviously, I saw through your act long ago. I knew you never really wanted to take over the Kiryuuin Group. But do not worry about a thing, because I'm going to admirably take over the family business in your place."

"Ha-ha-ha...," said Yuushou, laughing dryly, while she proudly puffed out her chest.

"You saw right through me, huh?"

"But of course. You have a habit of trying to distract yourself with something else whenever you cannot get what you truly desire. You're so easy to read."

"Am I really...?"

"Yes. When we were kids, you would always frolic theatrically in the sandbox whenever all the swings were taken. Whenever all the chocolate ice cream at the store was sold out, you would buy bags full of other types of ice cream..."

"Err..."

"And you haven't changed a bit. Even now, you surround yourself with girls who worship and wait upon you just because the girl you truly love won't give you the time of day."

"...?!"

Yuushou was speechless as a cold sweat began to drip down his back.

She knows? he thought.

"I have no clue who this girl is that you have feelings for, but showing off your harem isn't going to get her attention the way you want it to."

"...Oh, right," Yuushou said emotionlessly with a nod. Sumire shook her head and sighed. It was a complicated feeling to describe. He was both relieved and disappointed at the same time. Regardless, after letting out a deep sigh, he decided to put those feelings behind himself for now and move on. "Anyway, I know I said I wanted to study music in college...but this isn't something I can just decide for myself on a whim."

"Yes, you should first—"

"I know. I need to talk to my dad about it first... I'm sure it's not going to be easy to convince him, though."

"...I wouldn't be so sure about that."

"Huh?"

Yuushou lifted his chin, taken aback by her unexpected reply, where he found Sumire waving the letter that was inside the envelope.

"First, we're going to have to shave your head completely bald."

"...What?"

"You did something wrong, right? And when you do something wrong, you first need to shave your head, get on your knees, then bow for forgiveness."

Yuushou scowled after quickly scanning the letter, which read:

Yuushou Kiryuuin must confess to the entire school that he was responsible for every disturbance that occurred today.

"Don't tell me that...? In front of the entire school...?"

"That is exactly what I mean. You lost. Did you not?"

"Sure, but the conditions weren't that I had to shave my head and—"

"Are you a man or not?" interrupted Sumire while she vigorously poked Yuushou's chest with her index finger. She then tapped her finger with each word, each prod more piercing than the last.

"Shave. Your. Head. And. Bow."

Yuushou knit his brow defiantly, unable to bring himself to accept his cousin's demands, when...

"I. Mean. It."

"...Fine," said Yuushou, nodding obediently before Sumire's penetrating stare. After all, she was, for various reasons, his greatest weakness.

"H-hey, Alya? What's wrong?" Masachika asked the silver-haired maiden who was walking quickly ahead, but she simply continued to maintain her silence while leading him by the hand. She had been this way ever since Masachika rushed over to her as well, so there was no telling whether she was angry, flustered, or what. Then again, he did have an idea why she would be upset, but it didn't feel like that was what this was about.

"Come on, tell me where we're going. How was your show?"

Silence. That was all he got, no matter how many times he tried to strike up a conversation. Before he even realized it, they were walking behind the clubroom building, where not another soul was in sight. Only then did Alisa finally stop in her tracks, swiftly turn around, and glare at him in silence, making Masachika tense.

"You're mad, aren't you? Is it because I couldn't make it to your show? Or is it because I challenged Yuushou to that match without discussing it with you first? I'm really sorry about that. I know it's only going to sound like an excuse, but there's a reason for all this."

Alisa took a step closer, causing Masachika to take a reflexive step back, but it was already too late.

"Ah—guh?" he squeaked pathetically, for her arms were tightly wrapped around him.

"A-Alya? Seriously, what's wrong?" asked Masachika in genuine bewilderment, but Alisa still didn't say a word. She silently tightened her arms around him, hugging him even harder.

Huh? What's going on? What kind of emotion is this?

After all, this was the first time Alisa had ever even hugged him. Then again, it felt more like she was clinging on to him than hugging...

Wh-why isn't she saying anything? She's so soft, and she smells good, but she's really squeezing me hard... Is this really Alya? Did someone or something body swap with her? If I start getting giddy and let my guard down, is she going to open her mouth unbelievably wide and bite my head off?

The instant that final question came to mind—

"...?! Ow?! Ow, ow, ow, ow?!" shouted Masachika as she actually bit into the side of his neck.

"Seriously, what is wrong with you?! Were you taken over by some sort of parasite?! Are you a zombie?! Did I just get infected?!"

Once he yelled out whatever came to his confused mind, the sensation of teeth digging into his neck vanished, followed by something soft in its place, but by the time he looked down, Alisa was already burying her face into his collar.

"...Alya?"

"..."

U-uh... What is going on? She reminds me of a sulking child clinging to a parent...

Despite not even understanding what was going on, Masachika began to pat her back gently to calm her down, but before long, soft whispers in Russian began to tickle his ear.

"<You're my partner, you know...?>"

Alisa tightened her arms around him once more, and she continued to hold him quietly in her arms after that for a while until Touya eventually called Masachika's phone.

At least for now.

"After tallying up the votes, the award for excellence goes to the girls' kendo club for their play."

"Nice."

"Yeah, that makes sense."

"The sword fighting was incredible…"

"Sumire was so cool…"

"And the special award goes to the freshmen of Class D and Class F for their joint project: the maid café."

"…Yep."

"I know people might say they had the advantage, being two classes and all, but I can't believe they won by such a huge lead."

"Wait. You didn't go? Even though you're the president?"

"It was a little too…you know? For me."

"I caught a glimpse of how idol groups make their money…and I didn't like it…"

After the school festival came to an end, each class and club diligently worked to clean up while the school festival committee held their final meeting. Alisa had also finished her accounting work, so she joined the meeting as well…but she was hardly paying attention to anything anyone was saying.

Sigh… Why did I do that…?

She thought back to what she did to Masachika after his piano competition. Feelings, which even she didn't understand, pushed her to do something baffling. Now that her school festival duties had calmed her down, all she felt was regret.

Really, what is wrong with me? First, I hug him as hard as I can, and then I start biting him? I even kissed him… Ugh. It doesn't make any sense.

At that moment, she wanted Masachika to look only at her, and she wanted to be the only one with eyes on him. Plus, she was annoyed at how unconcerned he seemed for doing something so selfish…and before she knew it, she was wrapping her arms around him.

Sigh… Maybe I'm just really possessive?

Alisa was no longer in any position to deny that Masachika was special to her. Except for when she was very young, he was her first friend, her partner for the election, and the wizard who introduced her to so many new worlds. Masachika was surely far more special to her than she was to him.

Is that why?

Perhaps she wanted to be special to him in the same way he was special to her. Was that the cause of her possessiveness? Unfortunately, each one of these emotions was new to her, so she had no idea what they could be.

I guess I really am still a beginner when it comes to personal relationships…

Alisa managed to make new friends, thanks to the band, and her social skills improved as well, but that was also exactly why she knew that she still had so much to learn. She still wasn't comfortable with fake smiles, she still didn't know how to strike up a conversation, and she had a hard time judging how close she was to others—what good friends they actually were.

Yeah… I still can't rationalize what I did, though.

No excuses could explain why she suddenly bit him. It was incomprehensible. She wasn't a dog, and claiming inexperience or awkwardness wasn't enough to rationalize such a violent act.

Really, why? Why did I do that…? Then again, Yuki bit him, too, right? I remember seeing the teeth marks on his neck. Ever since I saw that, I've felt like…I wanted to scream…

After Alisa glanced at Yuki, who was focusing on the meeting without a care in the world, she shifted her gaze toward Masachika, who still had a cold compress on his neck to hide the bite mark, which filled Alisa with unbelievable guilt.

Sigh... I can't believe I did that... I really have to apologize to him later...but how...?

How was she supposed to explain herself and apologize when she didn't even know why she did it? Maybe she should just have him bite her back? An eye for an eye, as they say... Then again, that would make everything even more nonsensical than it already was.

Ngh... I want to disappear. Somebody, help... Anybody...

But right as she inwardly grumbled in the face of this unsolvable issue, the president of the school festival committee suddenly stood up.

"All right, guys! I know we ran into a lot of trouble today, but thanks to everyone's hard work, nobody got seriously injured, and the top dogs in the First Light Committee didn't have to come lecture us, either! We did it! So thank you! All of you!"

After he took a bow with the vice president, he grinned confidently and continued:

"It was a long month of preparation, but you did it! Now, go out there and enjoy the rest of the night festival together! Of course, don't go too crazy if you still have work to finish up, okay?"

The school festival president ended on a joke as he held his arms out wide.

"Now, let's wrap this up with a clap! Once I give the signal, I want everyone to clap once with me!"

Everyone in the room promptly stood up and got into the same stance as the president, with their hands in front of them.

"Yoooooo!"

Clap!

Countless hands clapped simultaneously, bringing an end to the sixty-sixth Autumn Heights Festival.

"Alya," uttered a voice from behind right as Alisa was about to leave the conference room, making her jump. But when she looked back over her shoulder to find Masachika behind her, she coldly replied:

"What?"

"Uh… Are you free? I need your help with something…"

Alisa hesitated. She frankly didn't have any plans after this, except for maybe helping her class clean up if they needed her help. Since she had finished her duties for the school festival committee, she didn't really have any other obligations…but she wasn't sure if she should honestly admit that to him. She pondered…until she realized that there was no use lying, since Masachika, who had been working with her this entire time, obviously knew she didn't have anything to do after this. Besides, it would be far better to apologize and settle things now instead of telling some ridiculous lie so that she could continue wallowing in regret alone.

"Fine," she replied over her shoulder with a nod.

"Thanks. Follow me, then."

Alisa proceeded to follow Masachika out of the room. As they walked down the hallway illuminated by the evening sun, she stared at his back while racking her brain for ways to apologize.

"I'm sorry for biting you"? But how would I then explain why I did it…?

Even the most far-fetched of explanations would do. She just needed something. The first reason that came to mind was the fact that Masachika had an official match against a potential rival without her, but he'd already explained the entire situation to her, the student council, and the president and vice president of the school festival committee after it was all over, so she didn't feel like it was right to bring it up anymore, since the issue had already been settled… Besides, there was an even bigger problem she had to face before that.

My anger itself is irrational…

There was no reason for it. Alisa simply acted on impulse after allowing her possessiveness to cloud her judgment.

I'm such an idiot.

Being physically close didn't mean they were any closer on an emotional level, and using her feminine wiles to see a genuine reaction wasn't going to get her any closer to catching a glimpse of what was in his heart. From the moment they first met until now, nothing had changed between them. Masachika was still right there by her side, and yet still so far away.

And one day…Masachika is going to leave my side.

Because he could do anything by himself and go anywhere he wanted. Once the time was right, he would most likely go far, far away as he followed his heart. And Alisa, who could not freely fly on her own, would surely not be able to follow after him.

I… No… I feel like I'm going to cry.

Her heart suddenly began to thump like a drum while she blinked…when Masachika came to a stop.

"…? Is this…?"

She tilted her head curiously after seeing where he had brought her, but Masachika paid no heed to her bewilderment and opened the door.

"Go inside."

When she stepped inside the craft club's clubroom, she saw a familiar female student waiting for them.

"Oh, great. You're here, Kuze."

"I'm really sorry to bother you like this, Professor Side Slit. I know you're busy."

"Yeah, you should be sorry. You owe me one."

"I'll pay you back tenfold when I become the vice president."

"Hya-ha-ha! Sounds like I'm gonna have to make sure you two get elected, then!"

Alisa shot a complex look at the two during their friendly exchange until the female student suddenly cast an eye on her.

"Anyway, shall we get started?"

"Huh? W-with what?"

"Don't worry about that. Just come over here."

"Wh-what?"

"Go with her," Masachika seemed to be saying to Alisa with his eyes when she turned to him for help, and before she knew it, she was taken to the same storage room that she'd had her pictures taken in the day before.

"Uh…?"

"All right, it's time to get changed. Go on."

"What?"

Standing in the direction the girl was pointing was a mannequin wearing a pure-white dress before the same window she'd posed in front of yesterday.

"Have fun! I'm fairly sure it should fit you, but if it doesn't, then I'll work as fast as I can to make sure it does. Oh, these are the shoes that go with it."

"Huh? What? Uh… What in the world…?"

"Let's do this!"

After the female student beautifully ignored her confusion, Alisa proceeded to change into the dress, still just as bewildered as she was when she walked through the door.

"Yesss! It's just the right size! Damn, I'm good. Yo, Kuze! We're done in here."

Right after flexing, as if she were proud of a job well done, the female student quickly left the storage room.

"…Uh… What am I supposed to do?"

Alisa began to rock back and forth uncomfortably, all alone in the storage room, but Masachika soon called her name, so she gave herself a quick check, then retired from the room as well.

"Whoa… You look really beautiful."

But Masachika's smile was met with a puzzled gaze, for his clothes were so bright that they were almost blinding, even in this dim room. He was dressed as a knight, his outfit predominantly white and blue, and his hair was combed to the side.

"Hey, don't just stand there. Say something," he said, laughing, as Alisa stood in a daze.

"Oh, uh… It's, uh…"

"On second thought, don't say anything at all! I know I look like an idiot."

Alisa almost said he looked handsome until he suddenly stopped her, making her swallow her words, so instead, she decided to put another thought into words.

"What is going on…?"

"Oh, this…"

Masachika awkwardly placed a hand on his neck.

"Remember the promise we made yesterday? I mean, technically, I guess it was a while ago...but we promised to check out the school festival together, right?"

"Ah—"

"I know. I'm really sorry. The festival is over. Not only that, but I didn't even get to see your performance, either...so I get why you were mad. Anyone would be," suggested Masachika, pointing at the cold compress on his neck. It was this gesture that proved how considerate he really was, and it made Alisa's heart flutter. He had realized that she was regretting her actions and that it was tearing her apart, and that was exactly why he was doing this. Masachika was telling her that she didn't need to apologize—that she didn't need to explain herself.

Ah...

Alisa almost wanted to cry all over again. Meanwhile, Masachika darted his eyes swiftly down to the side at the floor, as if he were giving her some privacy to shed a tear.

"So, uh... I know the night festival isn't the same thing, since it's basically just a closing party for the students, but I want to invite you to go with me...in my own way, just like you asked me to."

Once he cleared his throat, Masachika got on one knee, and after a moment of hesitation, he smiled softly.

"Just for tonight, I ask that you allow me to treat you not as a princess but as an individual," he pleaded in a joking manner as he gently held out his hand to Alisa. "Princess, would you do me the honor of being my partner tonight?"

It was an invitation to the night festival dance. The flashy, romantic performance sent Alisa's heart racing while she smiled.

"Come on... What are you doing? Who do you think you are? Sumire?"

"What? I'm being a perfect gentleman."

"How do you really feel?"

"Like the biggest idiot in the world."

"Pfft! Ha-ha-ha!"

Alisa could feel her heart fill with bliss while she laughed at his honest response. Although Masachika may have always joked around like this, at least right now, the only one he had eyes for was Alisa. The only one he wanted right now was her.

At least for now, he truly is my partner.

By some curious coincidence, they felt the same way. Although the present was but a fleeting moment, at least for this period of time, they shared the same emotion for one another. Alisa theatrically placed her hand onto his, not even realizing that their thoughts were one and the same.

"I would love to," she replied. She then grinned mischievously—

Out of nowhere, the soft sound of a camera shutter resounded, prompting Masachika to glare reproachfully in the direction of the noise.

"Hey, Side Slit. Don't take our picture."

"Don't shorten my name like that. Besides, you'll now have something to remember today by. Check it out."

Displayed on the female student's phone screen were Masachika and Alisa, smiling while they joined hands. Alisa bashfully curled in on herself, but when she glanced at Masachika, he was coincidentally glancing right back, and their eyes met before they quickly looked away.

"Whew. You two really are the perfect match. In fact, I'm sure everyone feels that way after hearing your passionate exchange onstage," the female student gushed unexpectedly in admiration.

"...What?"

But when Alisa knit her brow in wonder and looked back at the girl, she seemed genuinely surprised.

"Wait. Do you honestly not know what I'm talking about? Everyone at school is talking about what you said to Kuze onstage: 'I believe in you,' was it?"

"...Huh? Why—?"

Alisa suddenly began having flashbacks about what happened onstage as she stood in a daze. When Masachika told her to trust him and wait, Alisa had tightly clasped her hands before her chest and replied: *"I believe in you."*

...Her hands were clasped before her chest.

...Clasped around the microphone.

...Which was turned on.

“A-ah... Ahhh...,” she gasped, dreading what was to come, as the female student brightly grinned while giving her a thumbs-up.

“Anyway, as I said, it’s the talk of the school right now, so once you two go outside dressed like that, you’re going to be the stars of the night festival! I guarantee it!”

Her lack of awareness only made it sting that much more, overwhelming Alisa with embarrassment like she had never experienced before.

“N-noooooooooo!!”

Her bone-chilling scream echoed throughout the clubroom building that evening.

Хоть навсегда.

The Day Professor Side Slit Was Born

Back in middle school when Masachika was the vice president of the student council…

"All right, let's talk about the stage performances that are going to be held in the gym."

The atmosphere was strained the instant Masachika announced that they were going to start the school festival committee meeting.

Oof… Feels like I'm standing on pins and needles. It's not even my problem, and I'm still nervous.

But despite his thoughts, Masachika proceeded to carry out the meeting as the chairman.

"So, uh… After receiving every group's application, we calculated all the time we would need for everyone's project, and we're currently one hour over. The other stages are completely booked as well, so we're going to need for everyone to be flexible so we can shorten some of the performances…"

Even while Masachika tried to explain the situation, every representative for their respective club had their eyes locked on a single female student. Of course, one of the reasons for this was because she was why they had to call a meeting…but the other reason was undeniably her outfit.

Yeah, uh… Why is she wearing a qipao*?*

It probably wasn't only Masachika who felt that, either. Every single student most likely shared that sentiment, since only she was wearing an entirely red *qipao* among a sea of school uniforms. Plus, the slits went up really high on the sides, and sitting in a booth seat made that more apparent. But most of all, she was a relatively modest, innocent, beautiful girl, so the inconsistency between her personality and dress really brought it all together. More than a few boys weren't even trying that hard to hide their constant glances at her thighs peeking out from the slits.

Crossing her legs as if she doesn't know exactly what she's doing… Tsk. Who does she think she is? Some Triad boss's daughter? All she needs now is a massive bodyguard standing behind her, and it'd be perfect.

Once Masachika finished talking, the captain of the music club faced the Triad member and asked:

"Excuse me, uh… You're from the craft club, right? As far as I can remember, your club has never used the stage for any performance before. What changed?"

It was high-level roundabout criticism disguised as a question, but the captain of the craft club replied:

"Members of our club have been talking about how they've wanted to do something for years, but they've always been too passive to try to reserve any stage time, so I decided to apply."

The captain of the music club frowned at how cheerful she was being. There had actually been a mutual understanding for the past few years about which clubs got stage time during the school festival. The allocated time for each performance was essentially the same every year as well. The drama club and music club were especially adamant about keeping up with tradition and having the same spots reserved for their performances. Put simply, a select few were hogging all the stage time while claiming they should maintain tradition, even though the stage was open to anyone who wanted to use it.

That said, nobody ever complained publicly about the situation… until the captain of the craft club boldly came up with a plan of her own. In fact, their project was going to be so big that she claimed they needed an entire hour to themselves onstage.

"But the 'Spirit Collection' mentioned here seems…"

The captain of the music club grimaced while checking out his copy of the scheduled performances.

"Seems incredible, right? We're going to have models wear the outfits our club made and have a runway show!" the craft club captain exclaimed mirthfully as she suddenly rose to her feet with arms wide open like some sort of a stage actress. Of course, her movements naturally showed off the *qipao*...and the slits as well.

Ohhh, now it makes sense.

Her outfit was a sample for what was to come, and of course, every boy in the room was already daydreaming about it. They imagined beautiful girls dressed in risqué outfits confidently walking down a runway. Even the captain of the music club didn't seem to be an exception, looking away uncomfortably while he cleared his throat before calmly replying:

"There's no way you can do a runway. The installation and removal processes alone would waste so much time. I know they have portable folding stages, but you have to spend a lot of time adjusting the height and making sure everything is safe so that nobody gets hurt."

He stated his very reasonable opinion, which was based on experience, but the captain of the craft club still didn't back down.

"Then we can set it up the day before the festival, then take it down after the festival is over. I don't see any issue leaving the runway out for everyone else to use, either."

"Excuse me? You've got to be joking. A runway would just get in the way. We'd have far fewer seats for the audience, to boot! Right?"

He started making eye contact with the other club captains until the captain of the drama club, who "traditionally" had just as much say in this as he did, suddenly chimed in:

"That should work."

"Huh...?"

The captain of the music club was struck dumb by the betrayal, but it made sense to Masachika.

The craft club does make outfits for the drama club often, after all.

There were probably some behind-the-scenes negotiations that took place as well.

This qipao*-wearing captain is tougher than I expected.*

But while Masachika stared at the craft club's captain in admiration...

"What the...? Y-you can't be serious?" asked the music club's captain in utter astonishment.

"Why not? I bet the music club could make use of it, too. You know, like how professional musicians walk down the runway with their guitar or mic and show off to the crowd."

"No, but like… Well, sure, they do that, but…"

"Plus, I'm sure clubs like the dance club and juggling club could use a runway to try out a new act or something, too, right?"

The other club captains began to think seriously about the proposal. Even Masachika, who originally felt that such a ridiculous plan would never work, was starting to change his mind. He genuinely admired the hustle and was secretly kind of rooting for her, too.

"By the way, we can easily make the runway if we just borrow a portion of the high school's portable folding stage."

"Uh… How are we going to carry a giant stage all the way over here? They're extremely heavy, you know?"

"The school janitor will put it in his truck and bring it over for us if we ask."

"Mmm… Sure, but still, we don't even have time for the craft club's performance, since—"

"On behalf of the drama club, I would like to donate twenty minutes of our time to the craft club."

"…?!"

The drama club captain's second betrayal rendered the music club captain speechless.

"Thank you very much. I suppose we can make a compromise and shorten our performance by twenty minutes as well. Forty minutes should be enough…but we would still need someone to donate another twenty minutes to us…"

Everyone's eyes shifted toward the captain of the club with the longest performance: the music club…

"Man, that was impressive. Quite the negotiation skills you've got," Masachika complimented her genuinely after the meeting was over and everyone else was gone. The captain of the craft club stayed behind so they could discuss details in regard to the runway, since she somehow managed to magically pull forty minutes for her club's performance out of thin air.

"I couldn't have done it without your support during the second half there, Vice President."

"What? I didn't do anything special. It was your negotiation skills that sealed the deal. Not only did you prove that every club could benefit from this, but you also made sure to reap the most benefits for yourselves."

"Yeah..."

After bashfully scratching her cheek, the captain of the craft club stood up, took off a shoe, then placed her foot on top of the couch, revealing her beautiful, untanned thighs through the slit while leaving not much to the imagination. She thereupon placed a hand on her hip and declared:

"You know what they say: The greater the slits, the greater the reward!"

Masachika was taken aback, as if the secrets to the universe had been presented to him, and before he knew it, he was moved to tears and started crying uncontrollably. Okay, that last part was a lie, but he really was touched, and as his lips trembled with deep emotion, a term of endearment escaped him.

"P-Professor Side Slit...!"

Afterword

Hey, this is Sunsunsun, whose brain exploded after repeatedly writing afterwords that exceeded ten pages. Therefore, I decided to be a huge idiot and include a short story at the end, as if this were some sort of paperback comic book.

This is probably…no, almost definitely the first time a light novel has ever tried something like this in history. Yep. There isn't another author dumb enough to do something like this. I mean, it's probably rare just to find an author who doesn't keep count of how many pages he has written until after he's done, like, "Oh, crap! I still need to write a dozen or so more pages of material!" Plus, I doubt there are that many people who would go out of their way to write a short story just to make sure there are no ads at the end of the book, either. I bet there are going to be more than a few authors who are wondering why I'm in such a good mood after I submit my drafts to the editor…

Anyway, that's why I want to apologize to the few who believe that the afterword's the most important part, because this time, the afterword's going to be short! It's going to be short and hard to find! So starting next volume, make sure to start reading from the first page and not skipping straight to the afterword!

Anyway, I guess I should write something at least mildly interesting here, so let's talk about the class attraction that Masha and Chisaki did. That was actually something we did back when I was a student. So let me take a moment to apologize to all of those in the magician bar business for giving away one of your secrets. I made sure not to get into too much detail, so please cut me some slack. No,

I said "some slack!" Not "in half!" Nooo! Don't put me in the box and saw me in half! That's a real saw! Ahhh—

Ahem. Now, allow me to express a few words of gratitude. First, I would like to thank my editor Miyakawa, especially since I barely finished by the deadline, for always giving me great advice and for always looking out for me.

I would also like to say thanks to ever-so-busy Momoco for the beautiful, artistic (and not the least bit lewd) illustrations. I'm really sorry for always making such particular requests about the smallest things. With that being said, the lovely illustrations once again took my breath away, and I'm sure they're going to affect every young boy in puberty in one way or another. I personally enjoyed scrutinizing Alya's beautiful legs. For their artistic value only, of course. But still, thank you.

Next, I would like to express my thanks to Saho Tenamachi for her work on the comics, since they contributed to a huge influx of new fans. Thank you so much for always drawing everyone so captivatingly. The scene with the socks between Alya and Masachika was so incredible that it made me snort. Of course, I mean that in an artistic sense as well. No lewd thoughts here. Anyway, thank you.

Last but not least, I would like to thank everyone who was a part of this volume's creation and everyone who picked up a copy. Thank you so much! I am looking forward to meeting again when Volume 7 comes out. Until then.

By the way, who said there was only one short story?

THE SHORT STORY AFTER THE AFTERWORD

Yuri will save the world.

"Yo, Ayano! You better have those boobies ready for me!"

"As you wish."

"Mwa-ha-ha! Boing, boing! They're so soft!"

Ayano lay down on the bed while Yuki lay on top of her, rubbing her face in the maid's chest. However, once her master had calmed down enough, the maid asked:

"Is everything okay? This was rather sudden."

As far as Ayano knew, nothing happened to Yuki today that would have stressed her out that much, and yet she sought comfort. Therefore, it was only natural for Ayano to worry that something bad had happened without her knowledge.

Yuki slowly lifted her head out from between the booby pillows, then slowly got off Ayano while simultaneously and naturally unhooking the maid's bra (through the fabric of her maid uniform, to boot) as well, and it all happened within the span of a second. Yuki then immediately began to squeeze her maid's freed chest while tilting her head heavily to one side.

"I don't know… It's just… Work for the school festival committee has been really heavy lately. Everything has been so serious, so I just need to blow off some steam…"

"I hope this will help, then."

"It will. *Yuri* will save the world. It doesn't matter how brutal the war gets or how depressing the situation becomes, because once you have two attractive young girls share love for each other, everything looks beautiful in the end!"

"…"

Yuki's conversations were always a little difficult for Ayano to keep up with, but she still boldly continued to fondle her while paying no attention to how her maid was reacting.

"And boobs will save the world, too! Boobs can make anyone happy! In other words, world peace is actually achievable through the power of *yuri* and boobs!"

She then immediately took out her smartphone and called someone, and the instant that certain someone answered the phone, she yelled:

"You feel the same way, right, bro?!"

"What are you talking about?"

"Blah, blah, blah! Brrrt! Hubba, hubba! Boing, boing, boing!"

"Oh, definitely. Still, while two girls fondling each other's rack on the bed is nice, I actually prefer seeing two girls simply brushing each other's hair. Something about it hits just right."

"...?! Wh-what a convincing argument... I have been defeated... I was wrong, bro. It was foolish of me to try to combine too many fetishes into one."

"Yeah, sometimes keeping things simple is best. Yuri is good on its own, just like boobs are perfectly good on their own as well."

"Heh! Says the guy who has never even touched a boob in his life!"

"Hey, I thought we were—"

Yuki hung up before he could even finish his sentence, then got off Ayano and snapped.

"Yo, Ayano! Music, now! Play something elegant and relaxing... and nice and romantic but nothing too lewd!"

"Very well."

Although the requests were ambiguous and ridiculous, Ayano beautifully met her master's needs, selecting the perfect background music for the room. After Yuki nodded with evident satisfaction, she quickly slipped behind Ayano, wrapped her arms around her maid's stomach, then rested her chin on her shoulder while whispering alluringly into Ayano's ear with a mature expression:

"Oh my. Ayano..."

"L-Lady Yuki...?"

"*Giggle.* What's wrong…? Your hair is so messy."

Ayano's hair was really messy because a certain someone had been using her as a body pillow up until a few moments ago, but that thought didn't even cross Yuki's mind while she reached for a brush.

"What would you do without me? Come here and let me brush your hair for you."

"N-no, I could never ask you to do such a thing…"

"It's okay. You're my cute little sister, after all."

"Ah…"

Yuki strangely gave off the aura of a big sister as she gently grabbed Ayano's hair. Having said that, Yuki was tinier than Ayano, and that became especially apparent while they sat on the bed together, so in reality, there was nothing objectively big-sister about her at all.

"Your hair is so pretty… Just like a princess."

"Th-thank you… I have a lot of hair, so it becomes difficult to manage at times…"

"In other words, this beautiful hair is a monument of all your hard work," Yuki said, grinning confidently as she lifted up Ayano's hair…and slowly kissed her on the back of the neck.

"Ahhh! Lady Yuki…?!"

"*Giggle.* You're so cute, Ayano."

Her alluring whispers tickled the back of Ayano's neck, making her eyes widen.

"I—I…," awkwardly stuttered the maid.

"Hmm?"

"Would it be okay if I took a shower?"

"You trying to take this to the next level?"

Yuki flicked Ayano on the forehead, and she let out a cute "Oof." She then swiftly stepped away from her maid and cut off the music, once again returning tranquility to the room.

"That was a close one… We almost went beyond your traditional fan service scene and turned that into a sexy scene," said Yuki, deeply sighing.

"Fan service scene?"

"Yep. Some good ol' FSS," she replied, staring off into the distance until she suddenly snorted smugly. Ayano followed her gaze, but she didn't see anything, which only made her more confused.

"Um… Lady Yuki? What are you looking at?"

"Huh? Oh. A camera that's invisible to stupid people."

"…! I knew it, Lady Yuki. The world you live in truly is different from the one that unenlightened fools such as myself live in…!"

"It was a joke…," replied Yuki with an exhausted glare when suddenly, her phone began to vibrate. Displayed on the screen was a single text, reading:

By the way, yuri has to be natural. Nobody likes forced GL.

Alya, I look forward to continuing to work with you!